SPLASH

SGM ASHCROFT

THE HACK PAPERS
ISSUE TWO

ISBN: 978-1-3999-0639-5
Felt Side Publishing

SGM Ashcroft (sgmashcroft.com)
Cover design: designforwriters.com

For Iona and Otto, with love

LIST OF PLAYERS

Splash is the second book in *The Hack Papers* series, and more or less picks up from where *Hack* left off. Although *Splash* can be read as a standalone story, many of its characters feature heavily in *Hack*. Think of the books as being like seasons in a TV boxset. So, in the previous season of *The Hack Papers* ...

~✦~

Llew Sabler	Renegade newspaper reporter. Charged by police for defecating on an altar on a slow news day.
Thirza Kirkby	Llew's beautiful but sometimes violent fellow *Portsmouth Probe* reporter, who he secretly loves.
Emdel Black	Llew's oldest friend and housemate. Boffin. Broke Llew's heart by dating Thirza.
'Big' Al Barrett	Llew and Thirza's long suffering editor.
Rollo Baer	Wheelchair-using Southsea crook. Llew and Emdel helped him run an illicit mail-order porn venture.
Lucy Baer	Rollo's fifteen-year-old daughter. Damaged by mother's suicide. Talented writer.
Ma Baer	Rollo's mother. Bankrolled his move into crime.
DI Simmons	Charged Llew with altar crime, and suspected him of porn crime.

DI Bull	Simmons' police partner.
John Skinner	Owner of *The Tribune,* Portsmouth's main paper. Blackmailed gay men to appear in sick 70s porn films. Plotted to kill Llew to prevent Llew's exposé.
Daphne Skinner	Skinner's wife. Took ownership of *The Tribune* in a divorce settlement. Offered Llew a job.
Freddie	Skinner goon. Almost murdered Llew.
Herr Porno	Co-goon.
Nigel	Skinner's editor on *The Tribune.*
Henry	Llew's publisher on his first paper, the *Southampton Clarion.* A former Fleet Street executive.
Blanche	Landlady of the Barley Mow pub, for whom Thirza ditched Emdel.
David	Blanche's gay brother and Skinner blackmail victim.
Max O'Reardon	Catholic priest. Takes rap for Llew's altar outrage. David's partner and Skinner blackmail victim.
Bernie 'the shirt'	Llew's news tipster and Barley Mow local.
Alfred Ure	Ex-Royal Navy. Fellow pub tipster.
Glenn	Emdel's work colleague and porn library member.
Jason	Ditto
Darryl	Ditto
Bryan	Ditto

ONE

Portsmouth, England, 1997

I'VE ALWAYS LOVED A GOOD funeral. I never feel more alive than when someone else is being lowered into the ground. I find it heightens, in every way, the experience and delight of being me. But I don't feel like that any more, not after the latest one.

All the funerals prior to the most recent had been for peripheral figures in my life – great aunts and uncles so ancient and decayed that the end was surely a tonic for them, like some indefinite spa break. The only death to touch me, when I was younger, was that of our next-door neighbour, Mr Saunders. He was a haemophiliac and had perished from a nosebleed. He and his wife had no kids of their own, and so he'd spoiled me with sweets: aniseed balls, gobstoppers. Black Jacks. Sherbet Dib Dabs. Smiling Mr Saunders was forever proffering candied gifts over our garden fence. It was marvellous. But my free supply of confectionery had drained away along with the blood from his nostrils, and I cried for weeks. This remained my working definition of grief right up to the day Rollo Baer got himself killed.

Don't get me wrong, I wasn't that bothered about Rollo's demise. He and I had shared a grudging mutual respect, but that's about as far as it went. No, what cut deep was having to witness my girlfriend Lucy's suffering at the loss of her father. I hadn't seen anything like it before. Her loss was profound, and her pain became my pain. That's because we were in love and we shared everything. Well, almost everything.

One thing we hadn't shared, with Rollo at least, was the fact that she and I were an item. Lucy had long wanted me to tell her father about us, but I wasn't keen. Despite her claims to the contrary, I knew I was about as far from being Rollo's idea of a catch for his precious daughter as it was possible to get. He thought me a degenerate scandalmonger. I knew he would view me not as Lucy's boyfriend but as a contemptible toerag who was defiling her, and I feared he might try to carve me a new sphincter with a blunt box knife.

'I don't see why *you* can't break the news,' I countered whenever Lucy broached the subject, which she did with increasing regularity and fervour in the weeks prior to Rollo's death.

'Because it's not my place to tell him,' she protested, jaw muscles bunched.

'I don't get why we have to tell him at all,' I said. 'Why are you making such a big deal about this? It's not like we're engaged or anything. People don't announce that they're dating.'

'He knows I'm seeing someone and he wants to meet him. I've never kept secrets from Daddy, and I'm not about to start on your account.'

I could never summon a reply to that, so I let silence do the heavy lifting. But in the end, she snapped.

'Either you tell Daddy this week or you and me, we're history.'

'What? Jesus, Lucy! You've got to be kidding me.'

But I could see she wasn't.

My guts were in a Turk's-head knot of nerves on the day I planned to tell him. But I never got the chance to, for that Sunday evening firefighters discovered Rollo's charred remains in the still-smouldering shell of his rave venue. It would be a further three weeks before Hampshire Constabulary confirmed (via dental records) what everyone already knew to be true – that Rollo Baer was no more.

When I learned about Rollo's death, all I felt was relief. There was no thought of Lucy and how the news would destroy her. In those first moments all that mattered to me was that I no longer had to face the horror of presenting myself before Rollo as a potential son-in-law.

'It's normal to feel this way, given the circumstances,' I told myself despite the jabs of guilt that delivered a quite different message.

The closest I got to telling Rollo I was sleeping with his daughter was when I held Lucy's hand at his open graveside. Even then I was terrified he might spring from his casket to hurl me down into the hole they'd dug for him. And I swear he spoke to me through the ether. I even saw a snarl on his lip that twisted his porn-star moustache out of shape.

'*You* and my Lucy?' his disembodied voice growled at the sight of his daughter's hand in mine and her tear-smeared face nestled into the crook of my neck. 'No fucking way, Sabler. Over my dead body.'

But Rollo was forever silenced when the pallbearers eased him into the ground and he came to rest atop his beloved Ma. More than one-thousand of his and Ma's Metal Estate friends, neighbours and co-conspirators looked on as Lucy bent down, scooped up a handful of earth and tipped it from her hand. The hollow clatter of soil spilling on wood was followed by a wail, which issued from a place in Lucy that was unknown probably even to herself.

She was broken. Actually, broken doesn't begin to describe what happened to her. It was as if she had been disassembled and then spectacularly misassembled – in the dark, by a drunkard on roller skates wearing boxing gloves and a blindfold. She became a facsimile of her former self.

Before Rollo died things had been going so well – not just with me and Lucy either, but with *every*thing. Jesus, life had been near perfect. I had a girl I loved, a job I loved, an editor I loved, and I was working alongside Thirza, a girl I'd once loved to the brink of self-annihilation, but who was now a soulmate. In fact things were so good it made me nervous. Do you ever get that? The feeling that bliss is about to teeter over into something else entirely? You know, the way masturbation gives way to guilt moments after release? Or maybe that's just a Catholic thing.

Whatever.

Rollo's demise was just the start of it, and his wasn't the only death either. Had I known how dangerous things would get I might have sought refuge in prescription sedatives and taken to shuffling up and down Southsea esplanade in carpet slippers and sherbet leisurewear, muttering to myself. That would certainly have been a safer option.

To be honest, my head has only just stopped spinning from it all. I'm really not ready to start raking up all the dark stuff, not just yet. Instead, I shall go back to when life was blissful, and yet to tip over into something else entirely.

TWO

LUCY HAD BEEN FIFTEEN WHEN we first met. She'd just won a countywide writing competition and I had interviewed her about it for *The Probe*, the weekly newspaper I'd worked for upon arriving in Portsmouth. For the photoshoot she had sashayed into the family kitchen in school uniform and make-up. The sight of her conjured images of seventies British sex comedies in which comely women with heavy breasts played temptress schoolgirls.

'She's bloody fifteen,' I'd had to remind myself.

The thing is, six years on and she was still fifteen in my head. Try as I might, I could not shake the image of Lucy as a sultry fifth-former. Indeed, the harder I tried the worse it got, and so I gave up trying altogether. I came to terms with the fact that however long she and I ended up being together, she would forever be fifteen – even if her incontinence pants and soaking dentures suggested otherwise.

Lucy is in fact twenty-one – six years my junior, but at least ten my senior in terms of maturity, focus and drive.

'You're like a fucking infant compared to her,' Thirza never tired of reminding me. 'What the hell she sees in you is beyond me.'

As a soulmate, Thirza saw it as her job to mock, belittle and demean me at the drop of a hat. Bless her cotton socks, and her magnificent melons.

Thirza and Lucy became pretty close. Not only were they friends, they were also co-workers on *The Tribune*, Portsmouth's daily newspaper. It was John Skinner's old organ. Skinner, my nemesis, whose goons had so nearly succeeded in killing me, after he learned I was about to expose him for blackmailing half of Portsmouth's gay community into appearing in his depraved porn films.

By that time, Skinner was two years into a twenty-three stretch. To use good old tabloid speak, Skinner was 'caged' in HMP Parkhurst on the Isle of Wight, just across the Solent from Portsmouth. I liked to think he was little more than some lag's bitch, but I doubted it somehow. It was more likely that that psychopathic bastard had a kennel of his own bitches to service his every sexual whim. It would not have surprised me to learn he had the entire place in his pocket, like Noël Coward's con-in-chief Bridger in *The Italian Job*.

At least Skinner no longer had *The Tribune* in his pocket. Daphne, his ex, took ownership of it as part of her divorce settlement, and it was Daphne who hired me as investigations editor. She had wanted me as editor but I turned her down. She needed someone that could 'manage' half of her newsroom – most of them Skinner's overpaid cronies – out the door, yesterday. It would be carnage, for which I had neither the skills nor stomach. It was a job for a battle-hardened newspaper veteran, and even then that person would need a newsroom henchman to crack skulls, kick butts and generally terrorise Skinner's bootlickers into leaving. Or henchwoman.

Thirza joined *The Tribune* about six weeks after I had, having worked out her notice on *The Probe*, and it wasn't long before *Probe* editor Big Al – my über-understanding old boss – followed suit, taking up the reins as *Tribune* editor.

Daphne appointed Thirza as editor-in-chief, although executioner-in-chief might have been a more fitting title. When it came to ridding *The Tribune* of Skinner's people, it was Big Al's job to load the bullets and Thirza's to fire them – mostly at point-blank range into the faces of her victims.

As a condition of his appointment Big Al had insisted that Daphne also hire Henry, my old publisher from the *Southampton Clarion*. Henry was a seasoned national newspaper executive who had downsized his career in a bid to salvage his third marriage.

'I made it clear to her I'll need Henry,' Big Al had told me in the pub following his interview with Daphne. 'I explained that if she wants to shunt Skinner's people out the door without having to buy them off then we'll need someone who knows the legals on that front inside out.'

Henry hadn't taken much persuading. Despite his best efforts his marriage had crumbled anyway so he had little to lose by joining *The Tribune* and much to gain.

So it was that Big Al, Thirza and Henry were tasked with shifting no fewer than seventeen of Skinner's lackeys off the payroll – pronto. Not only were their salaries crippling Daphne's finances but they'd been in thrall to Skinner for so long, they could barely function as free-thinking entities.

'They freak me the fuck out,' Thirza confided a day or two after taking up her post. 'There's something about their eyes. It's like *Night of the Living Dead*, only in a fucking newsroom.'

On Henry's advice Big Al had begun the axing process by downsizing the lackeys' responsibilities. They were made to do the kind of grunt work even cub reporters loathe: police calls, parish news and, horror of horrors, the dreaded vox pop.

It was Thirza's job to implement this plan, and she began with Nigel, Skinner's former editor. I'd met Nigel years earlier at a *Tribune* executive barbecue that Skinner had invited me to in a bid to woo me across to the dark side. Nigel was a saturnine character whose gloominess most likely stemmed from having had his soul vacuumed from his body by Skinner. Nigel had played Goebbels to Skinner's Hitler. This made him de facto leader of the Skinnerites at *The Tribune*, and the obvious starting point for Thirza.

One day, Thirza sidled up to the Investigations desk where I was sitting with Lucy and two others.

'You lot,' she said. 'Hold on to your fucking hats. We've got countdown to lift-off.'

We watched her saunter across to Nigel's desk.

'Right, you,' she said, at a volume designed to ring across the cavernous newsroom, 'I want you over at Hayling Island doing a news trawl. Local police, library noticeboards, parish council, local businesses. The usual. And don't come back until you've got enough for the Hayling edition. Got it?' She pointed at Nigel as if picking him out from a police line-up.

Nigel stood up, his expensively tailored frame looming over Thirza. To the uneducated eye, it must have seemed a hopeless mismatch. But I knew better.

'Now you just hang on a damn second,' spluttered Nigel, running his tongue repeatedly across his outsized front teeth, which jutted over his bottom lip like a go-faster spoiler. 'Do you know who I am?' he asked as if he were a celeb who'd been denied entry to a swanky club.

'Right,' Thirza shouted without pause, arms waving above her head. 'Everybody, stop what you're doing. We've got an emergency here.'

The cacophony of clacking keyboards fell silent.

'We've got a chump here who doesn't know who he is. Can anyone help him out? What's his name?'

'Nigel,' called a lone male voice from afar. It was followed by a ripple of tittering.

'Right,' she said, still pointing at Nigel, 'now that you know who you are, maybe we can move on to what I just asked you to do. So tell me: what did I just ask you to do?'

Nigel's tongue went into swish-swash overdrive. 'Now you listen to me, I won't stand for this. I'll—'

Thirza flicked out her hand and Nigel crumpled into his seat, doubled over, clutching his ribs. She'd struck his solar plexus, so she was clearly in full-on attack mode. Even I was shocked. Downing a sex pest in the mosh pit was one thing, but a colleague at work?

'If you won't stand for it you can fucking well sit. Now you listen to me.' Thirza loomed over him. 'You might've been editor under your blackmailing, murdering scumbag of an old boss, but under this boss you're nobody. Got it? So if I tell you to go to Hayling fucking Island on a news trawl, what do you do?'

'I go to Hayling Island,' Nigel whispered.

'Speak up, *goffang*. I can't hear you.'

'I go to Hayling Island,' Nigel repeated more loudly.

'Right,' Thirza announced, turning full circle on the spot and wagging a quivering talon as she spun, 'there's a heap of people in this room who used to be something under that scumbag Skinner. We're sending all of you out into the districts to trawl for news. If anyone else has got a view on that, then let's have you, here and now.'

Silence.

'Good.' She hitched up her sweatshirt and slid a square of paper from her jeans back pocket, unfolded it, stomped across the room and pinned it to the noticeboard. 'This is a list of where we want you lot to go today ... and tomorrow ... and the day after that ... and the week after that. Get the picture?'

Hand on hips, Thirza scanned the room.

'What the fuck are you waiting for?' she shouted while clapping. Her face was red as a berry now. 'Get your sorry arses up and out.'

Skinner's lackeys sprang to their feet, grabbed their coats and huddled around the noticeboard just feet from Thirza. None of them dared catch her eye. Nigel was the last to leave the room, filing through a door that Thirza held open, ushering him through with faux deference. He paused at the threshold as if about to say something to her, but left without another word.

Having reduced their responsibilities, the next step was to reduce their salaries to match. Eight of the seventeen had quit at this point, having seen the writing on the wall. It was the younger ones who'd gone. They were mostly unmarried and unencumbered by kids or hefty mortgages. The nine who remained had been in Skinner's inner circle and not only had big homes to finance, but also public school fees to pay. They couldn't afford to throw in the towel so easily.

After having their salaries slashed, a number of them hit Daphne with threats of legal action. In response, Henry had *The Tribune*'s lawyers tie them up in a blizzard of legal paperwork.

'But haven't they got the law on their side?' I asked Henry in the staff canteen one lunchtime.

He tapped his trouser pocket, and smiled. 'The law is on the side of those with the deepest pockets, and our pockets are deeper than theirs. Their legal bills will hit four figures soon enough, and when that happens it won't be their mortgages that give or the fees for their kids' posh schools. No, the legal threats will dry up soon enough. You watch.'

'I don't get why they haven't clubbed together under one lawyer,' I said. 'It'd be far cheaper for them, wouldn't it?'

Henry put his index finger to his lips, before checking over both shoulders. 'Not so loud. Yes, group litigation would be far cheaper for them.'

'So if I've thought of it, why haven't they?'

'These aren't the brightest people, Llew. Skinner chose them for their compliance not their intellect, and thank goodness for that.'

Henry proved to be right, because having endured seven months of journalistic pond-dredging on a relative pittance, a further seven Skinnerites crumbled. Strapped for cash, they downsized their homes, sent their kids to the local comp and sought work elsewhere – on other local dailies, in PR and corporate communications. Big Al gave them all glowing references. He wanted them out the door but had no desire to destroy them.

'They were probably good people before Skinner got to them,' Big Al explained over a pint. 'And now they can be good people again, with normal jobs and normal salaries like the rest of us.'

So that left Nigel. The problem with Nigel was that he was independently wealthy, thanks to his generous father who by all accounts had been some high-flying City broker. This meant Nigel was able to maintain his old lifestyle even on the vastly reduced salary Daphne paid him. Also, despite Thirza's best efforts, it seemed Nigel was immune to the ritual humiliations she heaped upon him.

'He must have skin thicker than a rhino's,' I said to Henry one day while standing by the water cooler. We glanced surreptitiously at Nigel, who was ludicrously resplendent in his tailored three-piece suit and patent-leather shoes. 'How much punishment can one man take?'

'He's biding his time,' said Henry. 'He's building a case for constructive dismissal. He'll resign in his own time and then he'll sue. I've seen it all before. But it's no big drama. We'll settle out of court and consider it a victory. There were seventeen of the bastards don't forget. It could have been far, far worse.'

'So how long d'you think he'll last?'

'Not as long as he thinks.' Henry tapped his nose. 'Thirza's cooking something up as we speak. We'll have the last word on this, you'll see.'

*

'Right, Llew, here we go,' Thirza said, winking. 'You wanted to know what I had up my sleeve for that toothy twat over there. Watch this.'

She grabbed an old issue of *The Tribune* from a pile of papers beside her terminal and sauntered across to Nigel's desk, perching a shapely buttock on its corner.

'Good morning, Nigel' she said softly, all smiles. 'Can I ask you a question?' Then the smile disappeared. Thirza was a one-woman good cop, bad cop. 'What is this, exactly?' she asked, throwing the newspaper down on his typing hands.

Nigel continued to touch-type under it, not taking his eyes of his screen to look at either the paper or Thirza.

'Can you read it please, Nigel.'

He snorted, grabbed the copy of *The Tribune* and snapped it open.

'It's the piece with the big red ring drawn round it,' Thirza offered helpfully.

'That's the vox pop I did last week in Hayling Island about dog dirt on the streets, like you asked. What of it?'

'I'll tell you what of it.' She stood. Bad cop was about to spew forth, I could feel it. 'Look at the spellings of the first two names in your vox pop.'

Nigel eyed the paper. 'That's what they told me their names were. Look,' he added, thumbing through his notebook and holding up the relevant page for Thirza's inspection. 'Bernie O'Shay and Alfred Urr,' he said. 'See.'

My mouth fell open at mention of Bernie the Shirt and Alfred, our old Mow drinking buddies and news tipsters. Thirza, the crafty cow, had roped them into her plan to rid us of Nigel, and probably at no more cost than a few free drinks.

'Oh,' said Thirza, with more than a hint of am-dram. 'That's strange. Then how do you explain these?'

She produced what looked like a couple of sheets of letterheaded paper from a back pocket and handed them to Nigel. He read them.

'They're from a Mr Ure and a Mr O'Shea complaining that I spelled their names wrong,' Nigel said. 'But that can't be right. Look, it's all here in my notebook.' He tapped it again, a little more frantically this time.

Thirza snatched it from his hand.

'You ... big ... hopeless ... halfwit,' she said, punctuating her words with smacks to Nigel's head with the notebook. 'You can't even write down people's fucking names properly. YOU ... BIG ... GOOFY ... GORMLESS ... CRETIN.'

Thirza battered him about the skull with such ferocity that Nigel raised both arms in self-defence. She tossed the notebook on his desk.

'B-b-but ...'

'But fucking *what?*' Thirza screamed. 'You want me to contact these people and tell them they've been spelling their names wrong all this time?'

'B-b-but ...'

She perched on his desk, the same way she had earlier. 'If we can't trust you with a simple vox pop then we can't trust you with anything. We're moving you to the back office. You'll be in charge of stationery. Surely even you can manage paper clips and Biros.'

Nigel stood. 'This is an ... outrage.' His voice cracked, and his eyes glistened with tears. I felt for him, despite everything.

Thirza turned away from Nigel's desk and gave me a wink as she passed. I was left wondering if she didn't enjoy this kind of thing a little too much. Where, exactly, did she draw all that anger from? To think I'd once elected to go to war with her. Memories of that awful time sent a shudder through me.

I watched as Nigel gathered a few effects from his desk, clicked open his crocodile-skin attaché case and placed them inside. He slipped his camel-hair coat off a hanger he kept hooked on the mahogany hat stand that had once been in his old office, the one now occupied by Big Al. Then he pulled on the coat, picked up the briefcase and, with what little dignity he had left, walked out of *The Tribune* office for the final time.

Daphne received his letter of resignation three days later. I'm forever grateful to Nigel for doing the decent thing because it put Daphne in a good mood. She called me into her office later the same day.

'Close the door,' she said. 'Coffee?'

'No thanks. Given up.'

She poured herself a cup from the cafetiere atop an art deco sideboard adorned with a fancy patterned brass inlay.

'Is there anything you haven't given up?' she asked. 'First alcohol, now coffee. What's next? Sex?'

I studied my feet at her mention of sex. At that stage I had just started seeing Lucy. Daphne was anti-workplace romances, big time, because that's how she'd met Skinner. So I knew she wouldn't tolerate me sleeping with the junior reporter I'd only just hired to my team. In truth, I wasn't entirely comfortable with it myself, although not uncomfortable enough to stop doing it.

'So what can I do for you, Daphne?' I said, keen to nudge the conversation in a fresh direction.

'It's more a case of what you've already done,' she said, sitting in one of the four art deco armchairs in her office and gesturing for me to follow suit.

Jesus Christ, I thought. She knows about me and Lucy. Is she going to fire me?

'Why are you looking so guilty?' she cut in with a chuckle. 'Is there something I should know about?'

'Um, er, no.'

'You crack me up,' she said, cracking up. She smacked her palms against her shapely thighs, which that day were clad in glossy black tights that fed into a snug tartan miniskirt. Daphne enjoyed turning heads as she waltzed through the newsroom. 'On the one hand you're this *any*thing goes sort of bloke and yet you're so easy to embarrass.'

'I'm Catholic,' was all I could think of in reply.

'I just wanted to say thank you,' she said, leaning forward and placing an exquisitely manicured hand on my knee. She smiled into my eyes and left her hand in place. A warmth crept up my thigh. Where was her aversion to office romance now? In a panic I started thinking of boring things hoping to divert attention – and blood – away from my stirring member. Final reminders ... christenings ... traffic jams ... tidying up ... clothes shopping.

She sat back in her chair, taking her hand with her, and I breathed an inner sigh of relief.

'So what is it I've done?' I asked, crossing my legs, baffled by what had prompted her suggestive show of thanks.

'D'you know what today is?' she asked.

'Tuesday.'

'No, you fool. I'll tell you what today is – it's the first day of this paper's future.'

'What d'you mean?' I asked, head cocked like an inquisitive mutt.

'I mean that today is the first day there's officially none of *his* people on this paper.' She spat out the word 'his' like it was poison. 'For the first time, there's no shadow of him over this building, and I've got you to thank for that. It was you who suggested bringing in Big Al and Thirza. What they've done those two, it's a miracle.'

'There's no need to thank me,' I said, knowing she had every reason to thank me. 'I didn't shovel any of that crap. It was all Big Al and Thirza. And Henry. It's them you should be thanking.'

'Oh, I will, but first I wanted to thank you. How does an extra two thousand a year sound?'

'What? Really? God, thanks Daphne.'

The windfall left me wondering how much she was going to hand Thirza and Big Al. I was surprised, and vaguely disappointed, to find jealousy tugging at my guts.

'With all his people gone, I've now actually got a cash flow,' Daphne said, fetching herself a refill of coffee. God knows how much of the stuff she drank; she was rarely without a cup of it. Maybe it was a cocaine substitute. I knew all about drug substitutes, having swapped booze for endless cans of Coke. I was now ruining my teeth instead of my liver. 'D'you know what he was paying that buck-toothed idiot Nigel?' she asked, returning to her chair. 'Have a guess.'

'I dunno. Seventy thou?'

'One hundred and ten a year, and some of the others were on salaries not far off that. So yeah, I'm grateful, Llew. Really grateful.'

So with more cash on my hip, a great job as investigations editor and a girl I loved in my bed ... yeah, life was pretty blissful.

THREE

LUCY WILL MAKE A DAMN fine career journalist, I'm convinced of it. She has the full English of attributes: intellect, natural curiosity, a way with words, and she's great with people irrespective of class, creed or colour. Plus she's kind of beautiful, which only ever opens doors. Me, on the other hand, I'm just a nosy bastard, which isn't much of a USP for a news hunter-gatherer.

I guess I started the journalism ball rolling for Lucy. It was me who advised Rollo that Lucy should approach Big Al about a summer work placement on *The Probe*, back when she was between O levels and A levels. She had, and it'd gone like a dream for all concerned because, like I say, Lucy's got the lot.

After that initial stint, she spent every school holiday thereafter on *The Probe* learning the ropes. I was no longer with the paper by that time. I was working my way to the bottom of the tabloid heap, having moved to London to take up a position as a reporter on *The Insider*, a national red-top. It was a grubby experience, from which Daphne had rescued me.

By the time I moved back down to Pompey, Lucy was a fully fledged reporter in all but name. She had been shaped by Big Al and tempered by Thirza, and all she needed was an opportunity.

'Papers is all she wants to do,' Rollo told me when I bumped into him on my first Saturday back in town, while revisiting my old stamping ground in Southsea, near the offices of *The Probe*. I walked alongside him as he propelled his wheelchair along with heavily muscled arms.

'With her A-level results she could've had her pick of universities but she ain't interested. Her heart's set on papers,' he added, with an edge of distaste in his tone. 'Say, Sabler, if anything comes up on your rag, d'you think she'd get a look-in?'

'Well, I'm running my own mini-department at *The Tribune*,' I told him. 'And it just so happens I'm looking to hire one more reporter.'

'Brilliant. So that's a yes?'

'No, Rollo, it's not a yes. What I'm saying is we'll soon be hiring. Get her to send Big Al a letter and CV on spec. That way she'll be at the front of the queue. From what I hear, Big Al thinks the world of her, so who knows. But I'm not making any promises, okay? This is investigations we're talking about. It's hardcore – it's not beginner's stuff.'

'Just name your price, Sabler. I'll make it worth your while, if you know what I mean. You know I'm good for it.'

Jesus Christ, I thought, will you get your fangs out of my leg. But I suspected he'd never let go, never give me any peace – not where it concerned Lucy's interests. Still, I couldn't have him calling the shots like that.

'Keep your money, Rollo, and your TVs, fridges and stereos. If she gets the job it'll be because she's the best candidate, not because you've bought me off. And don't be giving me grief if she doesn't land it.'

I would liked to have rounded off that big, bold statement with '*Capiche?*', a word Rollo used to great effect when strong-arming folk. Hearing it coming from me, though, he'd most likely have pissed himself laughing.

'I've got ten grand's worth of flat-screen plasma telly in that garage right over there,' he said, pointing across the street. 'Ever clocked one?'

I shook my head. I'd seen one showcased on the telly, on *Tomorrow's World* or something, but that had been it.

'Forty-two inches. Even Branson's not got one of them beauties. No one has. I'm telling ya, it's like something from outer space. Interested?'

'Oh, go on then.'

It was as if someone else were speaking my words, like I was watching myself in some gritty police procedural.

Rollo reached out a hand. I shook it.

'Done,' he said. 'Say, where're you living these days?'

'Opposite South Parade Pier, just down from *The Tribune* offices.'

'Okay. I'll have it dropped round once my girl's on the payroll.'

Lucy joined *The Tribune* investigations team a few weeks later. She was interviewed by myself, Big Al and Thirza. Both of them knew and liked Lucy from her stints on *The Probe* in the school holidays, so she was pushing at an open door. But neither of them knew she was the daughter of a big-shot crook. Big Al knew nothing of Rollo Baer, his black-market welfare state or his role in the Skinner affair. And while I had told Thirza the truth about Skinner's porn, including a local crook's involvement in the affair, I'd been careful to keep Rollo's name out of things. Also, right from when Lucy had been doing work experience on *The Probe*, I'd advised her not to use the surname 'Baer' for story bylines. Just in case. She'd written under her mother's maiden name, Hobbs, instead.

Would either Big Al or Thirza have wanted anything to do with Lucy had they known who she really was? Probably not. Did hiding the truth from them bother me? Yes, especially with regard to Thirza. I'd given a solemn undertaking to never, ever deceive her again. If she were to learn the truth about Lucy, then Thirza and I would be history – for keeps.

So why did I lie to them? I think it was because when I looked at Lucy I saw a six-year-old girl who had discovered her mother dead in a bath of blood. I wanted to help her. At least that's how I justified it to myself. The plasma telly? That was just an aberration.

*

'Wow! It's a monster,' said Lucy, eyeing the plasma colossus that dominated my living room. It's even bigger than I thought it'd be. I tell you what, Daddy'd love one of these. D'you know, I bet he'd buy it off you. D'you want me to ask him?'

'Er, no thanks,' I said, with as much feigned insouciance as possible. 'You're all right.'

'I can't believe they just gave it to you, that PR company.'

'Yeah, well, they owed me a favour. A big one. I got their client on the front of *The Insider*.'

I'd told the story so often by then that even I was beginning to believe it. Hadn't I promised myself I was done with dishonesty and deception? Was I pathologically incapable of taking my own counsel? Maybe I didn't trust me. Perhaps that was it. But what the hell was I meant to do about *that*? See a shrink? A priest?

'It's so thin,' she said, inspecting the back of it. 'It's like half of it's missing. What's the picture like?'

I picked up the remote. A second later the TV burst into life.

'Wow! It comes straight on, like magic.' She was open-mouthed and her palms were raised as if in worship. 'So you don't have to wait for it to warm up?'

'Nope. Hey, where d'you want to go?' I asked, keen to get as far away from that damned telly as I could, as quickly as possible. I'd been unable to bring myself to watch anything on it since Rollo had had it delivered a fortnight earlier. Every time I walked into the living room that monster seemed to fix me with its evil eye, and it was even worse when I turned it on, because then I could feel it slowly extracting my soul. For his part, Emdel – my oldest friend, flatmate and an all-round brainbox – had been stuck in front of it pretty much solidly since its arrival.

'Where do I want to go?' Lucy repeated abstractly. 'What about your favourite local?'

'What, the Barley Mow? That's an old man's pub. You'd hate it.'

It was also the pub that Thirza lived above – with Blanche, its landlady. If Thirza saw me out drinking with Lucy she'd probably do her nut. Lucy had been on the paper for less than a week. What possible motive could I have for wining and dining her, other than the obvious? Not that there'd be much by way of dining in the Mow, unless you counted crisps or nuts.

'I know a nice little pub,' I added. 'Quiet, out of the way.'

'You're worried about being seen out with me, aren't you?' Lucy poked me and laughed. 'C'mon, admit it.' She continued poking and laughing. 'You are, I can tell.'

'Yeah, well, people might get the wrong idea, not least your dad. Have you told him it's me you're meeting?'

'Well, I would have, only—'

'And there we have it. What if he saw us heading for the Mow? He'd go nuclear on my arse, and don't try and tell me otherwise.'

'Oh, stop it. Daddy's just a teddy bear.'

Yeah, right, I thought, and about as cuddly as my cholla cactus.

'Llew, all we'll be doing is talking work. There's tons I need to learn about this job. I'm hungry for knowledge, and knowledge is power. You know that, right?'

'Yeah, and ignorance is bliss. C'mon, let's shoot. I'm taking you to the quiet pub. End of.'

*

Lucy's head was lying on my shoulder as we sat and watched the waves swish lazily back and forth over the pebbles. The May moon was bright and insanely large, as if it were on a collision course with Earth. It floodlit the becalmed Solent, its light casting a giant frosted triangular beam across the water. This narrowed to a point on the horizon, either side of which the lights of Ryde twinkled in the darkness.

'I'm sorry, Llew,' Lucy said, nestling even closer. 'This is why I usually avoid alcohol. I don't know why I drank so much tonight.'

'S'okay,' I said, feeling far from okay.

I still hadn't fully processed what had just happened. I'm not sure there is any processing that kind of thing. We had been walking along the beach, discussing our respective childhoods. Knowing what I did about her mother, I had tried changing the subject, but she had ploughed on regardless. Having mentioned her mother's suicide, she had begun crying, gently at first, but then – from nowhere – she had given a gut-wrenching howl, shocking dozens of gulls off their perches on the groynes and up into the sky. On and on she screamed until she had drawn a small crowd. They leaned on the promenade railings, looking down on her display of incoherent distress. Some were laughing, thinking it some kind of drunken joke. I tried to calm her, but she shoved me away. She was unreachable.

'But it's not okay, is it?' Lucy said, her voice muffled by the crook of my neck. 'Behaving like that. You must be wondering what kind of mad woman you've hired to your team.'

'I'm not thinking that at all. Look, Lucy, I know what it is to be messed up, believe me. That business with Skinner's goons? Did you know I was holed up in a B&B for weeks after that? Just over there, it was,' I said, pointing towards the looming Georgian terrace that flanked the promenade on the far side of the road. 'I was too terrified to set foot outside. If it hadn't been for Thirza I might still be in there now. That Skinner stuff? It still haunts me. Always will.'

'I *am* messed up, aren't I?'

'Look, I don't know you that well, and it's really not my place to pry into this deeply personal stuff of yours, but can I ask – have you talked to anyone about your problems?' She shook her head. 'Only, what you went through, and at that age, that's a lot for anyone to process, even with help.'

'I've got Daddy.' She said it almost as an afterthought.

'So you talk to him about what happened? The effect it's had on you?'

'Not exactly, no.'

'There must be someone you can talk to.'

She sat up and turned to face me. He tear-dampened hair was smeared across half her face like kelp. She peeled it back.

'I'm talking to you now, aren't I.'

'Well, yeah, but I meant someone who's qualified. Someone who's got training in—'

'All you need is ears, Llew.' She cupped my face in her hands and tugged at my lobes, sending shivers down each flank. 'I've just been waiting for the right pair, that's all.'

She stood up, readjusted her skirt and sat down again, crossed-legged, facing me. She rested her hands in her lap, palms up, and closed her eyes as if she was meditating. When she opened her eyes they had a faraway look.

'When you're a toddler,' she said, 'whatever is in front of you at any given moment, that's your entire world, right?'

'Yeah, I guess.'

'Nothing exists beyond that picture, until the picture changes and then that new picture, that becomes your new entire world. And on and on and on it goes, like you're building a jigsaw.'

'I hadn't thought of it like that.'

'So tell me – at what age are we meant to start joining together all those pictures into something that tells a story?'

'I don't know. Seven? Eight? It probably depends on the pictures.'

'Well, I'm twenty-one, Llew, and I can't make much sense of the world around me. I put on a good show of pretending I can, but inside … I'm lost. I can't see what my story is meant to look like. When I think I'm getting somewhere – when I think I'm starting to understand who I might be – I end up right back at the beginning, at that moment when I found my mother in the bath.'

She turned and stared out to sea, her gaze drawn to the silvery slash of moonlit surf. We sat in silence for a time.

'All I know about my story is that it has a beginning,' she said quietly. 'It's got no middle that I can see, and as for the end …'

She fell silent again and swallowed heavily.

I reached across and took her hands in mine. Her tears splashed my fingers like soft summer rain.

'I can't see where I'm headed,' she said, sniffling. 'I'm lost in my own story.'

I tried to think of something – anything – helpful to say, but it all seemed trite, and so I said nothing. Instead, I pulled her close.

'Llew,' she said, her voice muffled in the fabric of my shirt, 'I can't be alone tonight. I mustn't be alone,' she added in a whisper.

FOUR

'LET ME GET THIS STRAIGHT,' I said as Lucy lay beside me in bed reading the Sunday papers. 'Your dad's looking to break into the rave scene? *Your dad?*'

'Yeah.' She held up the paper to show me the feature she was reading, about the UK's huge house-music club culture. 'It's all he's been talking about for weeks.'

'Seriously? First of all, his taste in music stops at Elvis and Tony Bennett. Second, he hates drugs – despises them. And to cap it all, he's a recovering alcoholic.'

'He's says he'll be fine with people turning up out of their heads, but that he'll not stand for any dealing on the premises. As for booze, I don't think it's in his plans. He says the real margins are to be had on bottled water. Ravers on ecstasy drink tons of water, so he says.'

'And he knows all this how?'

'Er, well, you know the past few Saturdays when I couldn't see you?'

I nodded, all ears.

'Yeah, I was sort of out, with Daddy, at that big club up near the motorway. I drove him.'

She was forever ferrying Rollo about.

'*What?* You were out clubbing? With your dad?'

'It was research. He took a notebook and everything.'

'You're talking about that huge place up in Hilsea, on the site of the old aerodrome?'

'Yeah, Derek's. It's an old aircraft hanger. I'm telling you, it's cool. It was mobbed, even though it's a right old schlep to get there. There must've been over a thousand clubbers, all going bananas. Terrible name, though. Who calls a club Derek's?'

'Someone called Derek, presumably – unless it's some kind of postmodern thing. Anyway, what the hell? When were you going to mention all this?'

'Er, I just did.'

'So where's he gonna hold these raves of his, your dad? In his garages?'

'Very funny.'

'Seriously, where though? I bet that airfield place cost a fortune. All those licences for drink, safety, entertainment ... and then there's insurance, not to mention set-up costs. The sound systems they use in those places would put Motörhead to shame.'

'S'true,' she chirruped. 'The music's so loud it feels like it's coming from inside of you.' She beat her chest. 'It's brilliant.'

'So how will he afford all that? I know he's resourceful and all, and he can clearly run a business, legal or otherwise, but there's no way—'

'Daddy's not a crook.'

'I didn't call him a crook.'

'You implied it.'

'Look, I'm not going to tiptoe around you on this subject, okay. What your dad does is not legal, however you slice it. And you being part of *The Tribune* investigations team? That's a massive conflict of interests right there. Rollo is exactly the sort of story we ought to be looking into. But we're not, are we. We're complicit.'

I was running the best-funded investigative print journalism team outside of the nationals. We even had our own logo and motto – a sword crossed diagonally in front of a shield. *The sword of truth and the shield of fair play*. It was trumpeted atop every investigation we ran. And who'd been my most recent recruit to the team? The daughter of one of the biggest crooks in Southsea's history.

'Yeah, 'cos you're so squeaky clean, aren't you,' Lucy countered with a Thirza-style poke in the chest, minus the violent intent.

It was a fair point, well made.

'People change,' I said. 'I've changed. I'm not like that any more.' That damned telly loomed large in my head, every one of its wretched forty-two inches mocking my words. 'But your dad?' I added. 'He'll never change.'

She threw down the paper and thumped the pillow with a fist. 'I don't *want* him to change, thank you *very* much.'

It's difficult to convey much anger by slamming a newspaper down on a quilt, or a fist into a pillow, but somehow she managed it.

'Anyway,' Lucy added when she was done making forceful points with bedding materials. There was a slight pause, which she filled with a little cough and a sideways glance. 'I'm not exactly sure that he'll be bothering with all that licensing stuff.'

Of course he bloody won't, I thought. How could it be otherwise? This is Rollo bleeding Baer we're talking about, a man who wouldn't know 'legal' if smacked him about his lambchop-carpeted jowls with a rotting codfish.

'Right, stop there,' I said, holding up a palm like a traffic cop. 'I don't wanna hear any more. This conversation? We didn't have it. None of it happened. We know nothing about your dad opening an illegal rave gaff. Nothing. Got it?'

'What rave gaff?' she asked with a wink and a lopsided grin.

I was hit by a surge of affection for her. She truly is all things to all people, I thought. It's an amazing gift. I see a lot of myself in her.

*

Rollo turned his wheelchair full circle in the middle of the derelict hall, a fat smile on his lips.

'Well, whaddya think?' he said, looking from Lucy to me. 'Brilliant, eh? S'perfect, ain't it.'

'It's a shithole,' I said, nose scrunched as I sucked at the musty air. 'You've got me for an hour and not a second longer,' I told him. 'So what d'you want me doing?'

We were inside his proposed rave venue and I was there under extreme protest.

'Please,' Lucy had begged me days earlier, hands clasped in supplication. 'Daddy needs us to help him clean the place up.'

I had fixed her with a steely glare. 'So tell me, what happened to us knowing nothing about this rave crap of your dad's, eh? Now here you are, asking me to help him to prep the place for bloody lift-off. Are you out of your mind?'

'He's in a wheelchair, Llew, in case you hadn't noticed.'

'What's that got to do with anything? Dalek Davros had a body that ran on casters but that didn't stop him waging war on the universe.'

'Are you comparing Daddy to a Dalek?'

'I'm saying he's breaking the law, whether he's on wheels or not. Disability's not the issue here. My credibility as a journalist, that's what's at stake. My job – and yours by the way.'

'Oh, don't give me that old crap. You and Daddy were business partners for God's sake, unless you've forgotten. You were happy enough to pocket his money back then.'

'I told you, I've changed. That's not me any more.'

She sidled up to me, placing her hands flat against my chest and giving me a look of such plaintiveness that resistance was futile.

'Spare me the Princess Di eyes,' I told her. It's not gonna work.'

'Right, Sabler,' barked Rollo, rolling across the stinking hall towards me. 'We'll have you doing some honest work for a change – toughen up those girly hands of yours. See that pile of old carpets over there?' He pointed at a hillock of filthy carpets and disintegrating underlay. 'Lump all that in the hire van would ya, then take it up the tip.'

Eleven hours later I collapsed into my bed, having first showered off half a kilo of dust and filth. My hands were raw with blisters from the endless sweeping up, and all the humping and bumping I'd done had left my back feeling as though I'd been given an epidural of Araldite.

Lucy collapsed down next to me.

'Thank you,' she said wearily, brushing my cheek with a kiss. She draped an arm over my chest. 'Daddy really appreciates it.' I got another peck. 'And so do I.'

'Just don't ask me again,' I said. 'Ever. Okay?'

She gave me a three-fingered salute. 'Guides honour.'

'Mmm, I think I'd like to have seen you in a Guides uniform.'

'Pervert. But seriously, Llew, it means a lot, you helping out. And c'mon, admit it, you must be at least a little bit reassured, having seen the place and the area.'

Grudgingly, I had to admit she was right on that score; Rollo was nothing if not thorough. It was why he'd never been arrested for anything. The venue for his off-grid rave venture was an old Co-op dance hall in the run-down Fratton area of the city. But it wasn't just the hall that was derelict – the entire area was. The streets around the hall were deserted, the residents having been relocated. Row upon row of late-Victorian terraced housing sat empty, boarded up, awaiting demolition. It was part of the city council's urban renewal plan to reinvigorate a neighbourhood that had been in steady decline since the war. A shopping centre and supermarket were to replace the doomed homes. It all meant there were no residents within earshot of Rollo's proposed club – no residents to draw unwanted attention from the authorities by complaining about noise, drunken fights or cretins urinating through their letterboxes.

Even better – for Rollo at least – the old hall had last been used as a recording studio and practice rooms, meaning it was soundproofed, so any noise that did leak out wouldn't carry beyond the ghost streets. And as if all that wasn't enough, Rollo's venue was slap bang in the middle of the city, unlike Derek's, which was a taxi ride away, up near the M27.

'So how'd you come across this place?' I asked Rollo when I returned from my jaunt to the tip with the carpets.

'My mate Jimmy,' he said. 'You remember him?'

'As in Jimmy who stole Skinner's porn,' I said, 'and lied to you about it? As in Jimmy who almost got us killed? *That* Jimmy?'

Rollo looked away, and gave a little cough. 'Yeah, well, that junkie won't be turning me over again any time soon.'

Or walking properly, I thought, for Rollo had had Jimmy's legs broken as a little thank you for his deceit. I'd bumped into Jimmy during his convalescence. He was in a wheelchair, being pushed along the seafront by his elderly mother. His legs jutted out before him, a white-plaster V-shape, propped up on footrests.

'Anyway,' continued Rollo, 'Jimmy's Ma used to live in one of the streets round this here Co-op hall, one of them what they're demolishing. A few months back, shortly before they moved everyone out, I popped up here to visit her, 'cos I'd heard she was real upset about having to leave. Well, after I was done visiting her, I came out of her place and stood in front of this old hall for a bit, reliving some memories. And that's when I had the raves idea.'

Rollo went on to explain that his plans for the place included using the old upstairs practice rooms as chill-out areas.

'You know, with cushions and shit,' he said. 'For when folk get too hot or tired from all that raving.'

As I lay in bed next to Lucy, on the cusp of exhausted sleep, I tried wiping my mind of Rollo and his plans for the illicit club. I'd have no more to do with it, and Lucy had promised that neither would she. And yet as I drifted into sleep, fear settled about me like a mist. The reality was, there's never any wiping one's mind completely free of someone like Rollo Baer, especially not when you're sleeping with his precious daughter.

FIVE

WOMEN ARE EMOTIONAL CREATURES, AND for this I give praise to every single deity that may, or may not, exist. Why? Because if it were left to men, emotion would go the way of the dodo and the woolly mammoth. We'd be reduced to reading about it in books.

We need look no further than the nature of obsession to see the truth of this. A woman's obsessions invariably involve some sort of relationship, and relationships are driven by emotion. She will obsess about a man, a friendship, a familial tie, maybe even a pet. Humans are social beings, like bees and ants. We're designed to be outward looking, and it's no coincidence that evolution has entrusted this most important function to women, not men.

That's because when the male of the species becomes obsessed, the object of his obsession will be either sex (lust doesn't count as an emotion) or *stuff*. Things. Diesel locomotives. Real ale. Birds of Britain and Ireland. Tanks of world war two. The names of British football stadiums. Or, in Emdel's case, computer hacking.

I don't know much about computers. The internet had been around for four or five years by that time but I still didn't really get it. I didn't know how it works because I didn't care to know. It didn't interest me. What interests me as a man is, er, well ... sex and grammar. But for Emdel, how the internet works had become the centre of his universe. It was all he thought about. His idea of relaxing was to hack into some blue-chip firm's website.

'You don't hack websites,' I can hear him telling me as I write this. 'You hack servers.'

He was very particular about the terminology of what it was he did, which I totally get, because hacking was kind of his job then. As head of computer security at JCN, it was Emdel's responsibility to protect the company's digital assets from people like himself. What I couldn't quite fathom was whether Emdel became head of security because he was a hacker, or if he became a hacker because he was head of security. Perhaps it was a bit of both. Something else that's less than crystal was the legality of what he did.

It got to the point where most of my conversations with Emdel would go something like this:

'What're you up to there, Emdel?'

'Hacking Motorola's servers.'

'Isn't that kind of, you know, illegal?'

'It's how security works. A hacker gets into your system and then he offers to fix the vulnerability for you, for a substantial fee of course. But this is what JCN pays me to do. I'm like their own personal hacker.'

'Why don't you stick with JCN's computers? Why d'you have to hack into other companies?'

'I learn more that way.'

I'm not sure Emdel's reasoning would stand up in a court of law, but that really was pretty much all he did, both at work and home. And it didn't stop there either. He was also into social engineering, big time.

'What even is that?' I asked him when he first mentioned the practice.

'It's when you manipulate people into giving you information they shouldn't be giving you – like computer passwords or private telephone numbers,' he explained.

'Surely only an idiot would cough up that kind of info?'

'Really? I bet I can get your boss's password off her with a single phone call.'

'What, Daphne? No way. She's way too smart for that.'

'It's not a question of smart, it's a question of trust. People are basically very trusting. That's what the hacker exploits. The weakest point of any system is always the people using it. A tenner says that by this time tomorrow I've got her password. You on?'

'Too right I'm on. You've not got a hope in hell.'

Next day, Emdel slapped a scrap of paper down in front of me as I ate my tea. 'There you go – mrtibbs1964,' he said.

'What's this?'

'Our bet, yesterday. That's Daphne's password. I've now got full access to *The Tribune*'s servers. I could go in there and delete your entire website if I wanted. Or I could copy some choice emails and make them public. You might want to mention to your boss that in future she shouldn't be so trusting of strangers.'

I stared at the scribbled password like it was some kind of black magic. 'I don't get it,' I said. 'How'd you do it?'

He was right; it had been easy. He'd phoned Daphne, posing as a computer security consultant. He told her it had been me who suggested he call her – that he and I had a mutual friend, Emdel Black.

'I've heard Llew mention Emdel,' Daphne had said. 'What did you say your name was?'

'Scott McNair,' Emdel said.

'McNair? How funny. That's my surname. We might be related.'

'So you're not a McNair by marriage, then?'

'No, I'm divorced. It's my maiden name.'

'Get down, Sylvester!' Emdel had shouted. 'Ow!'

'Are you okay?' a puzzled Daphne had asked.

'It's just my cat letting me know he's hungry. I work from home.'

'Sylvester? Great name. I love cats. I've got a tabby.'

'Same here. Boy or girl?'

'Boy. Mr Tibbs.'

After that, Emdel had started banging on about computer servers and security patches and stuff he knew was way over Daphne's head. She'd lost interest and the call had fizzled out.

I looked at the piece of paper again. 'How did you know Daphne had a cat?'

'You mentioned it.'

'Really? I can't remember that.'

'And what about the 1964 part? How'd you get that?'

'I tried 'mrtibbs' and 'mcnair' with every year from 1930 to 1970. It took about ten minutes to crack. Most passwords are a combination of year-of-birth plus maiden name, pet's name or child's name. For blokes it might be a favourite sports team.'

'You should be working in a circus.'

'These are life skills,' he said. 'I run in-house training at JCN on social engineering so that our people don't fall prey to it.'

'Here's your tenner,' I said, slipping it from my wallet.

'Cheers. Hey, wanna watch some box? *Dirty Harry*'s on shortly.'

'Nah,' I said, swatting away his invitation like it were a bluebottle. 'I'm gonna read.'

'I don't get it,' he said. 'In our old gaff we had that shitty box with the fuzzy picture and you lived in front of it. Now you've got the best TV in the world and yet you never want to watch it. Why is that?'

'Because back then I wrote all my stories on a typewriter,' I said, scratching around for an answer. 'Now that I'm on a computer screen, watching telly feels too much like work.'

He shook his head, clearly unconvinced, and slipped away to watch a sneering Clint Eastwood blast holes in people.

SIX

LUCY WAS AS GOOD AS her word: she stepped away from helping Rollo prep his nightclub for launch. She also stopped pressurising *stroke* emotionally blackmailing *stroke* guilting me into helping him. She told Rollo she could no longer help him, explaining that her being a *Tribune* reporter meant she could ill afford to be associated with an unlicenced rave venue.

'I said it could cost me my job,' she told me. 'And yours.'

'Mine?'

'Yeah,' she said. 'Don't sound so surprised. You make it sound like he'd happily throw you to the wolves.'

Of course he would, I thought. The only reason he won't is because he knows if he did then his daughter might also end up as wolf food.

'D'you know what he's planning to call it, his rave venue?' I asked, keen to move things along before we got dragged into another ill-tempered debate about Rollo's shady career choices.

We were strolling along Clarence Parade, stabbing wooden forks into bags of vinegar-sodden chips.

'The Crystal Rooms,' she said. 'Apparently that was the original name of the place, back when it was a dance hall.'

'S'better than Derek's, that's for sure, but how's he gonna attract punters?'

I imagined the place with a big neon sign outside and of it being encircled by screeching cops cars before a single raver had even set foot inside.

'He's paying a few Metal Estate kids he knows to do some leafleting,' explained Lucy. 'The next few Saturday nights they're heading up to Derek's to hand out flyers to ravers waiting for taxis back into town. Here,' she said, reaching inside her tan moleskin jacket. 'Take a look.'

She handed me one of the flyers. 'The Crystal Rooms' it read. 'Pompey's new town centre rave venue. Secret location. Head for Besant Road, from 10pm, Sat 14th June. A pleasure steward will guide you to us. £5 entry.'

'A pleasure steward?' I said. 'What the hell is that? It sounds pornographic.'

'It's just someone pointing, but Daddy thought people'll be intrigued,' said Lucy.

'D'you think they'll come?'

'I would, wouldn't you? Why spend a fortune on a minicab to and from Derek's when you can walk to a brilliant club in town?'

'Yeah, that's assuming The Crystal Rooms actually is brilliant. I still say your old man is more tea dance than rave. I just can't see it going anywhere.'

What I had wanted to say was that I *hoped* it wouldn't go anywhere. Nay, *prayed*. I wanted The Crystal Rooms to be stillborn, a spectacular failure. I wanted Rollo's hall to be pulverised by a wrecking ball, and a soulless shopping mall called Fountains or Cascades built in its stead. I wanted a normal life – a life in which a 42-inch plasma screen didn't haunt my leisure hours; a life in which my reputation as a journalist wasn't forever hanging by a gossamer thread; a life that could be lived openly and honestly, without recourse to deception and deceit. A life in which my secret girlfriend's crooked father wasn't about to roll a hand grenade into the murky world of Pompey's nightlife.

*

'No, Lucy,' I said, pacing my bedroom, naked. 'One million per cent no. I'm not going, and nor are you. That's final. Why's this conversation even happening? You said you were having nothing more to do with The Crystal Rooms and now here you are, talking about going to the opening bloody night.'

'But Llew, listen, you don't understand, Daddy is—'

I loomed over her as she lay in bed and placed an index finger to her lips. 'Shh, shh, shh. Not another word.'

She lay there, eyes darting this way and that, propped up on her elbows, her body taut as a drum.

'Listen to me. I'm going to overcook some eggs,' I continued, digit still on her lips. 'And I shall burn some toast and make a cup of tea and then we're going to have breakfast in bed and talk about normal things, like normal people. Okay?'

*

I didn't dance until my fifth can of Coke, and even then it was more of a shuffle than a dance. As I plonked my feet here and there I realised that up to that point I'd only ever danced when drunk. Sober, dancing felt like a bad dream, like finding yourself naked outside Woolworths on Christmas Eve afternoon. Plus I didn't care for the booming music that was threatening to rearrange my internal organs. But Lucy had made me dance. She had wrenched me from my cushion in one of Rollo's chill-out rooms, where I had been sulking and brooding and suffering an endless stream of ecstasy-fuelled ravers telling me how much they loved me, man. In truth, being naked outside Woolworths was the better option.

I may have been shuffling on the dance floor but Lucy most certainly was not. She was going mental – like someone had plugged her into the National Grid. Everyone was. It was like some kind of collective dervish hysteria. I'd never seen dancing like it. Disco. Punk. Post-punk. Two-tone. New Romantic – it didn't matter what the genre of music was, the dancing was always choreographed and prescriptive, the moves preordained: hand-rolling, pogoing, windmilling, running on the spot, poncing. But this? This was visceral. People seemed to be breathing it, feeling it, living it. The only common thread was chaos.

'C'mon, Llew,' Lucy screamed in my ear so loudly she pierced my eardrum. 'You can do better than that. You're shuffling about like an old man.'

She grabbed my hands and dragged my arms up above my head before grinding into me, her hips gyrating like it was a Michael Jackson video. She was right – I may as well have been wearing a cardigan and smoking a pipe, so out of place was I amid the writhing, seething mass of steaming-hot bodies.

I pulled her head to mine. 'I want to go home,' I screamed. 'I'm leaving, with or without you.'

She bookended my cheeks with the palms of her hands and squashed my lips with a fat kiss. 'Okay, see you later. Love you.'

With that, she danced off into the throng, yee-hawing, one arm aloft and gyrating like crazy.

Leaving The Crystal Rooms was easier said than done. I had to walk sideways, arms up, to make any progress. Eventually I reached the foyer. It was one thirty in the morning and people were still queueing to get in. I took in the scene. The club was so full that Rollo's door staff were operating a one in, one out policy. Every now and then they'd talk urgently into walkie-talkies.

My eye was drawn to man in a turquoise shell suit and basketball shoes who was leaning against a wall. A girl in her late teens approached him and handed over some cash. He reached into his pocket and slipped something into her hand. I'd seen the same scene play out dozens of times earlier throughout the club. It had to be ecstasy. Quite why the dealers all wore sports gear was lost on me. They didn't strike me as cardio-fit sorts. I slipped past him, and out.

The cool night air was a tonic at first, but soon it was drawing the heat from me, chilling my sweat-slathered skin – and I hadn't even been dancing. Most everyone else in the joint had been sodden, as if caught in a downpour. When I left Lucy she looked like an entrant in a wet T-shirt competition.

During the mile-and-a-half walk from Fratton to Southsea I

pondered the night's events. Whichever way you sliced it, Rollo's rave venture was a runaway success. It was hard to say how many people had been crammed into the place, but I guessed it had be around five hundred. At a fiver a head, that was £2,500. Then there was drinks. Rollo was right – most people were guzzling water like they'd been wandering lost in the Kalahari for days. Water was a quid for a small bottle, and he must have sold thousands. People were buying two, three at a time. It was a licence to print money.

As for that liver-quivering sound system of his, that must have cost a pretty penny, but if the first night was to be any guide then it wouldn't take him long to recoup that outlay. As for overheads? He didn't have many. There was a DJ, and some people on the door and behind the bar, but that was about it. He had no licences to buy, nor safety inspections to pass, and although the club had mains power and running water, there was no way it was legit. The place was strictly off-grid. How he had secured power and water I had no idea. People like Rollo always seem to know a bloke who knows a geezer who can take care of that kind of stuff.

I did the maths. Jesus Christ, I thought, in ten weeks he'll have cleared twenty grand. If he gets lucky, he might pocket over a hundred and fifty thou in a calendar year.

You had to hand it to Rollo: he knew an opportunity when he saw it, and he had the wherewithal to act decisively and intelligently to wring every penny from that opportunity. He was also a master at operating in the shadows. On that opening night, as The Crystal Rooms had filled with ravers, Rollo was present and yet invisible. He was ensconced in an upstairs office at the end of the hall that fed into the chill-out rooms. He'd kept the door locked, but via a walkie-talkie he was in constant touch with his crew, orchestrating, deploying, advising and demanding. A puppet master; an Action Man with Pinocchio legs.

*

Lucy rolled in at 5 a.m. She looked ridiculously fresh and vital, as if she'd been for an early morning jog along the front. She kicked off her shoes and climbed up on to the end of the bed. Then she dropped to her knees and straddled me, pinning me under the quilt. It sparked flashbacks of Freddie and Herr Porno and that awful night when only my cactus had saved me. I shoved her off and she crashed to the floor.

'Hey,' she said, sitting up and rubbing an elbow. 'Don't be like that. I was about to seduce you.'

'For chrissake, you scared the crap out of me. And you might have come home with me,' I added, all surly. 'The only reason I went in the first place was to please you. And I hope you didn't walk home on your own.'

'Course not. I shared a cab with Daddy. Hey grumpy chops, I've got something for you.'

She pulled her cotton vest up over her head to reveal perfect half-grapefruit breasts that were exquisitely squished by a Wonderbra. She removed the bra, and pressed her breasts together with her hands.

'Helloooo, Llew,' she cooed, slow and smoky, gyrating like she had in the club. Resistance was futile.

Later, as we lay wrapped in a post-coital cuddle, Lucy revealed how Rollo had been furious at the end of the night. She was waiting for him in his office as he counted the night's takings.

'What the hell does he have to be angry about?' I asked. 'It couldn't have gone any better for him.'

'Did you see those guys in shell suits dotted about the place selling drugs?'

I nodded.

'Well, we saw those same men at Derek's when I took Daddy up there on his field trips. Actually, truth be told, I bought a little something from one of them on the sly.'

'You were on ecstasy? Well, that explains it.'

'Explains what?'

'The crazy dancing. You were like a woman possessed. In the Middle Ages they'd have burnt you at the stake.'

She levered herself up on to one elbow. 'Seriously, Llew, I'm telling you, you've *got* to try it. It's amazing. It makes you feel – I don't know – like you're at one with the world, like everyone's your friend.'

'Yeah, I know it does. I was on the sharp end of all that E-love in one of those chill-out rooms. It was interminable.'

'And the music,' she continued, looking to the heavens. 'The music feel like it's ... like it's coming from inside you ... like it's part of you. Honestly, you'd love it. I know you would.'

There was no way I was setting foot in that club ever again, and certainly not while off my face on E. My days of hedonism were behind me. Time for a sidestep.

'So what's your dad got planned for those dealers?'

'Yeah, so you know that judo club, the one that's based in the Scout hall near the Metal Estate?'

I nodded. Back in my *Probe* days I'd interviewed the guy who ran it. He was a Hollywood movie fight co-ordinator, and a tenth dan master. *The Bruce Lee of judo* had been the headline.

'Well, Daddy was at school with the guy who runs that place, and he's gonna to ask him if he'll do security – him and some of his black belt students.'

'So he's going to war with the drug dealers from Derek's? Is that what you're saying?'

'Kind of, I guess.'

'That makes no sense at all. I mean, you said it yourself. It's the ecstasy that makes people dance and drink water. Without it, you're left with a load of old stiffs like me, shuffling about like it's a school disco.'

'You know Daddy. He hates drugs – always has. He's had friends die from overdoses. Uncle Jimmy's a user, I'm sure of it.'

Uncle Jimmy? Jesus Christ, I thought. Some families.

'But you're right,' she added. 'It *is* the E that makes things tick, and Daddy knows that – but he's convinced that most people arrive at the place already high. I was.'

'Were you?'

'Yeah, I dropped it before we left.'

'Did Rollo know you were off your face,?'

'Of course he did. There's no hiding it, even when you're coming down. He made me promise I'd never do it again.'

'And did you – promise?'

'No. Truth is, I can't wait to do it again. He wasn't happy, but I had to be honest with him. It's kind of a rule we've always had, me and him.'

How novel, I thought.

'Anyway,' she continued, 'Daddy asked me where I got it, the E, and when I told him, his eyes lit up. See, he figures that when the judo guys have cleared out those dealers, then people will start stocking up on Es at Derek's on a Friday, so they can party at The Crystal Rooms the following night.'

'That's ridiculous. He's not got a crystal ball. He can't possibly know things'll play out like that.'

She gave me a smug little grin. 'Can't he? The money he took tonight? Llew, it filled a massive holdall. It was like something from a heist movie. I'd say he knows what he's doing.'

SEVEN

'BANDIT, YOU LOVELY BOY,' SAID Big Al, grinning and waving a folded sheet of paper in the air as he approached the Investigations desk. 'I've got something for you.'

A Consulate was glued to his lower lip. He was totally sold on their health benefits, claiming the menthol-impregnated filter 'helps shift all that gunk'. Somehow, the drooping ash at the cigarette's tip always remained attached as he walked and talked. It was a gift he had.

'What've you got there, Al?' I asked, looking up from my keyboard.

'Read it,' he said, handing it to me.

It was a sheet of folded A4 on which was printed a single paragraph of text: *You lot are always banging your drum about 'swords of truth' and 'shields of fair play', but you never investigate anything proper, like our corrupt police force, with all its Freemasons. Call yourselves journalists? You're bloody useless.*

'There was no name, or address?' I asked.

'Nothing,' said Big Al.

'D'you think it's a crackpot?'

'I don't think so. It's too specific. Besides, crackpots tend to use all caps.'

It was true: most crazy readers letters to newspapers tended to be written or typed entirely in capital letters, as if the person was shouting.

'So who, then?'

'Dunno,' said Big Al. 'Disgruntled cop, maybe?'

'You think? And what about the Masons thing? D'you know much about them?'

'What I know, Bandit, is that when it comes to the law, those bastards are everywhere. Back in the late sixties, when I was a reporter on a paper up in Humberside, I got a lead on a Masons–cop story and it was like smashing my head against a wall. Even my own editor told me to drop it. It was funny handshakes all round. I hate those bastards, the Masons. They stand for everything we don't: secrecy, lies, self-interest. Tell you what, Bandit, why don't you hit the library? Bone up on them, then we'll have a chat a bit further down the road, see if there's anything we can do.'

Big Al's ash skills deserted him in that moment. The sagging grey tip of his cigarette came free and tumbled down my face. I breathed some in and began coughing like a consumptive. Lucy laughed, as did Andy Devine and Larry Skirton, the other two members of my team.

Andy had been one of twenty-three applicants for a berth on Investigations and I had hired him because he was super-smart and super-qualified. He was a Cambridge modern languages graduate, fluent in French, German and Spanish, with conversational Italian for good measure. He'd joined from Reuters in London because his American girlfriend, an art therapist, had landed a job with the NHS in Portsmouth, and he had followed her down to the south coast. Andy was the very picture of urbanity, with a pinch of David Niven and a dash of Dirk Bogarde. The ladies adored him, and when you're asking awkward questions, that never hurts.

If Andy was silk, then Larry was sackcloth. He was tall and imposing, with intense eyes set beneath a heavy brow. He had the air of an enforcer, also useful when sticking your foot inside a closing door. I'd met him at a press conference held by a newly launched housing association, founded to help ex-servicemen, where he'd plonked himself down in the seat next to me.

'I suppose I better ask your bloody name,' he'd said. 'Hang on a second,' he added, slapping my chest with the back of his hand. 'I know you. You're Llew Sabler, the geezer who was up for crapping on an altar. Brother, I got some great mileage out of you. Did I ever.'

It transpired that Larry was a freelance journalist, specialising in crime. He spent most of his time in courtrooms, filling notebook after notebook with his one hundred and twenty words-per-minute shorthand. His customers were mainly the national papers, but he also sold pieces to radio and TV news teams along the south coast, pieces such as the degenerate hack who was arrested on suspicion of crapping on an altar, to drum up some copy on a slow news day.

'The charges were dropped,' I reminded him. 'The priest whose altar it was came forward, if you recall.'

'Yeah, then you got attacked, right, by that Skinner fella, but you nailed him with that blackmail yarn of yours. Good work, by the way. And then, as I recall, you kind of disappeared. *Pooof*. Just like that. Fella, you were hot property for a time. Everyone wanted a piece of you. You've no idea how hard I tried to track you down. Some ball-breaker on your old rag – what was it, *The Probe*? – threatened to sort me out if I bothered her again.'

'That'll have been Thirza.'

'Fella, I'm telling you, I flogged so much copy off the back of your antics it paid for the deposit on my flat. No word of a lie. I kind of feel like I owe you a debt of gratitude.'

'I'm glad I was able to help. Say' – I gestured at the sparsely attended event – 'this isn't your usual beat. Aren't the courts more your thing? Murder, rape, assault, fraud?'

'Yeah, well, my old man's a retired submariner. He never really settled back into civvy street. He's living on benefits in some low-life B&B in Gosport. I'm kinda hoping that if I can do this here housing mob a few favours – you know, with coverage and shit – I might be able to swing my dad a new gaff. Somewhere half-decent. Here,' he added, slapping my knee. 'Let me buy you a drink after. Seriously, I owe you.'

At the pub Larry was horrified to learn I'd given up booze.

'Never trust a man who doesn't drink,' he said. 'It means he's either uptight, a bore, or both.'

And so I'd gotten steaming drunk with Larry, and by the end of a marathon session he had accepted my offer of a job on *The Tribune*. It saved having to advertise the post, and with his courtroom know-how and fat contacts book he'd be a real asset to the team.

'It'll be nice being back in papers,' he'd said. 'Papers are my first love, and you never forget a first love.'

'Oi, Larry,' said Big Al, grinning at the sight of me spitting ash into a wastepaper basket. 'I hear it's your birthday, big man.'

'Yeah, that's right, Al. Twenty-nine years young.'

'Here.' Al fished out his wallet and handed a few notes to Lucy. 'John, you lovely girl, you're in charge of the kitty. Make sure these ugly herberts get back from the boozer in one piece.'

'Sure thing, Al,' said Lucy, smiling. She loved him calling her John, as she knew only favoured females were addressed that way.

'Thanks, Al,' I said, 'but I don't drink any more.'

'Course he bloody does,' said Larry, standing up and yanking his coat off the back of the chair. 'Right, you lot, let's foxtrot oscar. Those birthday drinks ain't gonna sup themselves.'

*

'Look at the state of you lot,' said Thirza with a shake of the head, her gaze sliding from me to Andy to Larry. She pointed a wavering talon at me. 'And as for you, I thought you'd given up drinking.'

I shrugged. 'Special occasion.'

Larry stood up and tiptoed across to her, cartoon-style. He slipped an arm about her shoulders.

'Hello, gorgeous,' he said. 'How's my favourite Rottweiler?'

She made a big show of throwing off his arm but her pretence at anger was betrayed by the hint of a smile. Larry was the only man I knew who could stick his head into the lion's mouth and have it licked rather than chomped clean off.

'Come and join us, Thirza,' Andy said, patting Larry's empty seat and giving her a smile straight from a movie poster. 'It's always so lovely to see you.'

Thirza's little grin blossomed into something else entirely. She had once confided in me that Andy was the only male who made her miss having sex with a man. 'He's like a bacon sandwich to a vegetarian,' she'd said.

'I'm only having the one, mind,' she said, sitting down. 'Fuckers,' she added, laughing.

*

'Oi, Thirza, you were meant to fetch them back, not join them,' Big Al said when he entered the pub, biting down on a fresh Consulate. 'I don't suppose there's any of my kitty left, is there?'

'Long gone,' said Larry. 'I'll get you one, Al. Have a seat.'

In Al's wake followed Lucy, Daphne and half of the newsroom.

'Right, everyone, listen,' Daphne announced. 'I'm picking up this tab, okay. We don't do this very often. Have a few on me. Enjoy yourselves.'

A cheer went up, and so began a long, joyous night, full of laughter and tall tales, one or two of which might even have been true. The drink flowed freely. After ten hours in the pub I should by rights have been flat on my back, having been dry for an age (my sodden introduction to Larry notwithstanding). And yet I was almost mystically sober. It was as if I had achieved the alcoholic equivalent of enlightenment. It's not often that alcohol transports you to such a place. More often, it lands you in a hedge, or a cell.

Maybe it wasn't the drink at all. Maybe it was the company. As I looked from Lucy to Thirza to Big Al and drank in the laughter all around me, I luxuriated in the warm glow of camaraderie. A perfect moment such as that is as fleeting as a mayfly's heartbeat. Reach out, and it's gone. And so it proved.

EIGHT

THE MUSIC POUNDED THROUGH ME – *from* me almost.

'It's un-bloody-believable,' I shouted at Lucy, a big stupid smirk on my face.

Lucy, writhing rhythmically before me, couldn't hear a word of what I said but she didn't need to. She knew what I was feeling. Everyone in The Crystal Rooms knew precisely what everyone else was feeling: ecstasy.

Hours earlier I had been sitting on the beach with Lucy, staring at the bright yellow pill in my hand, its little smiley face egging me on. She had already swallowed hers.

'I don't think I should,' I said. 'You read about people dying from this stuff.'

'One or two – mainly people who take too many, or who drink too much water.'

'I dunno. I've only ever smoked hash and had a little coke.'

'It's coke you should be worried about,' she said. 'It's addictive and expensive. Not like E.'

'But what if your dad sees us together? That'd be bad enough straight, let alone off my face on E.'

'Not gonna happen. He doesn't leave his office. He doesn't want to be seen. We've been through all this.'

'Ah, sod it.'

I popped the pill into my mouth and threw back my head to dry-swallow it like a pelican gulping down a fish.

'How long before it kicks in?'

'Well, we had those hot dogs – what, about an hour ago? So probably around nineish.'

I looked at my Timex: it was eight fifteen. The late evening July day still had some warmth in it. Families remained on the beach and in the sea, floating, splashing, swimming and paddling. The jingle-jangle of South Parade Pier amusements reached us on the briny breeze, along with the aroma of frying doughnuts. Lucy lay back on the pebbles, writhing a little to create a body-shaped hollow. I followed suit.

The wait was exquisite agony, a blend of terror and febrile excitement. At first I mistook those feelings for the effects of the drug itself, but when it kicked in, there was no mistaking it. It was like being whooshed up into the clean, cloudless sky among the gulls, who were circling on thermals rising from a Southsea that had been baked to a tee during a blistering hot day.

'Holy shit,' I said, grabbing fistfuls of pebbles as if that might help tether me to terra firma. 'Oh, my giddy aunt, it's like I'm on a roller coaster, and I bloody hate roller coasters.'

'Relax,' Lucy said, taking my hand. 'Don't fight it. Go with it.'

Those early moments were terrifying, but before long I had embraced it. I got to my feet and started swaying in time to the metronomic swish of the sea.

Lucy laughed, loud enough to turn nearby heads, both on the beach and in the water. 'So you can dance to waves but not to music?'

Two hours later and I was dancing for real – amid a seething mass of ravers doing likewise. I didn't want the music, or the feeling, to stop. Ever. But stop it did, and far sooner than expected.

All of a sudden, the mass of bodies before me parted to reveal two men posturing before one another, arms and legs spread, and up on their toes. One of them was dressed in a shell suit and had a knife. The other seemed pretty much a regular sort of guy. Shell Suit lunged at Regular Guy, who grabbed his weapon hand and levered him over his shoulder, slamming him into the parquet floor. Regular Guy had Shell Suit's arm locked in some kind of hold. He jerked it, the knife fell from Shell Suit's grasp, and Shell Suit issued a howl of pain that was audible above even the pounding music. Regular Guy hauled him up and, holding Shell Suit's arm at a crazy angle, steered him toward the exit.

Someone cut the music. The DJ addressed the floor.

'Sorry about this everyone,' he said, 'but we're gonna to have to ask you all to leave, nice and easy. Your safety's the main thing. The owner says to grab a flyer on your way out so you can use it for free entry next week. And please, keep the noise down outside. We don't want any visits from our friends in blue.'

'I'm going up to see Daddy,' Lucy said. 'Wait for me outside.'

On the way home, Lucy talked me through what had happened. On the stroke of midnight, in a prearranged move, Rollo's judo boys had taken out Dakin's dealers simultaneously – nine of them in all. But some of the dealers had been armed with blades and things had turned ugly. One of the black belts had been left with a six-inch gash in his forearm and was lucky it had missed the artery. It had been his blood I'd seen on my way out – big fat red splashes forming a trail from the building and on down the street.

I sighed as we walked, sorry that the drama had wrenched us from our highs. The come-down was quite different to having shock sober you up from booze. I felt bereft almost. The lovely woozy, fluid feeling I had enjoyed all evening was no more. All that was left was an elevated heart rate and a dry mouth.

'So much for your dad's crystal ball,' I said when she was done with the debrief.

'What d'you mean? He got rid of them, didn't he, like he said he would.' Her tone was defensive, as was her body language.

'Yeah, but at what cost? Those dealers were clearly a crew – like the Mafia, only in shell suits. Do you honestly think they're gonna take what happened tonight lying down? No chance. I'm telling you, this is just the start of it, not the end. Your dad's bitten off more than he chew this time. He should've left well alone. Everyone would've been happy – the dealers, the ravers and your dad's bank manager, if he's got one. But no, he goes and starts a bloody war instead.'

I stopped dead in my tracks and Lucy followed suit.

'Listen to me,' I went on, 'we're not setting foot inside that place again, d'you understand? Never. It's not safe.'

'Oh, come on, Llew. I think you're being overly dramatic.'

'You go near that club again and we're finished, you and me. I'm serious. We should be investigating that bloody club, not raving in it. My job could be on the line here. My career. And yours.'

I set off again. Lucy didn't follow.

'Are you coming?'

'Well done,' she scoffed. 'Now you've got me scared. Happy?'

'You should be scared. And so should your dad.'

We walked on in silence, me a few steps ahead. A while later, she went her way and I went mine without another word.

NINE

EMDEL SHOWED LUCY INTO MY bedroom where I was poring over minutes from the city council's planning committee. Trawling through Saharan-dry planning application approvals, denials and appeals was a chore, but if anything dodgy was happening, municipally speaking, then it would be in Planning. Most scandals are exposed by following the money.

'Some light reading?' Lucy asked.

'Why do they print this crap on green paper?' I asked, gesturing at the emerald sward of A4 spread across my quilt. 'It's a tough enough read as it is without the trippy colour.'

'Maybe that's the plan – to dissuade hacks like you from poking about.'

She sat on the bed next to me and gave me a peck on the cheek.

'I wasn't expecting to see you tonight,' I said.

She sighed, reached into her satchel-style handbag and produced a crumpled sheet of paper. 'Yeah, well, when I got home, I found this in the kitchen bin. It just caught my eye. Take a look,' she said.

'Shut the club now. Or else' it read. The message was composed of individual letters that had been cut from newspapers and magazines and glued to the page. They were a mix of typefaces, weights, sizes and colours – a bit like the cover of the Pistols' *Never Mind the Bollocks ...*

I turned to face her.

She held up a hand to stop me from speaking. 'Don't say it,' she warned me. 'Please.'

So I thought it instead: *I told you this would happen. I told you your dad had started a war.* 'Have you spoken to him about this?' I said instead.

'Course. I begged him to quit while he was ahead. There are four holdalls of cash in the airing cupboard under a pile of blankets and towels.'

'And will he? Quit?'

'What do you think? He said he'd never let anyone push him around in his life and he wasn't about to start now. I'm scared for him, Llew. Who d'you think might've sent that note?'

Really? I thought. Are you that blind? First Rollo steals Derek's customers and then he shakes down his dealers.

'Whoever's running those dealers your dad beat up would be my guess,' I said, as tactfully as possible. 'You said you saw those same guys in shell suits operating out of Derek's?'

'Yeah, that's right.'

'Then my best guess is that it's Derek whatever-his-name-is who's been busy with the glue and scissors.'

'Do you know anything about the Portsmouth drugs scene?' she asked, with notes of hope and desperation. 'Have you ever investigated it?'

'John Skinner had loose ties to drugs, but that's about the extent of my knowledge.'

'Llew, let's look into this. Not officially – only you and me, without telling Andy or Larry. We've got to find out more about this Derek character.'

I stood up quickly as if shocked off the bed by a big black spider. 'You're the bloody daughter of the man who's sparked this drugs war and you want me to turn the spotlight on that? Are you out of your mind? D'you want me to lose my job, is that it?'

She blew hard through her nostrils like a bull sizing up its target.

'Thanks for *nothing*,' she said. 'Some boyfriend you are. My daddy's life's in danger and you don't give a damn.' She snatched the note out of my hand and stuffed it in her handbag.

'You ought to be careful with that,' I said. 'That's evidence. And no one's threatening to kill him by the way. It's just a warning.'

She stormed halfway to the door, then turned. 'Oh, listen to you, the big brave man who's too frightened to tell anyone that I'm your girlfriend.'

'Spare me, not this again. Your dad hates me, okay. He can't even bring himself to use my first name.'

'But it's not just him who doesn't know about us, is it? Work's the same.'

'Emdel knows about us,' I offered helpfully.

'D'you know how it makes me feel, all this secrecy?' she said, ignoring my last offering. 'Like being with you is some kind of taboo.'

'Hey, you're a poet and didn't know it.'

I had forced the inanity from my lips. I'm not sure why. Diversion? Distraction? Dumbness?

Her lips grew thin and her face tight. 'Shut up. Shut up. Shut up.' She hissed the words, like an angry whisper, and her eyes grew wild and wide. 'D'you know,' she said, still hissing, 'right now I hate your guts to hell. I don't even want to be with you.'

'Well, maybe there's your solution right there,' I said, stung. 'If there's no us, then there's nothing to tell, is there.'

She stared at me for a few seconds.

'D'you know something? You're the biggest coward I've ever met.'

'Really?' I sat on the bed and picked up a wad of green paper as a prop to lend my feigned indifference added credibility, all the while anger burning hot inside. A coward? Me? How dare she. I had brought down Skinner's crime empire almost single-handedly, almost giving my life in the process. A coward?

'No wonder Thirza treats you like a doormat. I've seen jellyfish with more spine.'

'Now you're mixing your metaphors.'

I continued to flick through pages without looking up when what I actually wanted to do was fling the whole lot in her face.

'*You're a poet and didn't know it?*' Her tone was mocking and she pretend-stuck two fingers down her throat. 'You make me want to puke. Fuck you.'

'Fuck you too, and your dad.'

She slammed the door so hard it shook a piece of plaster free from the jamb.

A few moments later there was a tap on the door. Emdel let himself in.

'You two at it again?' he said.

'How could you tell?'

'So what was it this time?'

I couldn't tell him the truth. No one could know that.

'Same old same old,' I said. 'She wants me to tell Rollo about us, but I'm not keen.'

'I don't blame you. He'd kill you. He wanted to kill you even before you were knobbing his daughter. Hey, wanna watch some box? *Bladerunner*'s on shortly.'

'Yeah, go on then. Why not. That telly's kind of growing on me.'

TEN

THE SMOKE COULD BE SEEN for miles. I stood with Emdel on the promenade opposite our flat, rubbernecking. Black and thick, a billowing column of it climbed ever higher and was set in sharp relief against an otherwise white sky. It was late Sunday afternoon and Emdel had minutes earlier arrived home, having driven to work to retrieve some notes he needed for his hacking endeavours. He'd mentioned seeing a 'huge fire' on the way.

'So tell me, exactly where d'you think the fire is?' I asked.

'The area they're demolishing,' he said. 'You know, all those streets of empty houses. That's definitely where the smoke was coming from.'

'You mean Fratton?'

'Yeah, think so.'

After five years in Portsmouth, Emdel was still largely unfamiliar with its locales. I, on the other hand, could have drawn a detailed map of Portsea Island within six months of having moved there. Location – the 'where' of a story – never leaves you.

I dashed back across the road, to the flat.

Where're you going?' Emdel called.

'Car keys. I want a look-see at that fire.'

I dashed indoors, grabbed the keys and made for my latest ride – a Ford Mondeo that was the same shade of maroon as Emdel's jumpers. It was more reliable than the shit-brown Allegro had been and drier than the VW Golf, with its leaky sunroof. The car had three regular wheels and one sports alloy. The previous owner had had the others stolen but the bolts on the fourth wheel had frozen and the thief had been unable to shift them.

I bludgeoned my way from Southsea to Fratton in the Mondeo, earning a string of foul-mouthed abuse for my troubles. I swung into Besant Road, vacant and condemned. A little way up the abandoned road, the police had set up a cordon to prevent onlookers getting too near the scene of the fire. It was manned by a single constable.

'Officer,' I said, holding up my press card. 'Llew Sabler, *Tribune*.'

He ushered me through with a nod. There was an S-bend kink in the street, and it was only once I was past this that I was able to see orange fingers of fire rising from The Crystal Rooms.

I gave a little smile. Rollo would never quit the club for anyone, whatever they threatened him with. He'd not have given it up until the last possible moment, probably when the bulldozers were gunning their engines. And that would have meant months of worry that his illegal rave venue would inevitably appear on *The Tribune*'s radar and that Big Al would ask me to investigate. And then what would I do? Stall? Feed him disinformation? It was unthinkable.

But as I watched The Crystal Rooms burn I was sure I'd no longer have to worry about any of that. It was a fire in a derelict hall in the middle of a derelict district. Kids. In all likelihood that's what they would put it down to.

I would have hung around, soaked up the spectacle, but I had no wish to see Rollo, for he would be sure to roll up soon enough. The smoke was unmissable, and – like me – he would have a pretty good idea as to its source.

*

'D'you think a seat belt would've saved her?' I asked Emdel as we sat in front of the plasma TV, glued to a documentary on the death of Princess Diana, an event that had recently stunned the world.

'The driver survived,' he said, 'and he was wearing a belt, so I'd say yeah, it would've saved her.'

'To think that I used to sit on my dad's knee while he drove,' I said, adjusting the cord on my dressing gown.

'My favourite spot was in between the front seats,' he said. 'On a mound over the gear stick.'

'What if our dads had had a head-on crash?' I said. 'Who'd have had more chance? You on your mound or me on my dad's knee?'

'Well, you'd need to look at the mechanics of force to work out what—'

The ringing phone cut short his discourse on Newton's laws of motion. I picked up the receiver.

'Have you seen my dad anywhere?' Lucy asked a little breathlessly.

'No. Why would I have seen him? I'm a coward, remember? I'm trying to avoid him.'

It was a cheap shot and I regretted it almost as I was speaking the words. It had been the most we had said to one another since our falling out a couple of weeks earlier. When I spoke to her at work she either nodded her head or shook it, and if she had anything to say to me then she did so by email. It was excruciating.

'Sorry,' I said. 'That was uncalled for. Why d'you ask?'

'Because he should've been home hours ago,' she said. 'He went to the club for something or other and he's not come back. He's hardly ever late, and when he is he always lets me know. *Always*.'

The orange fingers of fire I had watched with a smile now filled me with horror.

'Llew, are you still there? Llew? *Llew?*'

As the breathless TV presenter dissected Diana's final moments, I pictured Rollo's – his desperate cries for help going answered as he dragged himself across the floor, choking and burning.

In a faltering voice, I told Lucy about the fire. Even Emdel heard the scream.

ELEVEN

'LLEW, LOOK, I KNOW SHE'S lost her dad,' Thirza said, 'but it's been three weeks now. She can't just stay at home indefinitely. When Larry's dad died he only took a few days off, and you know how cut up he was – *is*. It can't be one rule for her and another for everyone else.'

She was right; Larry was still grief-stricken, albeit it in a typically suppressed British kind of way, and yet he'd just got on with things. You had to feel for him. He'd managed to secure his father some badly needed new accommodation but it had been too late. Years of living in damp, mouldy digs had taken its toll, and Old Man's Friend, pneumonia, had claimed his father shortly after he'd moved into the smart new flat.

Thirza took a sip of coffee and gazed through the glass-fronted meeting room out on to the newsroom.

'We know about you two, by the way,' she said, still staring ahead. 'You and Lucy.'

'What? How?'

She rolled her eyes. 'Even Stevie Wonder could've spotted it, for fuck's sake.'

'Really? Oh. Well, I was going to tell you – y'know, when the time was right.'

'Yeah, yeah, yeah, whatever. Look, I only mention it because you're the obvious one to persuade Lucy to come in. She's gotta talk to us. It might well be she really is unfit for work, in which case that's another conversation. But either way, she needs to come in. Tomorrow. And that's from the top, by the way.'

'From Daphne?'

'Yep.'

'Does she know about Lucy and me?'

'I told you – everyone knows.'

So why hadn't Daphne said anything, given her distaste for workplace romances? Was it a good sign or bad?

'How did she take it?'

'Well, she didn't sack you.' No one did blunt better than Thirza.

'Anyway,' I said, 'about Lucy. The thing is, we've kind of fallen out.'

'Yeah, we noticed that too.'

'Jesus Christ, is nothing sacred?'

'Even if you're not with her any more, you're still her line manager, so try, okay.'

'I'll do my best, but I can't promise she'll listen.'

'Find a way. Get her up and out, like I did when you were holed up in that shithole B&B. Remember? Don't take no for an answer. No good'll come of her stewing at home like that.'

*

Lucy answered the door, glanced at me expressionlessly and disappeared back into the flat. I entered and found her in the same position she'd been in the only other time I'd visited since Rollo's death. She was lying on her father's bed, her face pressed into a bundle of dirty laundry she had retrieved from his wash basket, with socks and underwear among the clothes. She hadn't wanted to talk that first time, and it didn't look as if this latest visit would be any different. She had lost weight, and her once flawless complexion was now mottled and waxy.

Be firm, Llew, I coached myself. *Gentle but firm.*

'Lucy, look, I know it's difficult for you to hear this, but I'm afraid that outside of this flat, life is carrying on pretty much as normal. The sun comes up, the sun goes down, and *The Tribune* comes out every day. It's three weeks since you've been in to work. You need to speak to Daphne and Al. As your friends they're worried, and as your bosses they're concerned. They've asked you come in. Tomorrow.'

I waited not just for a response but for a sign that she had even heard me.

'It's over,' she said eventually, croaky and glassy-eyed.

'What's over, Lucy? What d'you mean?'

'The paper. It's finished for me. And for you.'

I blinked rapidly. 'What are you talking about? Finished?'

She sat up, still clutching Rollo's soiled clothes, and met my eye for the first time in an age.

'The police rang yesterday,' she said. 'Fire investigators say it was arson, and also that they found remains of the sound system and piles of melted water bottles. They know it was being used as a club. I told police about the note Daddy was sent, and some officers are coming round tomorrow. So it's over. All our lies? They'll soon be dust. Just like Daddy.'

There had been so many lies.

The latest concerned Rollo's death. There had been no hiding Lucy's grief, and so I had no choice but to tell work she had lost her father. But I said he had died of a cardiac arrest while shopping in Budgens for 'essentials'. I'm unsure why I embellished the lie in this way. To make it more believable to myself, perhaps, so it was easier to maintain? Or was it simply that I was a career liar, able to confect alternate realities at will?

But of course the biggest lie was Lucy herself. Thanks to me, the paper had unwittingly hired the daughter of a criminal with folklore status. With the police now involved, it was just a question of time before the paper discovered the truth about Lucy. In the case of Big Al and Thirza, the lie went all the way back to Lucy's work-experience days on *The Probe*. My goose had been cooked, along with Rollo's. I half-collapsed on the bed beside Lucy.

'I'll go in tomorrow,' she said. 'Like they want. I'll tell them everything. All of it. I couldn't care less. None of it matters any more.'

Not to you perhaps, I thought, before a wave of nausea got the better of me and had me scuttling for the bathroom.

*

She and I sat facing Big Al and Daphne in Daphne's office. The Venetian blinds on the internal windows were closed to screen out the newsroom beyond. It was a foul early autumn day, and rain stung the windows. The room was gloomy and quite matched my mood. Big Al and Daphne did their best to mask their shock at the cadaverous edge that Lucy's beauty had assumed in such a short time.

'We're so sorry about your father, Lucy,' Daphne said. 'It must've been a terrible shock, him having heart failure at that age.'

Lucy looked from Daphne to Big Al to me.

'Oh, God,' I said, slumping forwards under the weight of what they were about to hear.

'What is it, Bandit?' Big Al asked. 'What's up? You feeling alright?'

'I'm not who you think I am,' Lucy said, standing and taking charge.

She went on to tell the incredible story of Rollo's garages (making no mention of any porn, thank Christ), and then moved on to The Crystal Rooms, including the drugs war and the threatening note. When she was done, she sat down and folded her hands in her lap. 'I was never ashamed of him,' she added. 'I was proud. I *am* proud. I won't apologise for him.'

The concussive effect of her words left Big Al and Daphne stunned, and for a time the only sound was the ticking of the wall clock. Daphne was the first to recover.

She turned to me. 'And you knew all this?'

She needed only to see my face to know the answer.

'At least have the decency to look me in the eye,' she snapped.

I did, but boy was it painful.

'Why did you lie to us?' she asked.

'Because I didn't think Lucy would've got a look-in otherwise, given who her dad was. And she's brilliant. I thought she deserved a chance.'

Daphne leaned forwards in her chair. 'That wasn't your decision to make, was it,' she said through her teeth, poking my knee with a finger as she spoke.

I looked across at Big Al. He didn't look angry or hurt, just disappointed. Yet again I had failed this wondrous lunatic of a boss, a man who more than once had saved me from the most dangerous thing in my life: me.

'You should have told me,' Al said, pulling on a Consulate. 'Way back. You lied to Thirza too. Good luck with her when she finds out.'

Daphne placed her coffee on the table and crouched down in front of Lucy. She cupped Lucy's hands in hers.

'Sweetheart, we'll look after you until you find another job, don't worry about that. But I'm afraid you can't work here any more. With all due respect to your father and his memory, he's precisely the kind of person we should be looking into as a paper, and yet here we are, employing his daughter as an investigative reporter. If that was to get out, our reputation would be destroyed. Gone. Just like that. All the work we've done to restore this paper's name after what my husband did? It would all be for nothing. People would say that *The Tribune* hadn't really changed at all – that it was still rotten. You understand that, don't you?'

Lucy said she did.

'At least you had the good sense not to use his surname on your stories.'

'I made sure of that,' I added helpfully.

'What would we do without you?' Daphne said with a sneery smile.

'Can I go?' said Lucy, standing.

Daphne nodded and gave her a hug. It was a one-sided farewell; Lucy remained limp.

'John,' Big Al said, leaning in to give Lucy a peck on the cheek. 'If ever you need anything, just call. I mean it.'

She looked blankly at him, then at me, and left the room.

'That poor girl needs help,' Daphne said. 'She's clearly not right. And as for you,' she added, pointing at me. 'What's wrong with you?

What the hell were you thinking, lying to us like that?'

'I—'

'Please say you didn't know about the nightclub,' she continued. 'At least tell me that much.'

'I didn't know,' I said. The lie was a reflex, like closing your eyes when someone jabs a stick at your face. It wasn't as if I even stood to gain anything from it, because I'd be sacked regardless. 'I knew nothing about the club. She kept it from me. To protect me.'

'How sweet of her. So while you two were busy protecting each other, who was protecting us? Certainly not you.'

She wafted a despairing hand at me. 'You're suspended until I work out what to do with you. Get out of my sight before I throw this coffee over you.'

*

I found Larry and Andy sitting at our usual window table in the Rendezvous Café, with its views across the Solent – although not that day because the rain-lashed panes were frosted with condensation. Andy was nibbling delicately at a piece of toast, while Larry was demolishing a mixed grill. Grief certainly hadn't affected his appetite. The volume of food that man consumed was astonishing. 'I'm from farming stock,' he liked to say by way of explanation.

I sat down opposite them.

'Right,' said Larry. 'What's going down that's so big you have to meet us here?'

With roiling guts I ran through the Rollo-Lucy story again from scratch. Andy stopped eating as he listened, but Larry continued to bulldoze his way through the platter of food

'I'm sorry lads,' I added at the end. 'I've let you down. I've let everyone down.'

'Did she sack you?' asked Larry, swabbing away a dribble of grease with a napkin.

'Suspended.'

'Ach *nein*,' said Andy, always the polyglot. It was yet another thing the ladies loved about him, and the men.

'You're not gonna believe this, but I actually knew Rollo,' said Larry like it was nothing.

'What?' I gasped.

'Yeah,' he continued. 'Him and my older brother Vern were in the same class. They were pretty tight as it goes, and for a spell Rollo was round ours all the time. He was a dude, tough but decent. Once, he set about some older boys who were bullying me. No one touched me after that. But then him and my brother discovered girls and they sort of drifted apart. I still used to see him around, mind, as I had mates in the Metal Estate. He was always friendly. I felt for him when he had his accident. Later I heard what he did for the estate in the recession with those garages of his. I admired the guy. I can't believe he's gone.'

'Hang on,' I said. 'So what about Lucy? Did you know her too?'

'I knew of her, yeah.'

'You've known all along she was Rollo's daughter?'

'Yep.'

'And you said nothing?'

'You had your reasons, I had mine. She's a top girl. Why would I risk getting her into trouble? And I'll tell you this for nothing.' Larry cast about checking for earwiggers. 'Someone did for Rollo. Illegal club? Drug war? Arson? S'clear as day. Why don't we have a dig about, see what we can find? You know, for Lucy. For Rollo.'

I stiffened. I hadn't said anything about drugs in my account. I had glossed over it in my eagerness to get the sordid tale told.

'Larry,' I said. 'I didn't mention any drug war. How did you know about that?'

'Vern was working the door when it all kicked off. He's a boxer – knows how to handle himself. He told me about it. He waded in with those judo guys. He loves a scrap, Vern.'

Larry mopped a half-slice of bread around his plate, until the porcelain was forensically clean before folding the slice and chomping it whole.

I was reduced to shaking my head, too stunned for words.

'Is there anything else you two would like to tell me while we're at it?' said Andy. 'Hidden bodies, that kind of thing?'

'Look, lads,' said Larry, 'seriously, we owe it to Lucy to have a poke about in this fire business.'

'Be my guest, but it'll be without me. I'm history, remember.'

'What're you talking about?' said Larry. 'You can still freelance. I did it for five years. I'll throw some spadework your way. You're brilliant at that. Let's get whatever bastard did this to Rollo. Together.'

TWELVE

LUCY'S DOORBELL SOUNDED. I ROSE from the sofa and answered the door – to find myself staring at DI Simmons, the same detective who had been involved with the altar business. We blinked in mutual surprise.

'Mr *Sabler?*' he said. 'Have I got the wrong address?'

I assured him he hadn't – that it just so happened I was Lucy Baer's boyfriend and was there to lend moral support.

'Are you now,' he said, poker-faced. 'Well, fancy that.'

Jesus Christ, I thought, he's already making me feel guilty.

'Do you remember DI Bull?'

We nodded at one another.

'So you two are still a team after all this time?' I said.

'We're like an old married couple,' DI Simmons said wearily, like it was something he said a lot. 'Most of our colleagues have moved on and up, but clearly we don't know the right people.'

DI Bull pulled up a trouser leg and shook an imaginary hand, his fingers contorted into comical positions.

'Anyway, why are we telling you all this?' said DI Simmons. 'We're meant to be the ones asking the questions. Is Miss Baer at home?'

I ushered them in. We squeezed past a pile of microwaves that were stacked in the hall, still in their boxes. Rollo's presence remained very much in the flat. DIs Simmons and Bull traded knowing glances.

Lucy straight-batted everything they threw at her exactly as I had coached her. I didn't know if she'd been listening to my advice but clearly she had.

'No, I didn't know anything about the club,' she said in reply to the first question. 'I found the note after Daddy died. He'd thrown it in the bin. It just happened to catch my eye when I was emptying it.'

'Do you know of anyone who had cause to threaten your father?' asked DI Bull, shunting his circular glasses further up the bridge of his nose. Together with his age-shined suit and misaligned tie, they gave him the air of a down-at-heel college lecturer.

The pair of them were tag-teaming with practised ease. I inched forward on the sofa, anxious that they didn't catch Lucy off guard.

'Daddy was running an illegal nightclub, right?'

'Yes,' they chorused.

'So I'm guessing that there are probably people who weren't best pleased about that. Other club owners maybe? Mightn't someone like that have sent this?' said Lucy, holding up the threatening note.

'Why don't you leave the detective work to us, Miss Baer,' said DI Bull.

The two men stood up in unison as if they were telepathic.

'You've been very helpful,' said DI Simmons. 'And we're sorry for your loss. Mr Sabler,' he added with a nod. 'An unexpected pleasure.'

As I showed them out, DI Simmons paused by the pile of microwaves, tapping the uppermost box.

'Mr Sabler, if we were to run these product serial numbers through our computer, I wonder what we might find.'

I shrugged.

'We might be back,' he said, holding up the note, which was now in an evidence bag. 'And if these microwaves are still here—'

'—then next time we won't be turning a blind eye,' cut in DI Bull.

You even finish one another's sentences, I thought. You've definitely been together too long.

When they'd gone, I found Lucy back on Rollo's bed, curled up with his laundry.

'You did really well,' I said. 'You gave them nothing.'

'Just go, will you. I want to be alone.'

THIRTEEN

I COULD NOT GET ANY kind of read on Daphne's face. I suspect she'd make a formidable poker player. She sat opposite me in my living room, about to tell me my fortune. In truth, I was already resigned to my fate – I would be fired. I'd spent the previous couple of days pondering options for when I was sacked. Maybe I'd turn freelance like Larry had? He'd made a decent living as a court reporter for five years, so why couldn't I? But then he'd had one hundred and twenty words-a-minute shorthand. I'd struggle to take down a shopping list, let alone court proceedings. What about teaching? A posh private all-girls school wouldn't be so bad, would it?

'This business with you and Lucy is about integrity and honesty,' began Daphne.

As she mentioned those words, the plasma telly loomed large in my peripheral vision.

'Your decision to keep Lucy's true identity from us was horribly misguided and ill-judged. As for you sleeping with her? That's your business, but it doesn't make me think any more of you, that's for sure. So, what to do with you, Llew?'

Here it comes.

'Despite everything, Al and me feel that your motives for lying to us about Lucy were honourable,' she said.

Ooh. Sounds promising.

'So this is what we've decided. You're to be suspended for two weeks without pay and stripped of your role as editor of the Investigations team. That will be handed to Larry because he's more trustworthy than you.'

As she mentioned Larry's trustworthiness I pictured his brother wrestling with drug dealers in Rollo's club. It was all I could do not to smile.

'Thank you, Daphne,' I said. 'I was certain you were going to fire me.'

'I *am* firing you,' she replied.

The words barely registered, so little sense did they make.

'What? I don't underst—'

'All that stuff I just told you? That was before Thirza came to see me this morning. We had a very interesting conversation, she and I. Is there anything else you might want to tell me, Llew?'

What's she on about? She must know I lied about knowing nothing of Rollo's club. Thirza must've told her. But how the hell did Thirza know?

'What do you mean, anything else?'

'Oh, just a few trivial things – like you actually being guilty of taking a shit on that altar and letting that poor priest carry the can.'

Jesus Christ. Thirza's told her everything! My stomach heaved.

'And there there's my ex-husband's stolen pornography. I hear you're quite the entrepreneur. A mail-order porn business? A porn library? And all from your cellar? Impressive. But you had help, didn't you, running your little porn empire. Some local crook? I wonder who that might've been. Rollo Baer, perhaps?'

'Oh God.'

'Oh God is about the size of it,' said Daphne, standing. 'D'you know, I'd planned to ask you into the office to tell you all this, but I came to you instead for your own protection. Thirza would quite happily kill you right now. Slowly and painfully. You've been lying to her and Al about Lucy for years. You betrayed them, even though you promised her you'd never lie to her again about anything. Do you remember that, or do such things not even register in that warped brain of yours? I'll send on your P45.'

And with that, Daphne was gone.

I sat there alone and sank into oblivion. I had the sensation of falling from a great height. Looking down as I fell, I saw Thirza and myself walking laps of Southsea Common. She had rehabilitated me from the near-death trauma I'd suffered at the hands of Skinner's goons. Every day she had forced me further and further from the B&B in which I'd been holed up, hiding from the world. On and on she drove me, until she and I had walked the mile from South Parade Pier to the Common. She had fixed me, mended me. She had been the best friend anyone could ever hope to have, and I had decided to tell her everything. Well, *nearly* everything.

As I plummeted on through space, I heard myself speaking. I was telling her everything – about the altar business, about the stolen porn and how Emdel and I had profited from it with the help of a local crook – and I promised I would never lie to her again, ever. And then she spoke. She said that if I were ever to lie to her again, she would go to the police and tell them everything.

Except she hadn't gone to the police. She had gone to Daphne.

I snapped back into the present and looked about me.

All that existed was the plasma telly. It grew and grew, pulling me in, until the black screen threatened to suck me into its inky depths, down into a vortex of nothingness. I picked the thing up, ripping cables as I hoisted it above my head. I slammed it into the ground and stamped on the screen again and again until there was nothing left but white powdered glass.

'What the hell are you doing?'

I looked up, sweating and panting. It was Emdel.

'*The French Connection*'s on tonight,' he said. 'I was looking forward to that.'

FOURTEEN

WAS IT THE CALM AFTER the storm that had just passed, or the calm before the storm that was about to hit? It's difficult to say, but either way, for a couple of months life settled into a new, steady and uneventful rhythm – one devoid of drum-solo lunacy and guitar-windmilling madness.

I was able to draw breath, if not take stock. I'd had it with taking stock. It was taking stock, a few years earlier, that had led me to share with Thirza not only the truth about my role in the desecrated altar affair but also my involvement in sundry porn ventures. Had I kept schtum about all that, then I would still be at *The Tribune* with Larry and the team, instead of spending my working life surrounded by bespectacled androids with motherboards for brains.

Every single day in my new job at JCN there would come a point when I'd look around me and think: *What the hell am I doing in this place?* The logical – rather than metaphysical – answer to this question was that Emdel had swung a job for me, as editor of JCN's weekly staff newsletter.

'It'll be a doddle,' he'd said. 'Plus you already know a load of people. Glenn, Jason, Darryl, Bryan – they're all still there.'

'I was their pornographer,' I reminded him. 'Me knowing what they like to masturbate over doesn't make them my friends.'

'So how *are* you planning to pay your share of the rent then?' he asked. 'Bar work? Shelf stacking? Driving a forklift in a freezing cold warehouse, listening to Radio One all day?'

That did it, and Big Al had been kind enough to furnish me with a decent reference.

'Truth is, Bandit,' Big Al said, having visited me at home one night, 'you're a liability and a health hazard, both to yourself and everyone around you. I should be washing my hands of you, not giving you a bloody reference. But hey, everyone deserves a sixth chance, right?'

He chain-lit another cool-as-a-mountain-stream Consulate before jabbing it in my general direction. 'I know I'm wasting my breath but I'll say it anyway. Don't do anything stupid at this new place of yours.'

*

JCN management insisted on referring to staff as 'family'. The newsletter they hired me to edit was even called *Family First*, which I found unsettling because it sounded to me like the brainchild of some board-level Charles Manson cyborg freak.

But the most unsettling thing by far about joining JCN was that my finely tuned, micro-calibrated news antennae were suddenly useless. In newspapers I was able to source stories at will. Indeed, my news-sense was so strong it was practically a fifth force of nature.

Well-dressed woman with bruises? High-flying husband fond of battering his wife.

Middle-aged male busker sporting smart shoes? Frustrated chief executive reviving thwarted musical ambitions of yesteryear.

Movie memorabilia for-sale notice in newsagent window? Hard-up one-time special-effects man, responsible for some of British cinema's most iconic moments, including Sean Connery having his nuts laser-roasted in *Goldfinger*.

All these stories, and hundreds of others like them, I had found by keeping my eyes and ears open. Yet at JCN I may as well have been blind and deaf. I didn't have the first idea what constituted a story to these people. When I joined, it was my belief that the typical JCN employee was male, catastrophically single, socially inept and had an unhealthy obsession with pornography – ostensibly anal and gang-bangs. But I could hardly fill *Family First* with spit-roasts and cumshots, as popular as this might have been.

It was excruciating – scratching about in the dark, seeking something, *any*thing, that was fit for publication. My JCN discomfiture was compounded by me having a line manager, which was a profoundly different experience to having an editor, especially an editor like Big Al. My line manager's name was Geoffrey.

'Call me Geoff,' he kept insisting, but I never did because he neither looked nor sounded like a Geoff. Geoffs are men's men. They like to drink, tell bawdy tales and put their feet up on the desk. Geoffrey wore twill suits and sported not a tie but a dicky bow. And he was a church goer, a Methodist; he hummed hymns all day long.

If I was late for work – even by just a couple of minutes, which I was most days – he'd tap his watch and tut. He also insisted I kept a tidy desk. No one in the history of journalism has ever kept a tidy desk, and even by those standards I had been messy.

This meant that my idea of pathologically tidy was Geoffrey's idea of irredeemably slovenly. The state of my desk troubled him so deeply that he took to tidying it for me, filing stuff in my drawers when I wasn't there. I soon put a stop to that, by slipping a few hardcore gay porn magazines in said drawers, plus a half-empty tube of KY jelly, the other half of which I had squeezed down the toilet. He didn't go anywhere near my desk after that. In fact he even moved his own a few feet further back.

So no, I didn't call him Geoff. But in his defence, Geoffrey was fair-minded and patient. He had edited *Family First* himself before being promoted to Head of Communications. And all credit to him: he did succeed in re-tuning my antennae, mainly by switching them off.

'Geoffrey,' I said one day shortly after joining, 'I was chatting to—'

'Please, call me Geoff.'

'Right, anyway, I was chatting to some guy at lunch just now, who had nothing but sausages on his plate. So get this. It turns out that that's all he eats – I mean like, ever. He even takes a massive cooler full of sausages on holiday with him. So I was thinking, why don't we get a snap of him sat behind a mountain of bangers, knife and fork in hand, tongue lolling? That'd make a great splash, right?'

Geoffrey hadn't known what a splash was.

'It's the front-page story,' I explained, aghast at his ignorance.

He told me that no one was interested in reading about an employee with a protein-overload death wish. Geoffrey made me understand that at JCN, news was whatever the board told me was news, and that I would be told by email. 'Newsgathering' at JCN amounted to a daily trawl through my inbox for information about new products, new-joiners and new workplace initiatives. I was then to write up all this crap and send it upstairs. Board members would then rewrite everything by committee a dozen times over, thus ensuring that every 'story' had the requisite level of turgidity. Only then was it ready to grace the pages of *Family First* for everyone to ignore.

'Who reads this rubbish?' I said to Emdel, holding up my first issue of *Family First* by one corner as we sat in front of our new telly watching *Tomorrow's World*.

'No one.'

'What's the point of it then?'

'So that management can blow their own trumpets and remind us how lucky we are.'

'Well, you're lucky, that's for sure. You haven't got a manager who tidies your frigging desk the second your back's turned. Does anyone even manage you at all?'

'The head of IT, in theory, but to be honest he hasn't got a clue what I do. Just as long as I keep the black hats out of our system, then he's happy.'

'What the hell are black hats?'

'Hackers, the bad ones.'

'You mean there are good hackers?'

'Yeah, I'm a good one. I'm what's known as a white hat.'

He went on to explain that the hat references were taken from westerns, where the good guys wear white hats and the bad ones wear black.

'So a black hat'll take your system down, then offer to fix it for a big chunk of cash,' said Emdel.

'And the white hats?'

'Us white hats also hack into business and government systems, but instead of extorting cash we flag vulnerabilities so that they can fix them.'

'What, out of the goodness of your hearts?'

'No, in the hope of landing a job, or consultancy work. The bigger companies – like JCN – will often hire white hats as head of IT security. That's how I got my promotion. And us white hats, who work for the big firms, we help each other out by hacking into each others' systems.'

Sensing my bewilderment, Emdel switched into hacking-for-remedials mode.

'Okay, let's say I've hacked into a high-street bank's system, which I did last week, by the way. So, after I've found my way in I'll then contact the bank's head of IT security to let him know what I've done and how I did it, and then he goes off and codes a patch that'll stop anybody else from doing the same thing.'

'And by anybody else you mean black hats?'

'Exactly. It's a you-scratch-my-back thing. Most months I'll manage to hack into two or three companies, and most months at least a few of my fellow white hats will get into JCN's system. Then all of us plug those holes with code, and so it goes on, an endless cycle of hack-and-strengthen. Everyone's a winner – apart from the black hats, of course.'

'Jesus,' I said, shaking my head. 'There was me thinking you and your sort were C-3PO when all this time you were Clint bloody Eastwood.'

He huffed. 'That's you all over, isn't it – lazy stereotyping. Typical journalist. And technically we're not Clint Eastwood, by the way. Eastwood usually does some good but he's nearly always out for himself. He's a grey hat. John Wayne? Now he's the ultimate white hat.'

'Grey hat,' I repeated wearily. 'So how do brown hats fit into all this?'

Emdel stood up, blowing from his nostrils like a horse. 'Yeah, yeah, yeah. You're hilarious. I'm off to my room.'

'What the hell do you do in there on that PC of yours? Are you white-hatting?'

'Nah, that's for work. At work, I'm Wayne. At home' – he pulled an imaginary Stetson down over his eyes and squinted – 'I'm Eastwood.'

'I'm not even going to bloody ask,' I said, turning my attention back to *Tomorrow's World*.

FIFTEEN

IF SOMEONE SHUTS YOU OUT, you will hammer away only for so long before you decide it's time to walk. With Lucy, I hammered away for a month, during which time she went from letting me into the flat, and more or less blanking me, to not opening the door at all.

One day as I was thumping away – pleading through the letter box for Lucy to open up – a neighbour approached. She was middle-aged and wore utility clothing like it was still 1950. She introduced herself as Mrs Matthews and said she had been Rollo's cleaner after his mother, Aggie, had died.

'I've known that girl since she barely half filled a crib,' she said.

That girl? I thought. Not exactly empathetic.

'Don't worry,' Mrs Matthews said, tugging at her Playtex and wincing. 'I've got a key to the place from my cleaning days. I've been letting myself in, checking up on her, like. She's still alive, you'll be glad to hear. Been feeding her up too I has, and doing a spot of tidying. Thin as a rake she is, and the place is a pigsty. Her granny'd be turning in her grave if she could see the state of the place. Very house proud was Aggie.'

And so I had stepped away from the Lucy situation, knowing that at least Mrs Matthews had an eye on her, even if that eye seemed prying and distrustful. I gave her my phone number and asked her to call if she had any concerns, or news, about Lucy.

One night, some weeks on, my home phone rang.

'Mr Sabler?' came Mrs Matthews' strident tones. 'You asked me to ring if there was anything to know. Well, she's up and about. She's even eating.'

'That's good to hear,' I said. 'Does that mean she's healing, d'you think?'

'I don't know that she'll ever heal, that one. Not after what she saw as a tot. Her own mother, dead in the bath? All that blood? Shocking.'

Jesus Christ. You're like something from a Hammer Horror movie.

'No,' she droned on. 'I'd say she's brighter because she had a visit today. Some big streak of piss. Overfamiliar too.'

Larry. Had to be. He'd promised Lucy that he would keep her posted of any developments in The Crystal Rooms arson case.

When I was done with doomsayer Mrs Matthews, I called Larry's mobile. He answered within a single ring-tone. The thing was like an extension of his body.

'They've found someone,' he said. 'In connection to the fire.'

'Go on.'

'Well, it's been, what, ten weeks since Rollo died, and still no sign of an inquest. So I phones the coroner's office to see if an inquest date's been set. Nothing. So then I ask what's happening with the pre-inquest review hearing, 'cos normally they'll at least cough up some info about that. But again, nothing. Zilch.'

I had a reasonable grasp of the machinations of the law, but compared to Larry I was an infant. He had spent half his working life sitting in trials and hearings.

'Which means?' I asked.

'Which means the coroner is on pause with regards to Rollo's death because plod's building a case. So today I swings by the station and ask to see the record of recent arrests and interviews. And whaddya know? There it is, plain as day.'

I inched forward on the sofa. 'Who've they hauled in?'

'Take a guess.'

'Just bloody tell me, Larry.'

'Derek Dakin.'

He said the name like I should know it.

'Come on, Einstein,' he added. 'I thought you of all people would've known of Derek Dakin. He's the guy who owns Derek's, that club up near the M27.'

'Christ, yeah. Those dealers, the ones your brother helped beat up? Lucy said she saw them at Derek's. They're his crew, right? So d'you know anything about him, Dakin?'

'He's a slippery fucker, I know that much.'

Larry went on to say that some years earlier, he'd covered a drugs smuggling trial at Winchester Crown Court. Some yacht crew had been nabbed with five kilos of coke hidden in the hull. The boat had been registered to Derek Dakin.

'Get this. The crew all cop hefty sentences,' said Larry. 'But Dakin? He walks. Somehow his barrister wins over the jury with some bullshit story about the crew acting without Dakin's knowledge. The prosecution barrister was bloody useless. It was like watching Dakin being savaged by a dead sheep.'

'Will they charge him?' I asked. 'For the fire?'

'Well, they can't hold him for more than twenty-four hours without charging him, so we'll know soon enough.'

'Let's sit tight, then.'

We didn't have to sit tight for long. Dakin was released at nine o'clock the following morning without charge.

SIXTEEN

THE JCN CANTEEN WAS KILLING me – and just about everyone else – by stealth. I had never seen so much corpulence in one location than at JCN. It was almost as if the building itself was beginning to strain at the seams, its architraves and mouldings in danger of pinging off the walls like so many shirt buttons. In a little over three months I had put on nearly a stone and had to buy an entirely new wardrobe.

'Why don't they ever have anything healthy to eat?' I asked Emdel as I tackled a dollop of shepherd's pie encased in a lava flow of melted cheddar.

'Apparently they used to, but hardly anyone ever ate it so they stopped serving it. Besides, no one forced you to buy a dirty big bowl of spotted dick with custard for afters, did they. Or that bacon and egg roll you had this morning.'

He had a point.

'You could always bring in sandwiches,' he added.

'I don't do sandwiches. Unless it's hot, I don't count it as food. You know that.'

'Wassat, Llew?' said Jason, plonking himself down next to us. 'What don't you count as food?'

'Ignore him, Jason,' said Emdel. 'He's always moaning about

something. Today it's the food. So what did you get up to at the weekend?'

'Didn't do nothing, really,' Jason said through a mouthful of beef Wellington. 'Worked on Maureen Junior a bit.'

Maureen Junior was Jason's latest epic wreck of a car. It was an S-type Jaguar that was even more rusted and algae-slicked than Maureen Senior had been. Jason had still not fully come to terms with the demise of his spectacularly decrepit Rolls Royce.

'Jason,' I said, 'you do know that when you say "I didn't do nothing" it actually means "I did something".'

'Eh?' he said, looking from me to Emdel. 'What's he on about?'

'It's a double negative,' I persisted. 'It's like maths. Two negatives make a positive, so when you say—'

'What's this about double negatives?' asked Glenn, joining us and flipping his almost waist-length hair out from his shoulders.

'When're you gonna get that cut?' I asked him, extricating a foot-long strand of hair from the melted cheese. 'Can't you at least wear a bloody hairnet or something.'

'What's up with him?' Glenn asked Emdel.

'He's a miserable bastard, that's what's up with him,' Emdel said.

'Yeah? Well, you'd be miserable if you'd been doing what I've been doing all morning. While you were saving us from the perils of the black hats, I was taking photos of the tidiest desks in the building for some ridiculous bloody corporate shite they've got me promoting called Pride in Place.'

'What's this about tidy desks?' asked Bryan, sitting down next to us with his brother Darryl.

Although the company had a shirt-and-tie dress code, Bryan and Darryl had interpreted this very loosely. Bryan was sporting a denim shirt with a warlock-themed tie, while Darryl had plumped for a rhinestone-buttoned number and lace tie, which had a silver slide-guitar clasp. Unlike his brother, Darryl had moved on from Dungeons and Dragons and was now a country music loon. I hadn't seen him in a Stetson at work yet, but it was surely just a question of time.

'Llewellyn, you have an urgent call,' came a voice from behind me. It was Geoffrey, who, I noted, had somehow managed to find himself a salad, albeit one that was slathered in mayonnaise. 'Some chap called Larry.'

'*Llewellyn?*' everyone at the table chorused once Geoffrey was out of earshot.

'Don't bloody ask,' I said.

The fact was, out of the blue one day Geoffrey had taken to calling me Llewellyn, and had continued to do so every day thereafter. I could only conclude that it was a petty and mean form of revenge for me refusing to call him Geoff. And him a Christian.

I loaded a tray with what was left of my food.

'You not finishing that spotted dick?' asked Jason.

'You've already got one, you greedy sod,' said Emdel.

Jason reached for my bowl. 'There's nothing I don't love more than spotted dick.'

I declined to correct him, mainly because I had no idea as to the true meaning of his horribly mangled sentence. A phalanx of logicians would have struggled with that one.

*

My work phone sounded.

'Can you talk?' Larry asked.

'Not really. I'm at my desk.'

'I rang earlier. Why don't you get yourself a bleeding mobile?' he asked. 'Then you could step away from your desk. I don't get it.'

'Aside from you, hardly anyone I know has got one. Besides, who wants to be contactable all the time? Not me, thank you very much.'

'You're a journalist. You're meant to be contactable.'

'I'm not a bloody journalist though, am I. D'you know what I was doing all morning?'

Under my breath, I told him about the wretched Pride in Place initiative.

'No fucking way, fella. That's grim.'

'You're bloody right it's grim. Anyway, what's so urgent? Not you nagging me about mobiles, I'm guessing.'

'Listen,' he said, with a whiff of conspiracy, 'you're not gonna believe this. You know how Dakin was released without charge? Well, it seems there was something fishy about it.'

'Fishy how?'

'So this morning, in the post, we get an anonymous typewritten letter. It was addressed to you, actually. I think it's from a cop. In it, he – I'm assuming it's a he – says that by rights Dakin should've been charged, that there was enough evidence to build a case.'

'Bloody hell.' I thought back to the letter Big Al had showed me, alleging that the Freemasons were essentially running the city's police service. I asked Larry if he remembered. He said he did.

'And by way of proof,' he continued, 'our very own Deep Throat includes a photocopy of that threatening note – you know, the one Rollo was sent that Lucy gave to the police. Guess what? Deep Throat tells us that that note had the impression of some writing on it. It must've been taken from a ream of blanks that someone had written on. Deep Throat said he himself had done the old brass-rubbing trick to check the note for exactly that kind of thing.'

'So what did the writing say?'

'Get this. It was the postal address for Derek's nightclub. You can see it clear as day.'

'Jesus Christ. And they let Dakin go?'

'I said he was a slippery fucker and I was right. And now I know just how slippery.'

'What d'you mean?'

'It seems our Derek's got friends in high places. Mason friends. That's what Deep Throat says.'

'In the police?'

'Yeah, in the bleedin' police. The force is riddled with 'em, and it sounds like Deep Throat has had his fill of it. D'you know, it wouldn't surprise me if he's been passed over for promotion for not being one of them. I bet you any money that's what it is.'

I thought of DIs Simmons and Bull and their talk of how they were going nowhere fast in the force. And hadn't DI Bull mimed everyone's idea of what it is to be a Mason? The hoisted trouser leg? The funny handshake?

'Llew? Fella? You still there?'

'Yeah.'

'Remember I said I'd slip you some freelance spadework?'

'Go on.'

'I need you to do some poking about into Dakin – you know, his club and who he hangs with.'

'You want me to tail him?'

'I need you working the shadows, my friend. Your speciality.'

'The shadows,' I parroted for no reason other than it had resonance.

SEVENTEEN

I KNEW NEXT TO NOTHING about the Freemasons. DI Bull's trouser leg and handshake routine pretty much exhausted my knowledge of that shadowy organisation. So, with the old *know your enemy* mantra in mind, I went shopping for books on the subject. I should by rights have already done my homework, having been urged by Big Al to read up on the subject after the paper had received the anonymous letter about the Masons and local police. But I hadn't. In WHSmith I found just what I was looking for. Called *Inside the Brotherhood* – by TV journalist Martin Short – the book would become my guiding light as I journeyed deeper into Masonic murk and shadows. The shadows, where Larry said I belonged.

'Oi, Emdel.'

I was attempting to draw his attention away from *Terminator 2*, which we'd sat down to watch a while earlier.

'Now what?' he said. 'I don't want to hear any more Mason facts. Arnie's about to spring Sarah Connor from the nuthouse. This is the best bit.' He pressed pause. 'You and that frigging book. I swear you're more obsessed with it than I am with hacking.'

'Okay, here's a question for you: what would you say is the Masons' most closely guarded secret?'

I thought there would be no way he'd guess the answer. But of course, this was Emdel.

'I don't know,' he said, shrugging, remote cocked in hand. 'Their membership list?'

'How the bloody hell did you know that?'

'S'obvious, isn't it? If you've got a secret society, what could be more secret than who's in it? I mean, from the sound of it here's a bunch of blokes who all scratch one another's rings for mutual gain. So it stands to reason that they're not gonna want people to know who they are.'

'Backs, surely? You mean scratch each other's backs?'

'I mean rings,' he said. 'You say this Dakin bloke might've got away with burning Rollo just by him being a Mason? That's way more than scratching backs. That's scratching rings.'

'Yeah, I guess,' I said. 'Right, just one more and I promise I'll leave you to watch your film in peace.'

'It better be just the one or I'll flush that book of yours down the bog.'

'Right, here goes. So, each lodge keeps a record of all its members.'

'What the hell's a lodge?' he asked.

'It's their word for branch. They've got funny words for everything. Grand master, worshipful master, third degree – it's all a bit Dungeons and Dragons. Anyway, so each lodge keeps a list of members, which they send to the grand secretary.'

'The *who?*'

'He's the ring-scratcher in chief, up in London. So my question is this: what if *we* could get hold of that list – you know, for whatever lodge it is that Dakin and those cops are members of? That'd be a smoking gun, right? If we had that, then the story would more or less write itself. You'd have it all there in black and white. Cops and Dakin. Thick as thieves.'

'Hang on a second. What d'you mean, if *we* could get hold of that list?'

'Come on, genius, think about it. You'd be unearthing the biggest secret of the world's biggest secret society. It'd be like the Everest of hacking.'

Emdel rubbed his chin and stared into the mid-distance. With a sudden movement he aimed the remote at the telly, turned it off and stood up. He squinted at me, pulled an imaginary hat brim over his eyes and chewed on a non-existent cheroot.

'Okay, punk,' he growled. 'Let's go.'

'Punk?' I said, with a perplexed grin. 'That was Dirty Harry, not the Man With No Name.'

'Whatever,' he said. 'Both had guns and chased down bad guys – just like we'll be doing.'

I followed him into his bedroom. Where once his personal space had been dominated by a metric tonne of categorised pornographic videos and magazines, it now resembled nothing more remarkable than a home office, with desk, PC and monitor.

'Is this all you need for hacking? It looks like anyone's set-up.'

'It's what you do with it that counts,' he said.

I sat on the bed.

'Right,' he added, plonking himself down on a swivel chair opposite. He leaned back, foot on knee, hands folded in lap as if this were a counselling session. 'So what do we know for sure about Dakin?'

'Well, we know he runs a nightclub called Derek's, and that he wriggled out of a serious drugs rap some years back.'

'Forget the drugs thing. We'll start with his club. That'll be our *in*.'

He swung around and began tapping on the keyboard.

'There's no website for Derek's,' he said after much mousing about. 'There's a few mentions of Dakin's name on news sites in connection with that drugs case, but that's it.'

He slid a couple of phone directories off a shelf and thumbed through them.

'Right,' he said, 'Looks like Dakin himself is ex-directory, but the number for Derek's the club is listed here in the *Yellow Pages*, so that's where we'll start. We'll call his club and socially engineer Dakin's home address and phone number from one of his staff. He must have a manager. We'll target him, or her.'

'And how'll we do that?'

'Remember how I got Daphne's password out of her a while back? It'd be a similar deal, but a different tack. One of us'll have to phone Derek's during office hours and spin them some yarn in order to get Dakin's details.'

'Like what kind of yarn?'

'A plausible one – like we're specialists in cleaning products, or bar supplies, or lighting and sound systems. Basically, any kind of company that a club owner might need to deal with.'

'And say what?'

'That we're currently offering significant discounts. Everyone loves a bargain, right?'

'So we dream up a company out of thin air?'

'No, it's gotta be real, in case they check us out. So we use the name of an actual business, and the name of an actual employee in sales.'

He threw the *Yellow Pages* at me. 'You dig out a firm that fits the bill. Pick one that's got a website, as that'll make it easy for us to find the name of a sales rep. Most company sites these days have a page with staff contact details. Makes them look more human. You get me a company name, and an employee name and job title, and I'll do the rest.'

'So what'll we do with Dakin's phone number once we've got it?'

'If he hasn't changed his PIN then we'll be able to access his voicemails right off the bat. If he's got a pin in place then I'll have to spoof his caller ID to get at his messages.'

Emdel may as well have been speaking another language.

'Spoof?'

'It's very simple,' he said patiently. He had learned to be very patient with me down the years. 'Answer me this: how do you access your voicemail?'

'I don't. I haven't got a mobile.'

He sighed. 'Well, a normal person with a mobile will dial their number, hit the hash key, and listen to their messages.'

'So you don't need a password?'

'No. Your mobile phone operator assumes that because it's your own number you're calling there's no need for a password. So all I need to do is trick Dakin's operator into thinking that my call is coming from Dakin's phone and then it'll let me at his messages.'

'You can do that?'

'Yeah, I've coded a program to do exactly that. All I need is Dakin's number. The program calls his number, posing *as* his number, and then I'm in. I can rifle through his messages to my heart's content.'

'But I don't get it,' I said, scratching my head. 'This spoofing program. It's on your PC, right?'

'Yeah. What about it?'

'So how does it connect with Dakin's phone?'

'Straight from the computer.'

'That's possible?'

'Yep. It's called VOIP. It's the next big thing. Just last week I bought a top-of-the-range modem that lets me make calls using the PC. It's way cheaper than landlines, and way cheaper than mobiles. Everyone'll be doing it one day – just as one day everyone'll have a plasma TV like the one you wrecked.'

He'd loved that telly and hadn't forgiven me for destroying it.

'Huh, amazing,' I said. 'So do we even need Dakin's email address?'

'Absolutely. We need that so I can phish for his mail password.'

'Fish?'

'Yeah. I'll send him a bogus email. Make it look like its from his mail provider.'

'Saying what?'

'That there's been a security breach on the company's mail server and that all customers are being urged to change their password, just in case. But to change his password, he'll first have to enter his current password, and when he does that and hits send, bingo! We'll have full access to his email – incoming and outgoing.'

'He'll fall for that?'

'Wouldn't you, if you thought some stranger might be poking about in your inbox?'

'Jesus, Emdel, you ought to be working for MI6 or something. D'you pull this kind of crap at work?'

'Nah, this grey hat stuff's just for home, for fun.'

'Isn't this more, you know, black hat kind of stuff?'

'Darkish grey maybe,' he said with a little grin. 'Darkish grey.'

Darkish grey, I thought. Like shadows.

EIGHTEEN

LURKING IN THE SHADOWS PROVED a sight more interesting than filling *Family First* with pictures of tidy desks, beaming new-joiners and chalk-dry corporate news.

Getting hold of Derek Dakin's details had been simple. Posing as Dave McHugh, a senior sales rep with a major south coast wine and spirits wholesaler, Emdel had phoned to set up a bogus meeting with the manager of Derek's nightclub. On the call, Emdel asked in a casual aside if he might have the owner's contact details so he could send on a case of free samples ahead of the meeting.

'I only want to include those brands he likes,' Emdel had said. 'I'll also throw in a little of whatever you fancy – gratis, naturally, and only the best, of course.'

And with that, the manager had coughed up Dakin's home address, email address and mobile number.

'People love free shit,' Emdel explained. 'They can't help themselves.'

Minutes later, Emdel was spoofing his way into Dakin's voicemails.

'We mustn't access any new messages,' he said. 'Because then they show up as old messages when he hasn't even heard them, and that could spook him.'

Dakin had just three old voicemails and no new ones. All were recent. One was from the manager of Derek's with details of the bogus meeting Emdel had set up. Another was from a woman who we took to be Dakin's wife or partner reassuring him that the Indian restaurant they were going to that night didn't use peanut oil. And the third was from Dakin's pharmacist saying his EpiPen prescription was ready to pick up.

'Great,' I said. 'So we know he's got a serious allergy to peanuts. Hold the front page.'

'Here,' said Emdel, handing me a pen and notebook. 'I'll read out the messages, the time sent and the sender's number. You write it all down.'

'What, everything? Even that guff about peanuts?'

'Yep, everything. We'll make a log of all his messages. Build up a picture of him. Plus it looks like he's pretty sharp about deleting stuff, so if we don't make a record of senders' numbers then they'll be lost to us.'

'So what are you planning to do with the numbers he gets calls from?'

'Hack them, those of interest anyway. Not his chemist, obviously, but his wife for sure, and anyone else who sounds like a friend or associate.'

'Or accomplice,' I added.

'Exactly. Also the people leaving messages might not be quite so hot about deleting stuff. They might well have messages from Dakin.'

'Emdel Black, you are a very dangerous man, d'you know that?'

'I do my best. Now all we need is access to his email inbox.'

Dakin had yet to reply to Emdel's bogus security email.

'What if he doesn't bite?' I asked.

'Then I'll have to strong-arm my way in to his PC via his modem. But let's hope it doesn't come to that. That's the nuclear option. It'd be a lot of grunt work.'

In the event, Dakin answered Emdel's spoof message the following night. Within minutes, we were sifting through Dakin's inbox on Emdel's PC. I felt a crackle of excitement, like I was an intruder sneaking around Dakin's house in the dead of night. I even glanced over my shoulder at one point.

Like most people's email, Dakin's was choked with spam, and there was also plenty of mundane work-related stuff, much of which concerned staffing issues at Derek's. Then, about twenty-five screens in, we found it: an email from the secretary of Dakin's Masonic lodge – called Sagacity Lodge – advising him that his yearly membership was up for renewal. It was from a Peter Geraghty, who had signed off by saying, 'See you on Thursday as usual'.

'What the hell is sagacity?' asked Emdel. 'Sounds like some kind of disease.'

'It means wisdom,' I said. 'It's just more Dungeons and Dragons weirdness. Look' – I pointed at the screen – 'there's the address of their lodge. I know that place. It's an old Salvation Army hall not far from *The Tribune* offices. Hey,' I added, slapping his arm with the back of my hand. 'What are you doing Thursday night? Fancy a stroll up Eastney way?'

*

In the summer, Southsea residents weary of jangling amusement arcades, the scent of vinegar-sodden chips and the endless bustle of holidaying families and foreign-exchange students like to escape – by taking a constitutional up the coast to Eastney.

As its name suggests, Eastney fills the eastern corner of Portsea Island, the island upon which the city of Portsmouth was founded. To see the coast at Eastney is to glimpse Portsea as it must have been pre-settlement. There, the sea finds the land largely untouched and untamed – a pebbly and windswept wilderness, studded with tufts of marram grass and other pioneer plants. Eastney is a place of margins, where wilderness meets civilisation. Maybe that's why the Royal Marines built their imposing barracks there, on Gunner's Row, set back from the Solent behind an expanse of open parkland.

'Who d'you think would win in a fire-fight?' I asked Emdel as we passed the barracks. 'The Royal Marines or the Green Berets?'

'Marines, all day long,' he said.

'Based on what?'

'The fact they're British.'

'That's not exactly scientific, is it. Where's the rigour?'

'In my head it's scientific, only I can't be bothered explaining it. Anyway,' he added, pointing to the knapsack slung from my shoulder, which contained the work camera I'd borrowed from JCN, 'where are we gonna shoot from so they don't see us? It'll still be broad daylight when they're headed into their meeting.'

'Not sure. We'll case it out when we get there.'

I zipped up my jacket. 'Bloody hell, that wind's fresh,' I said. We're only a mile up the road from Southsea but it may as well be a different country. Aren't you cold?'

He shook his head. Emdel never wore a coat, ever – no matter what the weather. It was a point of principle with him. The last coat he'd owned I had burned, ceremonially, at the top of my folks' garden. It had been a thin, synthetic black affair with yellow stripes down each sleeve.

'Remember that petrol-pump attendant's jacket you used to live in, the one we burned?' I said. 'Boy, that thing stank. You can't ever have washed it, not once.'

'The one *you* burned, you mean. I loved that coat.'

'Is that why you've not worn one since? Out of mourning?'

'Yeah, that's right,' he said with a hint of irritation. 'How'd you guess. Right,' he added, pointing inland. 'We've got civilisation up ahead. Stop your gabbing and let's get serious.'

After passing a row of kaleidoscopically coloured beach huts, we swung left off the esplanade and walked in silence for a spell. Wind, pebbles and marram soon gave way to the low-rise streets of Eastney with its rows of Georgian terraced housing, corner shops and pubs. We turned into the road where the Salvation Army hall was. It was shortly before seven in the evening. We had maybe fifteen minutes before the Masons began rocking up to their weekly lodge meeting.

'There's no cover at all,' Emdel said, looking up and down the street. 'We'll be in plain sight. We need a plan. Um, what if we pretend we're American tourists taking pictures? Can you do the accent?'

'That'll never wash,' I said. 'Yanks don't visit Southsea, let alone Eastney. Besides, look at us – we're not fat enough. Your social engineering thing? That's all based on plausibility, right?'

'Yeah.'

'So what about this. We pretend we're doing a vox pop for my old rag, *The Probe*. I'll be the snapper, you be the reporter.'

'What's a vox pop?'

'It's when you quiz members of the public about some issue or other – like the amount of dog shit around the place.'

'I can't see any dog shit,' Emdel said, scanning the pavement. 'Maybe we could ask if they'd like more shit on their streets?'

We laughed, and then, for the first time in far too long, I deployed my news antennae, seeking anything that might qualify as a local story.

'Okay, got it,' I said. 'We'll ask them about the Marines – what they feel about having the world's finest elite troops on their doorstep.'

Hardly world-beating, but it felt good to know I hadn't lost the ability to conjure copy from nowhere.

'But how can I be a reporter without a notebook or a pen?' Emdel said.

'Look, over there,' I said, pointing. 'That shop's got a Post Office counter. Those places always sell stationery.'

We headed in and Emdel bought a spiral-bound notebook and a Biro.

Being a Thursday, most of the shops were still open and a fair number of people were out and about. We positioned ourselves opposite the hall and began stopping passers-by. Although my lens was pointed in the general direction of our interviewees, I had it trained on the entrance to the Salvation Army hall, and it wasn't long before Masons began turning up. All were white, and at least half of them were elderly – stooped and shuffling, some propped up on sticks. The rest were more or less middle-aged. All wore a dark-coloured suit and tie and carried a bag of some description, doubtless containing their prissy little ceremonial apron. I had no idea what any of our target Masons looked like, including Dakin, and so I snapped every one of them. Many cast a quizzical glance our way. One of them paused at the entrance to the hall, eyes slitty with suspicion. Then he crossed the road towards us.

'Can I ask what you're doing?' he said, his words as unyielding as his posture. He was an erect man of middling height and weight and impeccably groomed. It wasn't difficult to imagine him in a police uniform.

'They're from *The Probe*,' said the smiling woman that Emdel was interviewing. 'They're asking me about the Marines.'

He ignored her and looked to Emdel.

'What's your name?'

Emdel thanked the woman, who walked off. He then turned to Mason Erectus, notebook and pen at the ready. 'We're asking local people how they feel about having the Royal Marines on their doorstep,' he said. 'So what about you? Are you proud?'

I lifted the camera to my eye, focused, and fired off a few close-ups. Over his shoulder I saw more Masons arriving and I retrained the lens to catch them.

'May I have your name, sir?' Emdel asked him. 'For my paper?'

Mason Erectus made a grab for the camera, but I yanked it back just in time.

'What the hell are you doing?' I said. 'This was a free country last time I checked.'

'Give me that film,' he barked, taking a half step forward and holding out a soft-looking palm.

'Right, call the police,' I told Emdel. 'I've been assaulted and I'm being harassed.'

'I *am* the police, you idiot!' he said, up on his hind legs now.

'Really?' I replied. 'Well, that saves a phone call. You can arrest yourself, can't you. Listen up, Clouseau, we don't give a continental who or what you are. You've got no right interrogating us and demanding my film. This isn't Russia. Get yourself back across the road, to whatever it is you're doing over there in your Mafia get-up.'

I could see no more Masons approaching the hall. I nodded at

Emdel. 'We're done here. Let's foxtrot oscar.'

The pair of us turned heel away from Mason Erectus.

'You haven't heard the last of this,' he called at our backs. 'You mark my words.'

I spun around.

'My thoughts exactly,' I said, blowing him a kiss.

NINETEEN

'COMMENT ÇA VA, LLEW?' ANDY said, with a silver-screen smile.

'Yeah, savva, Andy, savva,' I replied, shaking his hand, then Larry's, who was sitting next to him.

We were meeting in an Eastney pub called the Live and Let Live, which Emdel and I had discovered on the way back from our Masons surveillance outing, having taken a wrong turn. It was tucked away on the corner of a cul-de-sac, in the middle of a maze of tight residential streets, and I could recall no one on *The Tribune* ever having mentioned it. We could not afford for anyone from the paper to see us together. It would arouse suspicions.

'You still off the sauce?' Larry asked me, dipping into his back trouser pocket for his wallet.

'Yeah.'

'Pint?'

'Go on then, you twisted my arm. I'll have a Razorback. Cheers.'

Larry got the drinks in. Behind the bar was a framed photo of the late Princess Di, adorned with a scraggly length of tinsel. Equally tired-looking Christmas decorations hung limply from the beams and walls of the pub, like they couldn't wait for the comfort of their cardboard box in the loft.

The shaven-headed landlord served him with a solemn air. There was stealth in his easy movements that had a whiff of ex-military. His upper body was heavily muscled, the way Rollo's had been. I found the similarity unsettling. I was still not entirely convinced Rollo wouldn't somehow find a way to punish me from beyond the grave for defiling his daughter.

'I hear you've got some photographs,' said Andy. He was not one for paper-speak. To the rest of us, photos were 'snaps' or 'pix'. He took a sip of red wine. It was the first time I'd seen anyone other than a woman drink wine in a pub, and yet it totally suited him – especially when he drew on his Panetela cigar.

'Yeah, I shot a whole pile of them.'

I plonked a backpack on the table, retrieved a plastic bag from inside and slid out a fat wad of photos, which I'd had printed as six-by-eights.

I riffled through them, stopping when I came to Mason Erectus. 'Look at this pompous prick.'

'So this was the chap who approached you?'

All men were 'chaps' to Andy. Women were *frau* or *fraulein*, depending on whether they were married or not. (He'd had to explain this distinction to me.)

'Yeah, that's him. Jumped-up tosser.'

'Let's have a look-see,' said Larry plonking two beers on the table. He hadn't bothered asking Andy if he wanted another glass. Andy could nurse a single drink all night long. 'You say this prick told you he was a copper?'

'Yeah.'

Larry studied the photo. 'I don't recognise him. My best guess is he's some low-ranking uniform – a constable, possibly a sergeant. He must've guessed what you two were up to, but if he had any kind of public profile I doubt he'd have risked coming up to you like that.'

Larry thumbed through the rest of the pictures.

'Right, where's our Derek?' he said. 'Come on, Dakin, come to Daddy.' He straightened up. 'Gotcha!' Larry held up a photo showing a thick-set man of average height with an Everly Brothers-like mane of dark hair, voluminous and swept back. He had been the only Mason to wear sunglasses. 'He hasn't changed much since the trial,' Larry added, 'though I see he's been at the Grecian 2000, the vain bastard.'

He worked his way through the rest of the photos.

'Him I recognise,' he said, holding up another snap. 'I think he's pretty senior. I've seen him more than once at police press conferences.'

Larry had been to dozens of such conferences down the years, and he said he'd have a trawl through *The Tribune*'s photo archive for pictures of past conferences.

'At those things they always have the officer's name and rank on display,' he explained, 'so hopefully we'll be able to put names to some of these Masons you've snapped. So, Llew,' he added, leaning forward, elbows on table, chin on interlaced fingers. 'Tell me. How'd you find out what lodge Dakin and his plod mates were in?'

'Yeah, well, that's between me and the shadows, Larry.'

'What kind of shadows are we talking about here?'

'I don't get your drift,' I said.

He sat back and looked from me to Andy. 'Okay. Let's say I've good reason to believe that Andy here is a kiddie fiddler.'

'*What?*' said Andy, almost choking on his pinot noir.

'Stay with me,' said Larry. 'I'm going off-piste here. So, one night I breaks into Andy's gaff and I take photos of stuff that prove me right, beyond any doubt, that Andy's a nonce. Then I take my pics to the cops, who charge Andy as a result.'

'Larry, old chap, might I be something other than a kiddie fiddler? A jewel thief, perhaps?'

'Fair enough,' said Larry, smiling at Andy. 'So let's say that Raffles here is staring down the barrel of a five-stretch for a jewel heist, all because of my photos. My question to you is this: where does that leave me – legally, I mean?'

'What, you mean because you broke into Andy's house?' I said.

'Exactamundo. I'll tell you where it leaves me – in the cell next to Raffles, and why? Because breaking and entering is illegal. My evidence could land me a two-stretch, even though it got Raffles banged up.'

'Yeah, nice story,' I said, 'but what's your point?'

'Most journalists will tell you that getting any kind of inside gen on the Masons is next to impossible,' Larry continued. 'Big Al told you as much himself. It's like trying to break into Fort Knox with a toothpick.'

He picked up a handful of photos from the table and waved them at me.

'And yet somehow you manage to hit the jackpot after what, a week? So tell me, how did you know Dakin would be at this meeting?'

I thought about lying – telling him I'd tailed Dakin – but that wouldn't wash because I hadn't known what he looked like.

'Okay. It's a fair cop. We hacked him – his email and voicemail.'

Larry threw himself back in his chair. '*That's* my point, Llew. I bloody knew it – I knew you'd cut a corner somehow. And who's *we*, by the way?'

I told him about Emdel.

'Well,' he said, 'you and your War Games pal have opened up a right can of worms with these pictures. When we publish them, our new Mason friends'll come after us, hard, and one of the first things they'll want to know is how the hell we got these snaps.'

'They're just photos,' I said. 'Anyone can take pictures of people walking into a hall.'

Larry gave a deep sigh. 'But they're not just photos, are they – they're the result of you hacking Dakin. Look, fella, these are coppers we're about to shit on, and from a great height. D'you think they'll take that lying down, mouths open? Of course they won't. They'll come back at us, hard, and so might Dakin.'

'So what do we do?' I asked.

'We cover our arses, that's what we do. We need a cover story, something that explains how we knew they'd be at that lodge meeting – something other than the fact you hacked Dakin, I mean.'

I recalled the lie I'd considered telling Larry moments earlier.

'What if we could show that we'd been tailing Dakin? You know, pictures of him leaving his home, his club, him out shopping. That way the Mason photos would look like the result of some good old-fashioned legwork.'

Larry stroked his chin and nodded. 'Yeah, that could work. Reverse engineering. I like it, Llew. Good thinking. I'll commission a PI I know. He'll have it done in a few days. But lads?'

'Yeah?' Andy and I chorused.

'This whole Rollo thing? It's gonna be big trouble. Think about it. You've got arson, manslaughter – possibly murder, who knows? And the likeliest culprit is a crook who may or may not have half the Old Bill in his back pocket. If Dakin has got cops suppressing evidence for him then you better believe it's just the tip of a very grubby iceberg. Buckle up boys. Things could get rough.'

TWENTY

SECONDS AFTER THE CORONER RETURNED a verdict of unlawful killing, Lucy leapt from her seat.

'Call this justice?' she shouted, pointing at the coroner. 'Why's no one been charged? This was arson. You said so yourself. So who killed my daddy?'

Rollo's friends and neighbours, who filled the courtroom, followed Lucy's lead, and the air rang with their incendiary language.

I tugged on one of Lucy's sleeves – Larry, the other – to encourage her to sit down, but it was no good.

'Miss Baer, please,' the coroner said, his voice mellifluous and his tone firm, but calming. He did not seek to suppress people's indignation, but instead waited until it had tapered to a low-level rustling and murmuring. I guessed that, down the years, he must have been faced with thousands of similarly distraught friends and loved ones.

'Let me repeat,' he told the now quiet room, 'it is not the job of this court to apportion blame in connection with the death of Mr Baer. The remit of this court is to determine who the deceased was, and where, when and how they died, and to arrive at a verdict on the nature of that death that is beyond all reasonable doubt. I shall say again, it is this court's verdict that Mr Rollo Baer was unlawfully killed. And with that, I have discharged my duties as coroner, and this inquest is now at a conclusion.'

Lucy sat staring ahead, unmoving. Larry, in full-on work mode, slid away to mingle with Rollo's friends and neighbours, notebook at the ready. After a few minutes everyone had taken their anger and frustration outside, leaving Lucy and me alone in the courtroom.

I took her hand, which sat limp and cool in mine. 'I don't know what to say, Lucy – apart from this isn't the end. You need to know that things are happening behind the scenes. Me, Andy and Larry are on the case. Dakin's not out of the woods, not by a long shot. I promise you that. Lucy?'

She withdrew her lifeless hand, stood up and left the room without speaking. I sat there alone for a time, too weary to move or think. I walked from the building, legs leaden.

'There you are,' said Mrs Matthews, approaching. 'This'll kill her, mark my words.'

Oh God, not her. This is all I need.

'She'll go the way of her mother, way things are headed.'

Enough. 'Have you actually got something to say to me? If so, let's hear it.'

She sucked at her teeth and folded her arms. 'She needs help, that girl, afore it's too late.'

Afore? You even speak like something from a Hammer Horror. I suppose I'd better ask.

'So what kind of help d'you have in mind. Grief counselling?'

She made a contemptuous blowing sound. 'The rope's half round her neck and he's talking about grief counselling.'

'Right, I've had enough of this. If you haven't got—'

'The sort of help that comes in white coats. That's what she needs, and she needs it now.'

'You can't be serious. You want her sectioned?'

'That I do.'

'And you're the expert, are you? On mental health?'

She bristled. 'I knew her mother – girl and woman. She were never right in the head, that one, nor's her daughter. Your little jokes'll not sound so funny when that girl's lying dead on a marble slab down the morgue. You're the closest she's got to family now, God help her. You do nothing and you'll have her death on your conscience for the rest of your days, mark my words.'

She pointed at me accusatorily, as if she were picking me from a police line-up, before stalking off. It left me feeling heavy and spooked. Did Mrs Hammer-Horror have some kind of voodoo powers? Had she cursed me?

After a few moments my thoughts turned to the dreadful things she'd foretold and I shivered. What if the evil old bag was right? What if Lucy really was so desperate that she might seek to end it all? It was unthinkable. I would never let that happen, but I knew in my bones that what would save Lucy was not men in white coats, but justice.

The inquest had been a huge blow for her, serving only to confirm that whoever torched Rollo's club, and him along with it, was laughing at her – feet up, cigar in mouth.

I'll get justice for you, Lucy. I'll get Dakin. Whatever it takes.

TWENTY ONE

MRS HAMMER-HORROR USED HER spare key to let me into Lucy's flat. I'd already closed my ears to her dark mutterings by the time I closed the door on her.

The flat was shipshape, and on the counter was a covered and untouched plate of ham and boiled cabbage. She might be an old witch whose cooking was nostril-twitchingly institutional but at least she was taking care of Lucy, and I was grateful to her for that.

I found Lucy in an easy chair in the living room, chin on knees, and wearing nothing but one of her father's shirts. It felt like an improvement on her being curled up on Rollo's bed, hugging his soiled crackers and socks.

'No wonder you're not eating if that's what she's cooking,' I said.

I sat on the two-berth sofa opposite her and placed my backpack on the floor between us.

'The old bag let me in. I hope you don't mind me coming. It's just I need to speak to you. It's important.'

She stared ahead at some indeterminate point.

'Look,' I said, 'I'll just say what I need to say and you listen, okay?'

She gave an almost imperceptible nod. I reached inside the backpack, slid out a paper folder and offered it to her.

'You might want to see this.'

She lowered her knees, placed the folder on her lap and perused its contents.

'What is this?' she asked.

'A file on Dakin – his emails and voicemails. We hacked him, me and Emdel. And there's some photos.'

I walked her through the Masons connection and told her that we thought this was how Dakin had managed to escape justice.

She held up my portrait of Mason Erectus.

'Who's this?'

'One of the Mason policeman. Keep going through the photos and you'll come to a man wearing shades. That's Dakin. Larry has ID'd seven of the coppers so far and some of them are pretty senior. He says *The Tribune*'ll be running a piece next week, once Big Al's done getting legal guidance, because obviously you don't take on the police and the Masons lightly, not on something like this.'

She looked up from the photos. She was still flat, lifeless. 'Will the paper say that Dakin is guilty?' There was a flicker of life in her words, of hope. I knew I mustn't extinguish it.

'*The Tribune* is walking a legal tightrope. The aim is to let Dakin and his Mason friends know that we're on to them. The paper's got a police insider feeding them info. The hope is that the story'll rattle some cages, maybe force them into a move, and that our insider then keeps us one step ahead.'

'You didn't answer my question,' she said with a little less hope.

'It's all we can do at the moment.' I went to her and crouched down before her. 'But we're on to them. We make a move, they make a move – but it's our game, our rules. One way or another, we'll get justice for your daddy. I promise you that.'

I heard myself gulp and hoped she hadn't.

'You promise?'

I nodded.

'When the story comes out, the police will be frantic,' I said, taking her hands now. 'Not only will they know they've a whistleblower in their midst but our story'll turn the public against them even more than they already are. A lot of people already think the force is rotten to its core, so this story'll have the cops squirming. It's all about turning the screw and waiting for something to give.'

'Something?' she said in a half-whisper, as if afraid to hope too brightly. 'Like what?'

'Like Dakin being charged, as he should've been in the first place.'

'And if that doesn't happen?'

'Then we turn to Plan B.'

I fished out a page, written in my hand, listing all the Dakin voicemails we had intercepted thus far.

'These are Dakin's mobile messages,' I explained as she read them. 'I know we haven't got much yet. Emdel reckons that Dakin uses another phone for all the shady stuff. The next step is to get hold of that number and see what we can find out.'

'Is that allowed?'

'No, it's very much not allowed. The voicemails and emails? All of it's illegal, so you mustn't say anything about it to anyone, okay?'

'Okay.'

I leaned forward and kissed her on the forehead. Her skin was cool and clammy. I packed up the backpack and slung it over my shoulder.

'I came because I thought it was important that you have some hope. I know the inquest was a low point. I've been worried about you.'

I laid a hand on her shoulder. She reached up and gave it a squeeze.

'Thank you,' she said with a reticent smile that at least hinted at hope.

TWENTY TWO

'HOLY SHIT,' SAID LARRY, AS he watched Emdel put the Caller ID program through its paces, using it to hack into Larry's voicemails. 'And you wrote this thing yourself?'

'It's actually quite a simple bit of coding,' Emdel said.

'Yeah, everything's simple to him,' I said. 'You spend enough time in his company and you'll end up feeling like the thick kid in class. Except with girls. Emdel's the remedial on that front.'

'Yeah, hilarious,' Emdel said with a scowl. He was touchy about the subject of women. He still had a picture of Thirza in his wallet, his one and only girlfriend to date – a girlfriend he had driven into the arms of lesbianism, one might add.

Larry patted Emdel's shoulder. 'Don't you listen to him, fella. You just gotta get out there, that's all – put yourself about a bit. There's no big secret to finding a bird, other than if you don't fill out the coupon, you'll not win the pools.'

'I'm more of a lottery man,' said Emdel.

'Same principle,' Larry said. 'Anyway you two, listen up. So this is how we're gonna play it ...'

I'd decided we needed to involve Larry in what we were doing. Emdel hadn't been keen, but I explained that Larry knew better than anyone exactly how close we could sail to the wind, legally speaking.

The Tribune was set to break our Masons story on the Friday of that week, and Larry had prepared a watertight defence should the police or the Masons – or both – begin questioning how the paper had come by the information that Dakin and a host of senior cops were members of the same Masonic lodge. Larry had commissioned a PI to tail Dakin, and now had grainy monochrome photos of him leaving his home and arriving at his club.

'So now, your snaps of those Masons looks like the result of a round-the-clock surveillance,' he explained to Emdel.

'But what about the dodgy quality of the photos?' I asked. Big Al must know you didn't use one of the staff snappers.'

'Course he does,' said Larry. 'I told him up front this was no job for a staff tog – that this was a stakeout, not some cheque presentation, and for that reason I'd be using a PI. So our arses are covered from all angles.'

'Is Andy on board with all this?' I asked.

'Are you senile or what?' said Larry. 'Raffles was sitting right next to you in the boozer when you handed over the snaps. Course he's on board.'

'That's not what I meant. I'm asking if Andy's okay about lying to Big Al and Daphne.'

'Let's just say that Raffles is about as okay with it as I am,' said Larry. 'I don't want to hoodwink them, but how else are we gonna nail that piece of shit Dakin and those bent cops? Besides, we're doing it for Lucy, same as you.' Larry gave a single clap. 'Right, so tell us about Phase Two. I'm intrigued.'

I nodded at Emdel. 'You're the expert.'

Emdel leaned forward in his swivel chair, elbows on knees. 'So, let's say that this *Tribune* story doesn't end up with Dakin being charged.'

'Which is more than possible,' said Larry. 'Those Mason cops'll stick together like shit to a blanket, and that's just the ones we know about. There'll be others – you can bet your life on it.'

'Yeah,' continued Emdel, 'so then we'll need something else on Dakin to give things a little shove. We already know that the one number we've got for Dakin will never give us anything. It's his clean phone, the one he uses for home and work. He must use another mobile for all his dodgy stuff.'

'Dodgy stuff like arson, you mean?' said Larry.

'Exactly. Now Dakin doesn't seem the sort who'd get his own hands dirty burning down a club, which begs the question: who set the fire and how did Dakin arrange it all?'

'You think he did it by phone?' Larry asked.

'There's only one way to find out. We need the number of his second phone.'

'And how d'you plan to get that?' asked Larry. 'He's not just gonna hand it over.'

'That's exactly what he's going to do,' said Emdel, smiling and looking my way. 'Isn't it, Llew.'

'Bloody hell, Llew, what've you got planned, exactly?' Larry said, looking at me hard. 'You've turned paler than an albino Scotsman.'

TWENTY THREE

THE TRIBUNE'S DAKIN SPLASH was a Big Al masterpiece. The banner headline read *Murky world of Mason cops*. A total of five inside pages were dedicated to the story, including a spread of my photos, with every police officer pictured being identified by name and rank. By chance, my poor lensmanship gave the images real impact. Their grain and slight blur, combined with the dark-suited, Reservoir Dogs-like Masons, reinforced the general sense of murkiness. The photos had originally been colour but the picture editor had rendered them into black and white, which upped the murk quotient even more. Each photo also contained an inset mugshot of that officer, taken from old police news-conference images that Larry had sourced.

And in a side panel on page three – out on his own – was Derek Dakin in shades and sombre suit. Constrained by law, the paper had been unable to say much about him, other than that he was a nightclub owner and had been cleared of drugs trafficking charges some years earlier. The subtext was clear: this man is no model citizen. And the juxtaposition of Dakin next to his Mason-cop buddies – he faced into them – also invited the reader to join the dots that had been so expertly positioned by Big Al. No wonder he had been in protracted talks with the paper's lawyers, for he had pushed what was permissible in law to the very edge. He was a master of inference and suggestion.

Those same dots would also be joined to devastating effect by the Mason officers who had been pictured and named. They would surely guess that *The Tribune*'s source was a fellow officer. Within the city's police, the story would sow mistrust and suspicion within the force – from the top to the bottom of their uniformed and plain-clothed ranks. As I had explained to Lucy, the pressure would build, and not just from within.

Public confidence in the police had rarely been lower than it was that year, 1997. Just a couple of months before *The Tribune*'s Masons story, the British government of the day had published an inquiry into Freemasonry in the police and in the judiciary. It had concluded that having public servants who are members of a secret society – a society whose raison d'etre is mutual self-advancement – is probably not such a great idea. The inquiry recommended that police officers, magistrates, judges and crown prosecutors should voluntarily register their membership of the Masons. People cried 'foul'. What Mason would voluntarily do this? None, was the consensus. The shadow of Masonic influence had even fallen over the inquiry itself.

Sections of the media – the Masons-free media, presumably – were outraged, as was the general public. Mason cronyism in public life became one of the hot topics of the summer. *The Tribune* steaming in with its murky Mason-cops exclusive would stir it up all over again in the national press and on TV and radio.

The cherry on top of *The Tribune*'s Masonic cake was Larry's double-page guide to Freemasonry. I had loaned him my copy of *Inside the Brotherhood*, and he'd used it to curate a spread of Masonic titbits to shock, appal and entertain the reader in turn.

His glossary of Masonic roles and ranks was mind-boggling: Grand Master; Past Master; Right Worshipful Brother; Very Worshipful Brother. It made the organisation sound like something Bryan and Darryl might dream up, having gotten stoned in a room containing members of their chess club, the Southsea Dungeons and Dragons

Society and the Ku Klux Klan.

His guide to Masonic language, meanwhile, was just as eye-catching. The fact that Masons referred to non-Masons as 'profane' might alone be enough, I thought, to convince many readers that Masons held the non-Masonic majority in contempt.

And to reinforce the link between the shady-sounding Dakin and his Mason-cop pals, Larry had written a piece about known cases of convicted Masons. The most shocking example was that of career criminal Kenneth Noye, who was convicted of handling gold bullion from the £26 million Brink's-Mat heist in Heathrow in 1983. Noye was a member of the Hammersmith Lodge and had been proposed for membership by two police officers. While Noye was serving time for handling the stolen gold, his fellow Masons – many of whom were serving police officers – had continued to pay his lodge subscriptions. How brotherly of them.

But for me, the most potent part of the entire *Tribune* exclusive was an editorial that had Big Al's classy stamp all over it. It was factual, simple and direct.

'When it comes to writing, less is more,' Big Al was fond of saying, and he had followed his own advice in writing the following:

'I will be honest and act with integrity at all times, and will not compromise or abuse my position.'

So reads Point One of the Police Code of Ethics.

Now picture an officer of the law – blindfolded, bare-breasted and with a noose around his neck – swearing on an open Bible that he will follow the vows of the Freemasons or risk having his throat cut and his tongue torn out by the root.

And what are these Masonic vows exactly? They are a code of mutual help – nothing more, nothing less. You scratch my back …

But whose backs are these Mason officers scratching? One another's? Those of criminals like Kenneth Noye? Are they upholding the Police Code of Ethics, or subverting it?

We simply don't know, and that's the problem. For this reason alone, serving officers should be barred by law from joining the Masons.

TWENTY FOUR

ONE OF THE FEW POSITIVES to working for JCN was that the company was minted. In a building full of PCs, I was the only person with a state-of-the-art Apple Mac. Plus I had screwed thousands of pounds' worth of training out of them, enough to make me a whiz with Photoshop and with page-layout software. I might be writing seven shades of corporate crap, but at least I could derive satisfaction from making it look nice on the page. Those skills also came in handy for other things – such as forging business cards.

In order to persuade Derek Dakin to hand me his secret mobile number, I would first need to convince him that I was who I claimed to be: Guy Tuck, Regional Sales Manager, Solent Drinks. It was a real company, and Guy Tuck actually was their Regional Sales Manager. Posing as Guy Tuck, I had set up a bogus meeting with the manager of Derek's nightclub.

'I still don't get why it's me who has to walk into the dragon's lair,' I'd protested to Emdel. 'You're the one with the social engineering skills.'

At that, Emdel had hiked up the sleeves of his maroon sweater and sighed through his nostrils.

'We're going round in circles here,' he said. 'For the last time, you've actually got better social engineering skills than me. You do it for a living. You can get anyone to tell you anything, and more importantly you can do it face to face. Sure, I can do it over the phone no problem, but in person? I'd be rumbled within seconds. But you're a natural-born blagger – that's a compliment by the way.'

'Yeah, thanks. I think. And what if he recognises me, the manager? Or Dakin himself for that matter? I was all over the papers just a few years back, remember?'

'Your photo was in a few papers over three years ago,' Emdel countered. 'When was the last time anyone recognised you?'

'Er, about three years ago.'

'Exactly. Plus you've got that beard now.'

I'd started growing the beard about a month earlier by mistake; all my disposable razors were blunt. It itched like crazy at the beginning, but I'd kept it because being unable to recognise yourself in the mirror can be an oddly alluring experience. And I was lazy.

To get to Dakin I first had to meet with the manager of Derek's. I'd hand him a case of free wine and spirits that Emdel and I had bought (and for which Larry had assured us we'd be reimbursed). We'd also bought a second case of top-quality wine and spirits. I would ask the manager if I might see Mr Dakin so that I could hand him his complimentary drinks in person. Having secured some face time with Dakin, the plan was to harvest Dakin's shady mobile number by establishing myself as a fellow miscreant.

'You're a miscreant anyway, so it shouldn't be that hard,' Emdel quipped by way of reassurance.

I would shoot the breeze with Dakin, before revealing the true reason for my visit: did he want thousands of pounds' worth of cut-price wine and spirits 'off the back of a lorry'? Emdel was certain Dakin would go for it, and that he'd give me his other number so we could make it happen.

But to pull it off, I needed to turn in a method-acting masterclass as Guy Tuck. I'd need to know Guy Tuck's job inside out – who his customers were, who his rivals were, who his colleagues were, and what the drinks market was doing. The rest I could blag – family, kids, interests, et cetera.

I'd also need an authentic-looking business card for Guy Tuck, complete with company logo. As I worked on the nearly completed card on my JCN Apple Mac, I failed to spot Geoffrey spectating over my shoulder.

'Llewellyn,' he said, 'who is Guy Tuck and what is Solent Drinks?'

'Oh, yeah,' I said, resisting the guilt-fuelled urge to shut down the Photoshop window I was working in. 'It's just a favour I'm doing a mate. He's setting up a new company and wants a business card.'

'Well, I'll thank you to do it on your time, not the company's,' Geoffrey said, tweaking his dicky bow. 'And you and I need to talk, by the way. Now, if it's not too inconvenient for you.'

Geoffrey led me to a nearby meeting room. I knew what was coming. In fact, I'd kind of been looking forward to it.

'Right,' he said, laying a past issue of *Family First* on the table. Circled in green highlighter pen was my article on the tidy-desk initiative. 'Please tell me what this is.'

I decided to play dumb.

'Er, it's a copy of—'

'You must take me for a proper Charlie. Do you, Llewellyn?'

'Do I what?'

'Take me for a proper Charlie?'

'I don't know what you—'

'Do not insult my intelligence by pretending you are not cognisant of what it is we are discussing here.'

Cognisant? And that's why you'll always be a Geoffrey.

'Okay,' he continued, unclipping one of the three pens he kept in his breast pocket – another driver of his Geoffreyness. He ringed the opening letters of the twelve paragraphs that the article was comprised of. 'What do those letters spell?' he asked, thrusting the publication to within six inches of my nose.

'S-P-U-N-K-T-R-U-M-P-E-T,' I said. 'I don't see what—'

'Spunk trumpet?' said Geoffrey.

Ah, NOW you sound like a Geoff!

'What were you thinking?'

'Er, actually I wasn't thinking anything,' I assured him, accessing my best serious face. 'It's just a random collection of letters. It could've happened to anyone. A spunk trumpet's not even a thing, is it?'

We to-and-froed for a few minutes, him accusing, me denying, until he lost patience and served me with the written warning that the board had demanded I be issued.

'This is an outrage,' I said to his back as he left the room. 'It's a poxy staff paper, not bloody *Pravda*.'

*

'So what is a spunk trumpet, anyway?' asked Jason as he spooned in another mouthful of jam roly-poly. A dribble of chocolate custard leaked from one corner of his mouth.

'It's like feeding time at the bloody zoo,' I said, looking from Jason to Glenn, who was tackling a double cheeseburger so towering he'd have needed to have dislocating snake-jaws to wrap his teeth around it. As it was, he tried eating it sideways, and the contents slipped from between the buns and splatted onto his plate.

'Glenn, you're not a python,' I said. 'Why don't you use a knife and fork?'

'Spunk trumpet,' said Emdel. 'S'funny. Took them long enough to suss it. I thought you'd gotten away with it. So who spotted it, d'you know?'

'The ten-year-old son of the MD apparently,' I said. 'The little tyke asked his mum what a spunk trumpet was.'

Everyone laughed, except for Jason. 'I still don't get it,' he said. 'What is a spunk trumpet?'

'Poor old Jason,' said Bryan, grinning and loosening his vinyl piano-key tie. 'Maybe he hasn't got one.' He nudged his brother with an elbow. 'Eh, Darryl?'

Darryl grinned. 'Yeah,' he said – an effusive response by his supremely taciturn standards.

I took in the glittering rhinestoned spectacle that was Darryl and shook my head. 'You look like Elvis in his Las Vegas days. Does no one ask you to wear proper work clobber?'

He just shrugged. Jason, meanwhile, thumped the table.

'Is anyone gonna tell me what a frigging spunk trumpet is!'

I felt dozens of pairs of eyes look our way, staring across the tumbleweed hush.

'You,' I hissed at Jason, 'are the biggest spunk trumpet I know, okay? Jesus.'

Emdel laughed so hard he almost choked on his Black Forest gateau. Glenn slapped his back with such force that Emdel's glasses flew off, landing in his dessert. Emdel fished them out and began licking the lenses clean of whipped cream.

'Jesus Christ,' I growled through my teeth, 'I swear to God, if I stay in this place a second longer I'm gonna lose my fricking mind.'

The only thing keeping me sane was the covert work Emdel and I were doing for Larry. The prospect of meeting Dakin might leave a cold pit of dread in my stomach whenever I thought about it but at least it made me feel alive and vital.

Without the thrum and buzz of a newsroom to sustain me I was like a junkie without his fix – twitchy, agitated and increasingly desperate. Too much longer at JCN and I feared I might throttle someone with an Ethernet cable. Geoffrey, probably.

'Ah, spunk trumpet,' said Jason, laughing on his own. 'I get it now.'

TWENTY FIVE

'HE ALMOST LOST AN EYE,' Larry told me. 'It might not look like it when you see him, but he was lucky. Fucking bastards.'

I followed Larry through the entrance hall of Portsmouth's general hospital. We took a lift, which opened onto two sets of double swing doors, each leading to a ward. Larry pushed through one set with me in his slipstream.

'He was such a handsome bastard too,' said Larry. 'I think that's why they chose him and not me. Wouldn't make much difference if they slashed my ugly mug, would it. Might even improve things.'

'Hey,' I said, tugging at his elbow. 'Stop a second, would you. I just want to gather myself before we go in. Is he talking?'

'Yeah, he's the same old Raffles – still speaking foreign, charming all the nurses. He's got them creaming their knickers. He's still in shock, of course.'

'Did he a get a look at whoever did this?'

'Some rangy fucker in shorts and a ski mask was all he saw. Andy gets a tap on the shoulder, he turns around and this great big streak of piss swings an arm, and then he's blind 'cos of all the claret. Some lady found him staggering about covered in blood. She waited with him till the ambulance came.'

'So how bad is it?'

'Forty-one stitches right across his face. Bastards. But we'll get 'em, you'll see. We'll skewer those scumbags.'

You'll have to find them first, I thought, but I decided to say nothing. I didn't want to dampen Larry's fury. He did his best work when riled.

'Who d'you think it was?' I asked. 'Dakin? The Masons? Surely not one of the cops?'

'My money's on Dakin. He can see we're closing in and wants us to back off. You ready?'

I nodded, and we swung into the private room Andy was in, and for which Daphne had paid. Big Al and Thirza were sitting at his bedside.

'Bandit, you lovely boy,' said Big Al, standing up. We shook hands. Thirza glanced up, and then away again almost as quickly, as did Daphne. Thirza had one of Andy's hands in both of hers. She'd been crying. I tried to recall the last time I had seen her cry but couldn't. She wasn't one of life's weepers. It suited her, I thought. The bloodshot eyes seemed to soften what could be a cold – if lovely – face.

'What the fuck are you looking at?' she said, glaring my way.

I gave her the twin palms of peace.

'Hey, Andy,' I said, tapping his shoulder.

Three quarters of his face was swaddled in bandages. A hidden hillock of dressings bulged over his right eye. With his left, he winked – or maybe he blinked; it was difficult to say. I smiled at him.

'*Ah, Llew, mon ami. Ça va?*'

'Yeah, savva Andy, savva. You?'

He nodded and smiled, and no one knew quite what to say, either to Andy or one another. It wasn't just because of what had happened to Andy; I was estranged from my former colleagues, and so we were reduced to non-sequitur small talk.

'Rain's forecast for later.'

'I see Pompey lost again.'

'Flowers are nice.'

Our unease was relieved by a nurse, who tapped on the door before coming in. She was middle-aged with warm, smiling eyes – precisely the kind of face I'd want to see if I was in Andy's position, I thought.

'Sorry folks, visiting's over,' she said. 'He's all mine now,' she added, smiling. 'I've been waiting all day to get this one on his own.'

'*Ma belle ange est là*,' said Andy, kissing the air and reaching out as if for a hug.

She blew him a kiss and giggled like a teen. 'I've no idea what he just said but it melted my heart anyway. Right you lot, off you trot.'

We said our goodbyes to Andy – the men with pats here and there and Thirza with a kiss on his forehead.

'Hey, you,' the nurse joked with Thirza. 'Lips off. He's mine.'

Thirza smiled. God, she was beautiful when she smiled. 'Take good care of him please,' she said. 'We love our Andy.'

'And so do we,' said the nurse.

We shuffled out of the room.

'Just a minute,' came the nurse's voice as we were about to exit the ward. 'I just wanted a quick word.'

She confirmed what Larry had said earlier – that Andy had been extremely fortunate not to lose an eye. He'd blinked at just the right moment, protecting it from the full vicious force of the blade.

'The bandages will be on for a while yet,' she said, 'but when they come off you must be careful not to stare or to look shocked. That'll just make it worse for him. He will look different, so you do need to prepare yourselves for that. And also be prepared for his behaviour to change, especially in the early days. An injury like this can have a big effect mentally. There's a kind of grieving process as the person comes to terms with their appearance. He might be a bit teary, and if he is, take him aside and encourage him to talk through his feelings. Or he may be very quiet. If he is, try not to tiptoe around him. Don't let him stew – just behave like you normally would towards him. And if he wants to joke about how he looks? Try not to feel awkward about it. Maybe even joke along with him, gently of course. Joking's just some people's way of coping. The one thing that Andy's got going for him is that he's male. Men tend to cope better with this kind of thing than women.'

It was too much for Thirza and the tears sprang forth.

'But he was so handsome,' she cried. 'He was so fucking handsome.'

The nurse took her hand. 'And he will still be handsome, my dear, if that's how you choose to see him. But please, you mustn't cry in front of him. It'll just make things worse for him.'

The nurse thanked us and returned to the ward, leaving us to exit the hospital in silence. As we exchanged muted goodbyes in the car park, Thirza lurched at Larry and grabbed two fistfuls of his jacket.

'You find the scum-fuck who did this,' she said, shaking him. 'Even if it means using that lying piece of shit over there. She released one fistful of his jacket to aim a quivering finger at me. 'Whatever it fucking takes. Just find him.'

'She's right,' said Big Al, looking pale. 'Let's get those bastards.' He looked from Larry to me. 'For Andy.'

'And Lucy,' I said.

'Yeah,' he said, removing his Michael Caine specs to wipe away a tear. 'For Lucy too.'

TWENTY SIX

DAKIN'S MANAGER EYED HIS FREE case of wine and spirits like a man whose Christmases had all come at once.

'I could get used to this,' he said, his smile broadening with each bottle he slid from the case. 'We get quite a few reps through here and the most I've ever had is a business card.'

'Talking of which,' I said, producing a bogus card from my wallet. It carried two phone numbers: one was the Solent Drinks switchboard, for the purposes of veracity, and the other was the number for a pay-as-you go mobile phone Emdel had bought.

Between the phone and the cases of drink, our bid to get Dakin's second number was proving costly. But now that I was operating with the tacit approval of Big Al, I could at least legitimately invoice the paper for my time. I'd heard from Larry that Daphne had been against my involvement at first, but one look at Andy's scar had been enough to change her mind. Of course, neither she nor Big Al knew what I was actually up to.

'And that's how we gotta keep it,' Larry liked to remind me. 'Or my job could be next on the line.'

The manager of Derek's tottered off to stash his precious freebies in the boot of his car 'for safekeeping'. When he returned he led me to one of the tables that surrounded the dance floor. Being a former aircraft hangar, the club was cavernous, with a ceiling as high as a cathedral. As we walked, the rubber flooring sucked at the soles of my shoes.

'Don't forget to wipe your feet on the way out,' the manager joked.

We sat. I watched a listless late middle-aged female cleaner push an automated floor cleaner around the place. She was lapping up and down the dance floor as if trimming the grass on a football pitch. Even in that huge space the stench of bleach was thick in the air.

'You get used to it,' the manager said, seeing my nose scrunch up. 'If the punters could see this place during the day I swear they'd never set foot in this shithole again. He doesn't give a damn about this dump,' he added, aiming a thumb over his shoulder at a distant door that I guessed must lead to Dakin's office. The manager picked at a strip of silver gaffer tape that had been stuck over a split in the red vinyl bar stool he was sitting on. 'Everything's falling apart. Even the wiring's dodgy. It's a miracle this place hasn't burned down, like that place across town. D'you hear about that?'

I told him I hadn't, hoping to coax from him whatever he happened to know about it.

'Yeah, The Crystal Rooms,' he continued. 'I heard it was twice as good as here. It must've been true, because our Saturday numbers were well down when that place was in full swing. Arson, they say. Funny that, don'tcha think?'

I suppressed my growing interest at his not-so-small small talk.

'Was anyone hurt?' I asked, trying to sound vaguely disinterested. 'In the fire, I mean?'

'Yeah, a man died,' he said. 'The owner.'

'Oh dear.'

'Rollo something or other was his name. One of them wheelchair users,' he added, as if paralysis was an injudicious life choice. 'D'you know, I recognised him from his picture in the paper. He was in here a few times, rolling around in his chair. Must've been doing some homework. He had some dolly bird with him. Right looker, she was. I would have, if you know what I mean. Got me right down, that did.'

'Down?' I asked, not entirely sure I wanted to know where this was headed.

'Yeah, 'cos there's me, right, who can't get seem to get any kind of bird, not even an ugly one, and then Ironside rolls in with this sexpot fawning all over him. Even cripples are getting more than me. It bugged me so much that one night when he came in I very nearly asked him what his secret was.'

Now *that* I would like to have seen, I thought.

'Anyway,' the manager added, leaning back, 'you haven't come here to hear about my sex life, or lack of it more like. So tell us about Solent Drinks. What can you offer us?'

I handed him the company's catalogue. Emdel had blagged a copy by phoning them and saying he was a business studies undergraduate studying the drinks trade.

'I've circled our bestsellers,' I told him. 'Most of them are mid-range products. That's the sweet spot for most of our clients.'

He tapped the brochure and winked, indicating it was a done deal. I wondered how the real Guy Tuck would react when the manager of Derek's called to fine-tune the deal. And what would the jaded manager make of it all when he realised he'd been had? Who cares, I thought. I'll be long gone by then.

He stood and offered me his hand. 'He'll give you ten minutes,' he said, pointing at the same distant door. 'You're honoured – you're the first rep he's seen since I've been here. I guess *that* helps,' he added, nodding down at the second case of drinks I'd brought with me for Dakin. 'Here,' he added, checking over his shoulder for eavesdroppers even though the only other person near us was the cleaner, about a goalkeeper's kick away. 'A word to the wise about my boss. Dakin'll make out like he's your best mate, like you're the most important person in the world to him, but first chance he gets, he'll fuck you over.'

'Look,' I said, shaking my head. 'I'm sorry, but I've got to ask. Why do you stay here if it's so bloody awful? I mean, Pompey's a seaside town – there's tons of other nightspots you could work at.'

He rubbed his thumb against the first two fingers of one hand, did a zipping motion across his lips with the other and winked. I half expected him to mime 'book' or 'film', and tap out syllables on his arm. I nodded knowingly; he was trapped. Sex-starved and trapped.

You'll make someone a lovely husband, I thought as I picked up the case of drinks. The bottles chinked as I tottered towards Dakin's office. I placed the box on the floor and knocked.

'Come,' came a voice from behind the door.

I opened it a crack, picked up the box and used it to shunt my way into the room. Dakin was sitting behind a forbidding ornate dark-wood desk that had a green-leather surface inlaid with a swirling gold-leaf border. It was the kind of desk that belonged in a National Trust property, not the office of a skanky club a stone's throw from the M27. I recognised Dakin from the photo I'd taken of him arriving at his Masons meeting. My stomach lurched. I'd forgotten about those bloody photos. Emdel and I had been standing just across the road from him. What if he recognised me? My beard itched in that moment as if to remind me of its purpose.

Dakin stood up, arms outstretched like the Saviour.

'Ah,' he said with a toothy smile. 'He comes bearing gifts. And what do we have here?'

I plonked the box on the desk and he began lifting out bottles. He had a copy of that day's *Insider* newspaper on his desk, I saw. The *Insider* was my old paper – the national tabloid for which I had briefly worked. They'd had me and all its other reporters celeb gamehunting every second of every day. At the time it had felt like a never-ending deer stalk, but now that I knew some of Emdel's hacking tricks, I realised that in truth we'd been shooting fish in a barrel.

'All my favourites,' Dakin said, beaming at a bottle of twelve-year-old single malt. He offered me his hand. 'Someone's done their homework. That's what I like to see.'

I handed him a business card.

'Guy Tuck,' he said, reading it. 'Well, take a seat, Guy Tuck, and tell me all about yourself.

I riffed on my true-life backstory, because lies are always more convincing when marbled with truth.

'Very good,' he said with a smile so broad I thought his face might split in two. 'So what brings you here today, my friend?'

'Yeah, well, about that.'

'Ahhh,' he said, leaning across the green acres of his desk. 'Why do I get the feeling all of a sudden that your company doesn't know you're here?'

'That feeling would be correct, sir.'

'Sir?' he said, laughing. 'Oh, I like you, Guy, I like you. Manners. You can't put a price on manners.'

'So, yeah, um, well, you see—'

'Come on,' he said. 'Out with it. You're amongst friends here.'

'I might have something for you in about a month. A consignment of drinks.'

He leaned back in his matching National Trust chair. 'I'm listening.'

'It's a bonded warehouse, Southampton way.'

The bonded warehouse had been Emdel's idea. 'I saw it on *Beverly Hills Cop 2*,' he'd explained.

'What the hell is a bonded warehouse?' I'd asked.

'S'where they keep duty-free stuff, for export and things. I've looked into it. There are some bonded places near Southampton docks. It's a better story than you offering him drinks that've fallen off the back of some truck or other.'

Emdel and I had even driven to Southampton to check out the warehouses for real.

'There's a bonded storage place near Southampton docks,' I told Dakin. 'My oldest mate does security there. During the day there's someone on the gate, but at night it's just my mate. He's got keys.' I pulled some photos from my suit jacket pocket. 'Here,' I said, leaning across the desk. 'This is the place.'

He thumbed through them, nodding. 'So, Guy, tell me, why me? Of all people, why d'you come to me with this?'

We'd debated what I should say if Dakin asked me this.

'Tell him that you overheard some drunk men in a pub toilet talking about Dakin,' Emdel had suggested. 'You know, when you were taking a dump. It's plausible, without you having to give descriptions or names.'

And so that's what I told Dakin.

'A pub toilet?' he said, shaking his head. 'Which one?'

'The men's,' I said to buy myself a few seconds. It hadn't occurred to us that he might ask which pub I'd been in.

'Are you taking the piss?' he said. 'I meant which pub were you in, not which toilet.'

'The Red Cross Knight, in Stamshore,' I said. I'd been in there just once, years earlier, during my first stint in Portsmouth, when I'd been working for *The Probe*. I'd interviewed the landlord for a story because we'd heard that the pub was so rough at weekends the landlord would get his Alsatian dog reeling drunk and set it loose on troublemakers. It was exactly the kind of pub one might overhear such a conversation.

'You're breathing quite hard, Guy,' Dakin said, running his tongue along the inside of his upper lip.

'Yeah, well, I'm nervous,' I said, still following the script. 'S'the first time I've ever done anything like this.'

'And why *are* you doing it, exactly?'

'I'm in debt to the wrong sort of people. I need some cash, real quick.'

Dakin nodded with the air of a concerned priest taking confession. He stood up and walked across the room. He opened another door, one I hadn't spotted.

'Jay,' he called out.

Dakin retook his seat.

A rangy man – six-five, at least – strode into the office towards where I sat. He was early thirties and wearing a T-shirt and shorts. He grabbed my ears and hoisted me to my feet. I gasped with pain and shock.

'Tyek it off,' he barked, in a North East accent as he tugged at my suit jacket. I did. He frisked every inch of it before casting it to the floor. He ripped open my shirt, sending buttons flying in all directions.

Dakin tutted.

'Troosers,' Jay snapped. 'Off.'

I unbuckled my suit trousers and stepped out of them. He patted them down and threw them to the floor on top of the jacket.

'At least put them on the chair,' Dakin told him.

Jay picked up the suit and dumped it in a heap on the chair in which I'd been sitting.

'Shoes,' Jay ordered, clicking his fingers.

I removed my brogues. He felt inside them, then retrieved a penknife from his jeans pocket and levered the heel off each one before frisking my besocked feet.

'He's clean,' he said. 'No bugs.'

I stood there in my boxers. There was no longer any need to act; I was shaking.

'D'you know,' Dakin said, pointing at me and stroking his cleanly shaved chin. 'Your face is familiar. Where've I seen you before?'

'I've been in your club a few times,' I lied as conversationally as my pounding heart would permit.

'Nah, that's not it,' he said. 'I'm rarely on the floor.'

I shrugged and forced a smile. 'Maybe I've just got one of them faces.'

I thought that saying 'them' instead of 'those' would make me sound like someone else, and might mean Dakin would be less likely to place me. It's amazing what terror makes the mind do.

'Maybe, maybe not,' he said, picking up my business card and placing it next to the phone on his desk. 'Let's just see if you are who you say you are.' He picked up the handset.

'Hello,' he said. 'Solent Drinks?'

Jesus Christ, we hadn't thought of this. If the real Guy Tuck answers, I'm a dead man.

'Yeah, I'd like to speak with Guy Tuck, please.' There was a pause. 'Okay, thanks. Nah, I got no message. I'll try him later.'

He replaced the receiver in its cradle. 'Seems that you're out meeting a customer. Put your clothes back on, Guy. He nodded at Jay.

'You can go.'

Jay left the room the way he'd entered, ducking under the lintel.

Dakin opened a desk drawer and pulled out a metal box. He unlocked it and handed me five ten-pound notes.

'Get yourself a new blouse and shoes. Sorry about him. He's northern,' he said as if that explained everything.

He fished out a bunch of keys from a tweed jacket that was on a hanger hooked on the back of the same door Jay had ducked through. Dakin retook his seat and unlocked a second drawer. He produced a clam-shell mobile phone and punched in some numbers.

'I've just called your mobile,' he said. 'You've got my number now, okay?'

I nodded, too shaken to force a smile.

'It's in the glove compartment, my phone,' I said, apropos of nothing. 'S'why you can't hear it ringing.'

'I want to know every tiny little detail about this job of yours,' he said. 'And I mean *every* detail – right down to the size of your mate's grundies. I've got this far in life without doing any choky and I ain't having some hard-up drinks rep blot my copybook. This is my job now, understand? I call the shots. I ask you to jump, you ask "How high?" Got it?'

I nodded as I tucked in what was left of my shirt. I looked as if I'd been mugged, which was precisely how I felt.

'Good boy, and thanks again for the drinks,' said Dakin, winking and combing a hand through his unnaturally dark thatch.

He stood up and we shook hands. His were soft and well tended – not the sort of hands that would set a fire, I thought. More the sort to dial the number of someone who would do it for a fee.

'Thanks for your time, Mr Dakin. I really appreciate it.'

'Lovely manners,' he said, striking another Saviour pose. 'Lovely. P'raps you could give that northern monkey of mine a few lessons. Gawd knows he could use 'em.'

TWENTY SEVEN

'YOU READY?' EMDEL ASKED ME. 'Cop a load of this.'

We were sitting shoulder to shoulder in front of the PC in his bedroom. One mouse click later and a strange male voice issued from a pair of beige satellite speakers Emdel had recently added to his set-up. The voice was addressing Dakin.

Ah wants me brass, leek we agreed, it said.

'He sounds the same as Dakin's man, Jay,' I said. 'That's a Geordie accent, right?'

'Geordie is Newcastle,' said Emdel. 'This number's a Sunderland area code.'

'It's a landline?'

'Yeah,' said Emdel. 'Not the brightest move, eh? Dakin chews him out for it later. You'll hear.'

'He sounds just like the Yorkshire Ripper hoaxer. Remember him? '*I'm Jack*,' I said, in a risible Wearside accent. 'But what's he saying exactly? Can you even understand it?'

'It took loads of listens before my ear tuned in,' said Emdel. 'He's demanding some kind of payment from Dakin.'

It had been three weeks since I'd secured Dakin's second phone number. I'd grown deliriously tired in that time, having become fearful of sleep because of a recurring dream in which Dakin was speaking to the real Guy Tuck on the phone as I looked on in my underpants. The dream would then jump-cut to me being marched by Jay across an area of scrubland. We'd stop, he'd force me to my knees, and then I'd awake with a start and in a sweat, breathing hard like I'd been running a race.

In those three weeks, Emdel had got nothing from Dakin's second phone. Then the voice I now thought of as belonging to 'Hoaxer Jack' also called Dakin. Emdel logged Hoaxer Jack's number and waited for Dakin to listen to the message, hoping he wouldn't delete it straight away. And he hadn't. He'd kept it for no more than twenty minutes, enough time for Emdel to access and record the message. Even better than the message, Emdel now also had Hoaxer Jack's number, which he had since hacked. Unlike Dakin, Hoaxer Jack was not fastidious about deleting old voicemails. Among them, Emdel found one from Dakin:

Listen to me, you fucking northern monkey, you ain't getting no more dough. You loused up the job. I had cops crawling all over me, and then the fucking papers. You ever call this number again, you're brown bread. Got it? And what the fuck are you doing using a landline, you moron.

Emdel had also found a series of other messages on Jack's phone from another man with a Wearside accent. He'd hacked that number too. Using messages from across the three numbers, Emdel was able to build a narrative.

'I'm gonna play you the messages in the order they were left,' Emdel said, 'so that you get some sense of what's going down here. You've already heard Jack hassling Dakin for money, and you've heard Dakin's response. Next, there's this message on Jack's phone:

Ah nee't tuh speak wi' yee aboot that Portsmooth job.

'He's got the same accent as Jack,' I said. 'So who is it, and what the hell's he saying?'

'It's some associate of Jack's – got to be. I call him Kermit because he sounds like a right muppet. In that message, he's telling Jack that he needs to speak to him about the Portsmouth job. This next one is Jack replying to Kermit.'

Nar yee faffin cannit hev haff up front, yee cheeky cunt. Yee git quartor, leek wuh agreed.

'It's like another bloody language,' I said.

'So Kermit's asked Jack for half his money up front for a job he's doing in Portsmouth,' Emdel explained, 'and Jack's telling him to fuck off – that he'll get quarter, like they agreed. Here's the next one.'

Divvint crack tuh wor agyen aboot brass. Get yor arse doon tuh Portsmooth next week an' git it done, or you'll git done.

'Right,' Emdel said in full-on translator mode. 'Kermit's clearly not getting the message, because he's still hassling Jack for more money up front. So Jack's telling Kermit to get the Portsmouth job done, or else. Now, hold on tight for this next one. You're gonna like this.'

A've telt yee already, the client wants the fucker smoked alang wi' eez club. Yee agreed tuh that, an' yee ain't backin oot noo, neet if yee knar what's canny fo' yee.

'Did you get that?' Emdel asked, wide-eyed.

'My God. Is he saying what I think he's saying?'

'Yep, he's talking about burning down some club and the owner along with it. Kermit's getting cold feet. Smoking guns don't get much smokier than that. Plus, the timing of the messages ties in perfectly with The Crystal Rooms fire.'

'Holy shit. Are there any more?'

'Yeah, so this next one's a couple of months after the fire. It's from Jack to Kermit.'

Yee caal this numbor agyen an' yas a deed blurk.

'He's warning Kermit not to call him again or he'll kill him,' said Emdel.

'So I take it Kermit's been hassling Jack for the rest of his cash,' I said.

'Exactly, and why d'you think Jack won't pay him what he's owed?' Emdel posed the question as if I were sitting a phone hacking oral examination.

'Because Dakin is refusing to pay Jack.'

'Q, E fucking D.'

'What I don't get,' I said, 'is why Jack didn't just do the job himself?

Why'd he farm it out to Kermit?'

'For the same reason Dakin farmed it out to him – to put some distance between himself and the crime. It's murder we're talking about here.'

'And why's Dakin's refusing to pay Jack, d'you think?' I asked. 'I mean, Rollo died in the fire like Dakin wanted.'

'Dunno. Maybe there's ways to torch stuff without sending sniffer dogs into a frenzy?'

Emdel was referring to the fire investigators' specially trained cocker spaniels who, amid the smouldering ruins of The Crystal Rooms, had detected traces of accelerant – petrol, the investigators had concluded.

'It could be that,' I said, 'or maybe Dakin's simply a skinflint and is blaming Jack for the fact we're on to him, so he doesn't have to pay him the full amount. I could believe that of him. You should see his club. It's falling apart.'

'So what d'you reckon Dakin's goon's link is to Jack and Kermit?' Emdel asked.

'Jay? I suppose Jack could be a relation, or a friend. Whether Jay knows Kermit at all, who knows? Whatever the truth of it, everything points back to Dakin.'

I blew hard as the enormity of what we had discovered hit home.

'Right,' I said, 'burn everything onto a CD and I'll give it to Larry.'

'Dakin is *so* screwed,' Emdel said, smiling and rubbing his hands together.

'Maybe, but if anyone finds out where these messages came from,' I said, pointing from him to me, 'it won't just be Dakin who's screwed. He's not the only one playing with fire here.'

TWENTY EIGHT

'JUST DON'T STARE AT HIM,' Larry warned me down the phone. 'You'll want to, but fight the urge.'

'Is it that bad?' I asked.

'Yeah, it is. It's like someone's got a red marker-pen and run it across his face. Except worse – much worse.'

'Okay, I'll try not to stare. So how's he been, Andy, since he got back to work?'

'It's playing out just like that nurse said it would. He keeps cracking jokes about the way he looks, only of course no one feels much like laughing. Anyway, he's heading back to his desk, so let's change the subject. I'll have a listen to that CD of voicemails you posted. From what you say, it sounds like fucking dynamite. And I've got some news of my own – Deep Throat's been back in touch. Seems our Masons story ruffled more'n a few feathers, just like we hoped. Anyway, I'll see you tonight down the Live and Let Live.'

*

It was an inclement late-spring night and the Live and Let Live was quiet. It was the kind of pub that suited quiet. It had a serene, almost church-like vibe. As I walked in, Larry and Andy were at a table to my right, sitting opposite one another. Larry was facing me and waved. All I could see of Andy was his back. Seeing Larry wave, Andy turned around.

Don't stare. Don't stare. Oh, Jesus Christ!

'*Ah, cómo estás*, Llew?' he called across.

'Yeah, comma sa, Andy, comma sa. You?'

'*Si, soy bueno*,' he said, smiling.

His smile made the scarlet slash seem even more grotesquely out of place amid his soft, warm features. I focused on his eyes, like Larry had suggested. It didn't help much.

'Another drink?' I asked.

I took the order and approached the bar.

'Here,' the landlord said, 'what happened to your mate over there?' His massive forearm rippled as he pulled our drinks, the muscles animating a globe-and-laurels tattoo. I recognised it as the Royal Marines insignia.

'He was attacked,' I said.

'Lucky bastard.' He said it like it was the most normal comment he could possibly have made.

'I'm sorry?'

'You wait,' he said, drawing another pint. 'Once that scar dies back, the ladies'll go mad for him. He's a right handsome bastard too. He'll clean up. He'll be like James Bond and Blofeld rolled into one. Irre-fucking-sistible.'

What man in his right mind, I wondered, would choose to look like a disfigured Donald Pleasence, even if you did throw in some Sean Connery?

'Are you serious?' I said.

'Deadly. Seen it all before. Lost limbs? Now they're the pits. People're squeamish about that shit, and if he'd lost the eye then it'd be the same deal. But what he's got there, that's the Holy Grail of scars that is. You mark my words – give it a few months and he'll be filling his boots. Be sure to tell him.'

'Er, yeah, thanks,' I said, taking my change.

I sat next to Andy, worried that having to face him across the table might prove too taxing first time out.

'So what do you think about the new look?' Andy said, tapping my arm and striking a country-casuals catalogue pose.

'Well, the landlord reckons you're a lucky bastard – his words exactly. He said that with that scar you can expect to clean up with the ladies.'

'Really?' Andy said. He seemed genuinely intrigued.

'Honest. Maybe you should have a word with him later?'

'I might do that. Thanks.'

'Like Raffles needs any more help with the ladies,' said Larry, taking a long draft of ale. 'They're crawling all over him as it is. Anyway, let's get down to business. Deep Throat. He's been back in touch.'

'What about the voicemails?' I said. 'Don't you want to start with those?'

'I'll get on to that,' Larry said.

'I just wasn't expecting second billing,' I said. 'What we got from Dakin is explosive. Have you actually listened to them?'

'Yeah, Llew, I've listened to them. Just hear me out, okay?'

Larry went on to reveal that *The Tribune* had received another anonymous typewritten letter – this time addressed to Larry, not me, suggesting that whoever sent it must know that I was no longer with the paper.

'What did it say?' I asked, sneaking another look at Andy's scar.

'It seems they've reopened the Dakin line of inquiry,' said Larry. 'Deep Throat said our story put the wind right up them – said they saw those pictures of Dakin and the Mason cops as a veiled threat.'

'Which is exactly what it was,' I said. 'Big Al's a genius.'

'That's not all,' Larry continued. 'Deep Throat said that last time, the only evidence they submitted to the Crown Prosecution Service was that threatening note Rollo got.'

'But isn't that pretty much all they have?' I said.

'Get this,' said Larry. 'The version they submitted was a photocopy, taken before Deep Throat had done all that brass-rubbing malarkey, meaning the CPS had no way of knowing that the note was linked to Dakin. No wonder they chose not to prosecute. Now though, it seems our Mason friends have told the CPS that they've since discovered that the note is connected in some way to Derek's. So it's game on, and it's all thanks to those photos you took, Llew.'

'And what about the voicemails?' I persisted. 'They do more than connect Dakin to Rollo's death. They pin it squarely on him.'

'Yeah,' said Larry, looking from Andy to me, 'and they're so fricking hot that the CD you gave me is practically burning a hole in my desk drawer. What exactly d'you suggest we do with them, Mr Media Law Expert?'

'Blow it wide open – like the *Daily Mail* last February, when they splashed those racist pigs who killed Stephen Lawrence across their front page. "Murderers", they called them, in one hundred-point type.'

Larry shook his head. 'Nah, nah, nah. You're comparing apples and pears. Those scumbags the *Mail* skewered had just been acquitted on some technicality and the general public was disgusted. Dakin's not even been charged. If we accuse him of murder, he could sue *The Tribune* out of existence.'

'You can't defame a murderer by calling him a murderer,' I said.

'You fricking well can if he hasn't been charged,' said Larry. 'And then there's the voicemails. It wasn't exactly legal what you did.'

'What I did? You were sat right there with us when we were discussing it.'

'Yeah, I know, but I thought you'd only be digging about for stuff that pointed us in the right direction. I didn't think for a second you'd come back with a smoking gun – that's pointed at our own heads.'

'So what are you saying? That I've wasted my time?'

'Fella, calm down. All I'm saying is those voicemails are a nuclear option. We've already got the police to reopen the case, so let's be happy with that for now. We'll sit tight and hope that justice finally takes its course.'

'Justice?' I said. 'I wouldn't have broken the law to get those voicemails in the first place if I had any faith in justice. D'you know what I had to go through to get Dakin's second number? When he phoned that drinks company I nearly shat my boxers. I thought I was toast.

I've hardly slept since. It's like the Skinner crap all over again. And to cap it all I was strip-searched by some gangly Northerner.'

'*Gangly?*' said Andy, turning to face me. 'How gangly?'

'Very, like a basketball player. He was even dressed like one. Shorts, baggy T-shirt.'

'Shorts?' Andy said. He'd turned pale, throwing the livid scar even more into relief.

'Jesus, Andy, you don't think that—'

'Did he have a scar on his right knee like he'd had surgery?' Andy cut in.

'I can't remember his knees, Andy. Sorry. My own were knocking at the time.'

'Maybe the man who did this' – Andy tapped his scar – 'is the same one who searched you. I mean, if Dakin really did sponsor the attack on me, then that would make sense, wouldn't it?'

Only Andy would use a word like 'sponsor' in that context, I thought.

'You're damned right it would,' said Larry. 'If we could somehow get a look at his knee then we'd know for sure. We could tail him, get close. He sounds like the type who lives in shorts. Shouldn't be too hard.'

'Larry,' I said, 'we're not undercover cops. And anyway, what if we did find out he's our man? Then what?'

'Then you come see me,' the Marine landlord said, appearing as if by magic, like the mysterious shopkeeper in *Mr Benn*, the seventies TV show for kids. He pulled up a seat. 'Me and an old oppo of mine would be only too happy to sort out the toerag what did this.' He looked at Andy, keeping his gaze on him long enough to make Andy shift uncomfortably in his seat. 'Like you says,' he went on, 'it's a waste of time going to the cops. Mason filth.'

'Er, yeah, right ... actually, I'm not at all comfortable with this,' Larry told him. 'This is a private conversation. That's kind of why we were whispering, you know.'

'Son, nothing's private in here,' he countered. 'S'why they call it a public bar. You want privacy, go down the beach. But I'll tell you this: whatever's said in here, stays in here. You have my word on that.'

'Yeah, okay, great,' said Larry, nodding dismissively. 'Thanks, but no thanks.'

'It ain't up to you,' said the landlord, fixing Larry with a Marine death stare. 'You ain't the one what got slashed.' He turned to Andy again with a look that was borderline adoring, I thought. 'The offer stands.'

'Thank you,' said Andy, shaking the landlord's hand and watching it vanish in the other man's expansive mitt.

The landlord nodded and slapped Andy on the back, giving him a big smile.

'He's so gorgeous I almost want to kiss him myself,' he said. 'Listen,' he added after a pause, 'when you're cleaning out scum, sometimes you gotta get a bit dirty yerself, and there ain't no one what knows that better'n an old soldier. Can I get you gents another? On the house.'

TWENTY NINE

I NO LONGER KNEW WHAT Lucy was to me. Over the years, she'd been many things. First, a mere news item, then the sultry schoolgirl daughter of my criminal accomplice. Next, she became a colleague, and then my girlfriend. But what was she now? We hadn't split up, not officially, for it wasn't just me she had no wish to see, but everyone. She had split up with the entire world.

What I did know for sure was that I missed being with her. I missed her kooky little lopsided grin and the zesty scent of her billowing hair on my pillow. I missed waking up next to her, and marvelling at how she somehow managed to make even snoring seem sexy. But most of all I missed the way her eyes shone with affection, mischief and vitality. After Rollo died, it was difficult to say what it was that was in her eyes. Sadness? Not exactly. It was more like nothingness – like looking into a doll's eyes.

Those were the eyes that greeted me when I sought her out to reveal that the police had reopened The Crystal Rooms arson case. I let myself in with a copy of Mrs Matthews' spare key, which I'd had cut after my previous visit, before returning the original to her. The less I had to see of that old crone the better.

I found Lucy on the sofa, her doll's eyes watching children's television – *Postman Pat*. She was wearing nothing but one of Rollo's favourite patterned shirts. Her chin was rested on her bare knees. I glanced down at her sex, which was on full display. She'd painted her toenails, I noticed, but so badly it was as if she'd held the applicator in her teeth.

I sat down next to her. At no point did she acknowledge my presence; I may as well have been a shadow. But that all changed when I told her about the latest development. She turned to me and something like interest flickered in her eyes, like she had tuned momentarily back into her regular signal.

'They're going to jail him – Dakin?' she said, getting to her feet, hands clasped to her chest. She looked down at me on the sofa.

'Let's hope so,' I said. 'The pressure's on now, thanks to *The Tribune*. The police know they're being scrutinised. But listen, Lucy' – I looked up at her – 'I know how much this means to you, but try not to get your hopes up too much. We're still talking about the same bunch of rotten coppers here.'

'So you're saying that nothing the paper does will make any difference?'

'No, I'm not saying that.'

'What, then?'

'Just that it might be a long road, with bumps in.'

'Bumps?' Her eyes clouded over with something dark. 'Bumps?' she repeated, shaking her head. 'I want justice, and you're giving me bumps. Cowards are weak,' she said out of nowhere, jabbing a finger my way. *You're* weak. A weak man. Not like Daddy.'

She'd stung me into paralysis; not a single thought formed in my head.

'You're crying?' she said with a malevolent little giggle. 'Weak man.'

Hurt catapulted me off the sofa. I grabbed her by the shoulders. '*Weak?* I've been out there risking my life for you, and for your dad.'

She batted away my hands. 'You work for a stupid computer company. What can you do?' She batted away my hands.

'What can I do? I'll tell you, shall I. I've got proof that Dakin killed your precious daddy. One hundred per cent guaranteed. And how do I know? Because while you've been in here watching cartoons and sniffing your dad's underwear I've been out there, putting my neck on the line. But d'you know what? I wish I hadn't bothered.'

I stalked off.

'What d'you mean, proof?' she called at my back. 'Llew, stop. Tell me. I'm sorry. Come back.'

Mrs Matthews was loitering outside the front door, spectre-like.

'I heard shouting,' she said. 'What's going on?'

Lucy followed me out. Mrs Matthews looked her up and down. 'You might want to put on some clothes.'

I turned to Mrs Matthews. 'You want to call those doctors of yours?' I said, cocking a thumb at Lucy. 'Be my guest.'

And that's how I left things with Lucy. Like I say, I don't know what she is to me any more.

THIRTY

'LLEWELLYN, A WORD PLEASE,' SAID Geoffrey, adjusting his dicky bow.

He led me to the same meeting room he always did. It was small, dark and airless, with no windows.

'You know there are other meeting rooms, Geoffrey,' I said. 'Ones that feel less Stasi-like. Why can't we use one of those?'

He ignored me and ushered me in. He opened the box file he had tucked under one arm and tipped the contents on to the table – slips of paper, dozens of them. Here we go, I thought. Play it straight, Llew, play it straight.

'I'd like you to read these, if you would be so kind,' he said, sitting back and folding his arms.

'What are they?'

'Just read them, Llewellyn.'

I selected one. 'I believe JCN should ... ban dicky bows as acceptable work attire,' I read.

'And another,' he said, giving his dicky another tweak. 'Keep going.'

I picked up a second slip. 'I believe JCN should ... have topless photos on page three of *Family First*.'

Geoffrey nodded for me to continue.

'I believe JCN should ... put something people want to actually fucking read in *Family First*.'

'I believe JCN should … stop its Nazi purge against fruit and veg before the entire work force has a collective coronary.'

I waved that last slip at him.

'That's actually a very good suggestion,' I said. 'D'you know, I've put on a stone and a half since joining JCN, and I notice you're not getting any thinner either, Geoffrey.'

He slammed the table with the flat of both hands. 'Enough! I've had enough of you and your infantile behaviour. There are forty-nine suggestions here, and forty-three of them are clearly from you. And some are pure filth.'

I guessed he was referring to my suggestion that JCN have team-building days in a well-known brothel in Fratton. I'd visited it once, purely in a journalistic capacity. The madam had festooned the premises in the colours of Portsmouth FC when the club went on a run deep into one of the cup competitions. I'd wrapped up the article with the timeless words: *I made my excuses and left*.

I decided now was the time to give Geoffrey a Bafta-winning turn as Mr Outraged. I stood up, blew hard and paced about the tiny room like a cornered animal – before shocking him with some table-slamming theatrics of my own. He cowered and gave a little puppy whimper.

'No!' I bellowed, leaning across the table into his space. 'It's me who's had enough of *your* endless accusations. All baseless. How dare you. This is harassment. I warned you the suggestion-box story was a bad idea. I told you this would happen. People hate it here.' I grabbed a fistful of slips. 'Of course they're gonna write stuff like this. And you're blaming me? Take a look around out there, Geoffrey. Have a good look at people's faces. You'd get more smiles down the local funeral parlour.'

Geoffrey cleared his throat. 'Erm, I think you should go home, Llewellyn,' he said, looking down at the table. 'You know, calm down a little. We can talk about this tomorrow.'

I glowered at him before doing a passable storming-from-the-room routine, making sure to slam the door as an exclamation mark. I grabbed my jacket from the back of my chair and left the building. As I made for the car park I met Emdel coming the other way. He'd left his sandwiches in his car. Even he had grown weary of JCN's artery-furring lunchtime cuisine.

'Where are you off to?' he asked.

'Home. I've had a run-in with Geoffrey.'

'Another one? Did he find the KNOB GOBLIN you snuck into that story about the works choir?'

'Nah, looks like I've got away with that one. It was the suggestion slips he was balling me out on.'

'Brothel team-building?' said Emdel, smiling. 'That was genius – so good it should've been mine.'

A few weeks earlier, he and I had spent an evening typing out employee suggestions for the JCN suggestions boxes that were dotted about the building. We'd been sure to distribute the slips when no one was looking.

'You haven't been fired, have you?' he asked.

'I don't think so. He can't prove it was me. I went mad at him – you know, for effect. I thought he was gonna cry.'

'Maybe you should reel it in,' he said. 'Give the poor bloke a break before he has a stroke or something.'

'It's me who's gonna have a stroke,' I said. 'I can't be here any more, Emdel. This place is turning me into … I dunno – someone else.'

'I know what you mean,' he said. 'I've had my fill of it as well. I'm thinking of doing consultancy – you know, IT security.'

'Sounds like you're as bored as me. Say, fancy a little something to spice things up a tad? A bit of *spying*, maybe?'

'Spying? You serious? On who?'

I told him about Jay and the scarred knee story.

'We need to get a look at his knees?' Emdel said, parroting me. 'That's just weird.'

'You up for it or not?

'Yeah, sure,' he said. 'Why not. Let's talk tonight.'

THIRTY ONE

'RIGHT,' SAID LARRY, 'LET'S DECIDE this thing. All those in favour of phoning the landlord …'

Every hand in the room shot up – mine, Emdel's, Larry's and Andy's.

'Okay,' Larry continued, 'let's do it. No point hanging about or we'll get cold feet. You got a *Yellow Pages* in this gaff?' he asked Emdel.

He fetched one and handed it to Larry, who in turn offered it to Andy.

'Raffles, I think you should make the call. It's you he was offering to help, not us.'

Andy nodded, took the phone book and thumbed his way to the number of the Live and Let Live. He stood, and made for the phone on the other side of the room.

'Don't use the landline,' Larry said. 'Too risky. If this thing goes tits up and the Old Bill somehow get wind of it, we don't want the rozzers finding Llew's number on the landlord's phone bill. Call from that payphone across the road just down from the pier.'

Andy tore off a yellow scrap of paper, reached inside his sports jacket for a pen and wrote down the number in an immaculate cursive script. He was quite possibly the only person on the planet who elected to join numerals together.

'How much did that thing cost you?' I asked, nodding at his Montblanc fountain pen.

'Three hundred and fifty pounds,' he said. 'Give or take. Little gift to myself. It's the Ferrari of fountains.'

'Christ almighty,' I said. 'I didn't pay much more for my car.'

'It shows,' said Larry.

Andy slipped from the flat.

'No going back now,' I said. 'We *are* doing the right thing here, aren't we?'

'Course we're bleedin' not – not in the eyes of the law anyway,' said Larry. 'But fuck the law, right? They're not gonna help Andy, are they? As far as they're concerned, Andy's the enemy. Dakin's goon could probably walk into the local nick, admit his guilt and they'd still not charge him. They're more likely to buy him a drink. It is what it is.'

Looking back now it seems crazy we agreed to commission a revenge attack on Dakin's man Jay with such little fuss. For all we knew, the landlord was capable of anything – murder, blackmail or extreme violence against one or more of us. Even the little we did know about him – tattoos, muscles, military training and a penchant for off-piste justice – ought to have been enough to scare us off, and yet we voted as if deciding what kind of takeaway we wanted.

'What d'you think the landlord meant when he said he'd "sort out" Andy's attacker?' I asked the room, almost as an afterthought. 'That could mean anything – from breaking his jaw to killing him.'

'When we meet with him that'll be my first question,' Larry said.

'And then there's his motivation,' I said. 'What's in it for him?'

'That'll be my second question.'

After that, we sat in silence, waiting for Andy's return. The doorbell sounded. We sprang up in unison and made for the hall. I opened the door.

'Saturday, nine a.m., Live and Let Live,' Andy said. 'He wants the three of us there. He said to go round the back – that he'd leave the kitchen door open.'

'What about me?' said Emdel, sounding like a schoolboy who

was missing out on a class trip. 'It was me who almost got beaten up identifying Andy's attacker,' he added plaintively.

'The landlord doesn't know you exist,' said Larry, 'and it's better we keep it that way. If we were to rock up with you in tow he might pull the plug. I would. So no surprises.'

*

We sat around the landlord's kitchen table watching him fuss over a plate of biscuits. He'd arranged them in three perfectly concentric circles. The outer ring was comprised of Custard Creams, the middle one was Bourbons, while the inner was pink wafers. In the centre, like a bullseye, was a lone Jammie Dodger.

'I decide who gets the Jammie Dodger,' he said, his solemn and weighty tone perfectly matching our mood, even if it was preposterous in the context of his comment. 'In fact, I've already decided. Andy, you get the Dodger. Go on, my old mucker. Tuck in. It's all yours.'

'You're too kind,' said Andy, artfully plucking the Jammie Dodger from the plate.

The landlord returned to his kitchen counter and prepared tea, which he served in a floral bone china teapot with matching cups, saucers and milk jug. He poured the tea through a strainer, his little finger cocked. It might have been afternoon tea with a great aunt.

'Help yourselves to milk,' he said, taking a seat at the table. 'I prefer mine black, like my women.' He laughed heartily at his own joke.

I offered him a humouring smile, as did the others. He took a sip of tea and picked up a Custard Cream.

'Didya know that the pattern on a Custard Cream is actually tiny little ferns?' he said.

We shook our heads.

'Them Victorians were obsessed with ferns,' he continued. 'Back in the day, some ferns were worth more'n gold, and they used to risk life and limb collecting them, clambering up cliffs and whatnot. S'funny, ain't it? There's history all about ya wherever you look. Even in a biscuit.'

'It's a Baroque masterpiece,' said Andy, studying a Custard Cream at close quarters, having secreted the Jammie Dodger under his saucer.

The landlord laughed even louder than he had at his earlier joke. 'I love this guy,' he said, pointing at Andy. 'Right,' he added, reaching for a Bourbon, 'down to business. First up, I wanna be sure that you've got the right man. That's very important. Convince me.'

I told him about Jay's extreme height, his preference for shorts and the scar on his knee that Andy had seen in the split second before being blinded by blood.

'He was about to slash you and you was looking at his knees?' the landlord said, giving Andy a look of bewilderment.

'His legs were so long, white and thin,' Andy said. 'He looked kind of preposterous.'

'The scar?' I said. 'I saw it on his knee. It's definitely him.'

It had in fact been Emdel who'd seen it, but Larry felt we should make no mention of him whatsoever.

It had been a hair-raising experience for Emdel. I'd dropped him at Derek's one Saturday night and he'd hung around the door of Dakin's office for a couple of hours, nursing a drink and trying to look like he was on the pull. Emdel said eventually the door swung open to reveal Jay wearing a T-shirt and khaki shorts. He followed him into the toilets and stood next to him at the urinal, glancing furtively at Jay's knees. Thinking Emdel was giving him some kind of gay come-on, Dakin's man had rounded on him.

'He pinned me to the wall and had his hand round my throat,' Emdel told me in the car on the way home that night. 'He called me a dirty little queer fuck. But at least it gave me time to get a good look at his knees. The scar is as clear as day.'

I relayed this story to the landlord, swapping places with Emdel.

'He pinned you to the wall 'cos he thought you was queer?' the landlord said, shaking his head and surprising us with his unalloyed outrage.

'And he spat in my face,' I added. Emdel had told me that the spitting had been one of the worst experiences of his life.

The landlord slammed his fists on the table, making us – and the bone china – jump.

'I oughta kill this guy,' he said in a fierce whisper, as if the words had leaked out in error. 'Leave it with me, lads,' he added matter-of-factly.

Larry put up his hand like a third-grader. 'Er, yeah, thanks, but can we just ask, you know, what are you going to do to him exactly?'

'Fair question,' the landlord said. 'I'm gonna scare him right and proper so he'll think someone wants him dead. People like him always have enemies. I'll drive him off, out of the area, for keeps. Classic psywar tactics.'

'When you say *shake him up*,' I said, 'what do you mean, exactly?'

'Me and my oppo'll grab him, hood him, gag him and drive him to a local woods I knows. We'll lash him to a tree and leave him there overnight. Woods at night play all sorts of tricks on a man's mind, even when he's not lashed to a tree. By morning he'll be crying like a baby, and when we rock up in balaclavas he'll think his number's up and he'll start babbling. He'll tell us everything, anything – whatever he thinks'll save his neck. Guaranteed.'

'Oppo?' said Larry. 'You mean there'll be someone else involved?'

'Affirmative.'

'Who?' Larry asked.

'You don't need to know that, son. All you need to know is that this is a two-man mission, and that him and me have got each other's backs for life. We're brothers-in-arms.'

I put my hand up. 'You said *it works every time*. If you don't mind me asking, how often do you do this sort of thing?'

'Now, now, you don't ask them sort of questions – know what I mean? All I'll say is life's real battles ain't fought in combat with a gun. The enemy's everywhere. You tell me, what's the difference between this Jay toerag and some Mick bomber with a fistful of Semtex who's looking to butcher men, women and children? In fact, this scumbag's worse, 'cos at least the Provos believe in something.'

'What do you want in return?' asked Larry, more pointed than before and with no raised hand. 'You must want something.'

'Normally, I does it for the love of it,' he said, popping another

Custard Cream into his mouth – his fifth. 'You know, a bit of civilian soldiering to keep me honest. But with you lot I do want something, as it goes.'

'Which is?' asked Andy, the concern in his voice chiming with that in my gut and that on Larry's face.

'You're paper people, right? Reporters? So I do this for you and you go to town on the MoD in your rag.'

'The Ministry of Defence?' Larry and Andy chimed in stereo.

'Yeah, them bastards. My brothers-in-uniform? I'd die for 'em, as they would for me, but those pencil-pushing motherfuckers? They don't give a shit about any of us. We're just numbers. When they're done with us they flush us out like pieces of shitty bog roll.'

The landlord told us that down the years he'd lost more soldier friends to suicide than he had to enemy action.

'Some of the stuff we see in uniform – what they have us do? There ain't nothing can prepare you for that. Then back on Civvy Street it's sink or swim, with no help from no one. Nightmares, cold sweats, flashbacks. You name it, we suffer it – alone, and more frightened than we ever was under fire.'

He added that many of his comrades had been 'damaged goods' even before enlisting.

'Plenty of 'em was escaping violent dads, junkie mums, pervert uncles, you fucking name it. So when years later they gets spat out by the army they're more fucked up than ever. They need help, support, guidance. And what do they get after years of service, putting their life on the line for Queen and country? Fuck all.'

'No problem,' said Larry. 'That's just up our street, right lads?' Andy and I nodded our agreement. 'I'll sit down with you and you can talk me through everything.'

'I'd rather do it with Andy,' the landlord replied in a tone that brooked no argument. 'It should be his story. S'only right, ain't it.'

'Fine,' said, Larry, not quite managing to mask his disgruntlement.

'Good,' said the landlord, reaching for a pink wafer. 'So, like I say, leave it with me.'

THIRTY TWO

THE REOPENED ROLLO INVESTIGATION WENT nowhere. Again.

Dakin walked. Again.

The Crown Prosecution Service decided that the new evidence didn't pass the threshold required to bring charges. It was Deep Throat who let us know this, with another of his typewritten missives.

Larry called me at work on my mobile with the news. I had relented, finally, and bought a mobile phone. Things were hotting up too much to be uncontactable. I stepped outside, ignoring Geoffrey's tut-tutting and head-shaking. I'd protested my innocence in the suggestions-slips affair with such vehemence I'd deterred him from taking disciplinary action. In fact, I'd scared him off full stop. I'd reduced him to a head-shaking shell of a line manager. Maybe Emdel was right about me leaving JCN before Geoffrey had some kind of breakdown. He had developed a facial tic, I'd noticed, and had begun muttering to himself. He'd also taken to wearing a tie instead of a dicky bow, which I took to be another sign of his distress.

Outside, Larry walked me through the latest developments. While being interviewed under caution, Dakin had been shown the threatening note, the one that had been brass-rubbed to reveal its connection to Derek's nightclub. Dakin's lawyer had claimed that, it being a nightclub, Derek's received mail every day from all manner of suppliers, as well as from young people looking for bar work. He had argued that the threatening note sent to Rollo could just as easily have been sent by any one of dozens of sales reps or job hopefuls. The CPS had agreed with him and so Dakin hadn't been charged.

'But Dakin's the only one with a motive to send such a note,' I said. 'Rollo's club was a direct threat to his profits. Any idiot can see that. Why would a supplier or some student looking for bar work send a note like that? It doesn't make any sense. This screams Masons to me. D'you reckon the CPS is full of them too?'

'Probably,' said Larry. 'Dakin being pulled in for questioning again? I reckon it was all for show – so Deep Throat would report it back to us, and make it look like due process was being followed. I think the whole thing's bullshit. Bottom line is, we've nowhere to go. We've done all we can.'

'No we haven't,' I said. 'The voicemails. The nuclear option, remember? *Your* words.'

My mobile hissed with the sound of Larry's sigh.

'We can't use them, Llew. I took them to Al and Daphne right after I found out Dakin had walked for the second time.'

'You did?'

'Don't worry,' he said, hearing my alarm. 'I told them we didn't know who'd sent them in but that it was probably Deep Throat. Anyway, Al says the risk of going public with the voicemails is too much, and he's right. Dakin's been questioned twice now and has walked, twice. If we accuse him of murder then he'll sue the paper into liquidation.'

'But they'd *have* to charge him on the strength of those voicemails, wouldn't they?' I said, aghast at what I was hearing. 'I mean, Jesus, you've got three blokes talking about burning down a club in Portsmouth, and the owner along with it. What more could they need?'

'You'd bet your life on that, would you? After all the funny handshake bullshit we've uncovered? And that's just the ones we know about. Like you say, the CPS is probably riddled with Masons too.'

It was my turn to sigh. It was the only answer he needed.

'Exactly. You can't expect Daphne to risk the future of *The Tribune* on a long shot.'

'So Dakin gets away with murder,' I said, deflating inside and out. 'That's what you're saying?'

'It makes me sick to my stomach every bit as much as it does you, but yeah, that's what I'm saying.'

'Not as sick as it's gonna make Lucy,' I said, trying hard not to think about the effect such bombshell news would wreak on an already troubled mind. 'Listen, could you do me a favour? Would you go round to Lucy's? Let her know?'

'Me? Why not you?'

I told him what had passed between us.

'I don't know if we'll even see each other again,' I said.

'I'm sorry to hear that. Yeah, sure, I'll go see her, the poor girl.'

'Hang on,' I said, holding up a finger as if Larry could see I'd had a bright idea. 'What if we send the voicemails to the police? You know, anonymously. Maybe that would jump-start the whole thing.'

'You don't really believe that, do you, Llew?'

'It's worth a try, surely?'

'Do it if you want, but I'm telling you, nothing'll happen. They'll get filed in a bin – or worse, some Mason cop'll tip Dakin off that he's been hacked, and then he'll come looking for *you*.'

'Dakin doesn't know me from Adam,' I said, a nanosecond before recalling that Dakin had said he thought he'd seen my face somewhere before.

'If only we knew who Deep Throat was,' Larry said, wistfully. 'Then we might be able to do something. He's the one cop we know we can trust. If we could go to him with those voicemails then he could get a court order allowing him to intercept voicemails on the same phone numbers Emdel did. He could make it look like the result of detective work – that he'd found those scheming Geordies himself. That way the voicemails could be used as evidence without *The Tribune* being involved at all.'

'They can do that, the cops?' I said. 'Listen in on messages? I thought they weren't allowed to, not for evidence.'

'Damn right they can. They can't intercept calls for evidence – that's what you're talking about. But voicemail? That's not counted as interception. Voicemail's like email. All a cop needs to earwig your messages is a signed order from a judge. A few years back I covered a trial where some armed robber was caged on the back of his voicemails.'

Caged. Only a journalist would use such a word, I thought. Adjectives of that ilk were like badges of belonging for hacks like Larry and myself, and we wore them with pride.

'Anyway,' he continued, 'it's all hypothetical ain't it, 'cos we've haven't got a fucking Scooby who Deep Throat is. We're done. Kaput.'

I thought of those 'profane' DIs, Simmons and Bull, and their anti-Masons tirade when they'd visited Lucy. I smiled to myself.

'Maybe,' I said. 'Or maybe not.'

THIRTY THREE

'WILL YOU GO VISIT HIM?' Jason asked me, looking up from his copy of that day's issue of *The Insider*, which was propped up against a litre-jug of cola that he and Glenn were sharing.

'Didn't your folks tell you it's rude to read at the table?' I said.

Jason shrugged.

'And no,' I continued, 'I'm not going to visit him. It was probably me who put him in hospital in the first place. If I rock up with grapes and chocolates it might finish him off.'

'You saved his life,' Glenn chipped in, between mouthfuls of beef Wellington. 'That means you two are forever connected.'

'This isn't Hans Christian bloody Andersen,' I said, forking a gravy-sodden dumpling around my plate. 'Geoffrey had a coronary and I performed CPR. That's all.'

'Glenn's right,' said Bryan. 'You saved his life. That means you two are like a solar and a planetar. Your fates are forever intertwined on a spiritual plane.'

'Yeah,' added Darryl, his double-denim rhinestone ensemble twinkling in the canteen's fluorescent lights.

'Oh, for chrissake,' I said, throwing down my fork with a ceramic clink. 'It's not Dungeons and bloody Dragons either. He needed help. I helped him. End of story.'

'People are looking at you,' said Emdel, pointing around the canteen with his knife. 'You're a hero, like Superman or something.'

'Right, that's it – I'm off,' I said, picking up my plate of partially eaten dumpling stew. 'I'm clearly not gonna get any sense out of you lot. But what's new.'

'Hang on, Llew,' Jason called out, when I was a half-dozen steps away from the table. 'Come and have a look at this. You're famous.'

I turned around to see Jason waving his copy of *The Insider* in the air. I went back and placed my tray on the table.

'What are you talking about?' I asked.

He held up the paper for my inspection.

'That bloke what you got jailed?' said Jason, 'John Skinner? He's dead. Heart attack. They found him in his cell. There's a photo of him, and one of you as well. You look tons younger without that beard.'

I snatched the paper off him. *Ex paper-boss porn fiend dead,* read the headline. It was a page-three lead. They'd used Skinner's death as an opportunity to indulge in some trumpet blowing. *Fearless former Insider reporter, Llew Sabler,* the caption under my picture read. Their piece recounted my role in Skinner's downfall. They made it sound as if I'd been working for them at the time, rather than *The Probe*.

'Good riddance to bad rubbish,' I said, handing Jason back his paper.

'You really are quite the hero today, aren't you,' said Emdel. 'Saver of lives. Jailer of villains. No wonder people are staring at you.'

I looked around the canteen and all eyes were indeed on me. I left the tray on the table and got out of there as quickly as possible.

*

Geoffrey was asleep in his hospital bed when I arrived. He was rigged up to a heart monitor. He had a good colour. In fact, I had never seen him look healthier. On his bedside cabinet was a puzzle magazine, a bag of Werther's Originals and the same issue of *The Insider* Jason had been reading earlier that day.

I'd been sitting at his bedside for about ten minutes, doing a word-grid puzzle, when I was joined by a late middle-aged lady. She was a living, breathing, walking Women's Institute cliché. I'd never seen a more wholesome-looking female. She was tall, too – five-ten, at least – and elegant in an understated way. Whatever the line in the sand was before twin-set and pearls, she had drawn it.

'Muriel,' she said, offering me an impeccably manicured hand. 'Geoffrey's wife.'

'Llew,' I said, taking it. 'Geoffrey's underling.'

She stared at me open-mouthed.

'Please, there's no need to say anything,' I said. 'I'm here to tell your husband that I'm sorry for the way I've been with him and that I've decided to resign. I won't lie: I hate JCN, but taking it out on him? That was unfair. I feel terrible. This is all my fault. I'm very sorry. I should go now.'

I put the puzzle magazine and pen back on the bedside locker and was about to leave.

'My dear,' she said, laying a hand on my upper arm. 'You saved him. If it hadn't been for you, I'd be a widow now. So thank you. Stay, please, won't you?'

We talked as Geoffrey slept. I told Muriel what had happened when her husband collapsed at my feet just as the two of us had been about to discuss my latest 'story' for *Family First* – a piece on considerate parking. (A number of able-bodied employees were in the habit of using the disabled bays, myself included.)

'You don't look well, Geoffrey,' I'd said. 'In fact, you look terrible. Maybe you should sit down?'

That's when he had thumped to the ground. I'd been in the St John Ambulance from the age of nine to fifteen, providing rudimentary health care at events such as non-league football matches, banger racing and school sports days, where it was not unheard of for out-of-condition dads to keel over during the dads' race. I had once watched a senior St Johner resuscitate one such dad, and the scene was forever lodged in my mind: tilt back head, blow into mouth, push fast and *really* hard on chest twice per second. The St Johner I'd watched had broken two of the dad's ribs with his compressions, as had I with Geoffrey. I'd felt them crack under the heel of my palm – heard them too. Some woman from Accounts who'd been watching fainted and banged her head, knocking herself clean out. They'd taken her off in the same ambulance as Geoffrey.

'How are his ribs?' I asked Muriel.

'Tender and bruised,' she said with a warm smile. 'You must have applied some force.'

'We were taught that it's almost impossible to press hard enough,' I said, 'although when the ribs go, you've got to be careful not to puncture a lung. But even a punctured lung's better than no heartbeat. CPR's not for everyone, that's for sure.'

'Are you really going to resign?' she asked.

'I think so. It'll be better for both of us.'

'You know it's funny, you calling him Geoffrey. I've always known him as Geoff.'

I felt guilty for having denied her husband that simple request: *Call me Geoff*. How petty and mean-spirited I had been. I'd even dragged him down to my level, forcing him to call me Llewellyn.

Geoffrey stirred. 'I heard my name,' he said. He looked up at Muriel. 'Darling, how lovely to see you.'

She stood up, leaned over him and planted a kiss on his forehead, before cradling half his face in her palm. It touched me, the obvious love they had for one another. For some reason, I hadn't believed Geoffrey capable of love. In my eyes, men who wore dicky bows and elbow patches were desiccated relics, with as much life-blood as a bag of flour. Had my brain been tabloidised? I wondered. Were all my world views so narrow and stereotypical? I hoped not, but feared so.

Geoffrey looked from Muriel to me. I'm not quite sure what it was I saw in his eyes. A blend of horror and gratitude perhaps? That would make sense, given I was the man who pushed him to the brink of death, only to then save him. His eyes twinkled.

'Llew,' he said, reaching out a hand. 'Thank you, my friend.'

I shook his hand and smiled. 'You're very welcome, Geoff.'

THIRTY FOUR

I HAD BEEN SITTING IN my car for a little under five hours and my buttocks were numb. It was a foul day, with rain gusting in off the Solent. The car was steamed up, meaning that every time someone entered or left the police station across the road, I had to open the driver's-door window to see anything. Pressed to my eyes were a pair of opera binoculars I'd stolen from a 1970s school theatre trip (*Billy Liar,* Theatre Royal, Drury Lane, with Michael Crawford). All this meant that with each coming and going the rain swept in, leaving my thighs sodden and itchy.

In movies, stakeouts are invariably sun-kissed, with cops parked up some place in Florida or LA under a palm tree for shade. Big-screen stakeouts have lashings of banter, plus there's endless junk food to ease the tedium. But I had no wise-cracking partner to keep me entertained, nor to fetch coffees, burgers and hot dogs. The boredom was crushing, and this made me want to eat, the way long-haul flights make you want to eat. Trouble was, I'd not brought anything like enough sandwiches, and so I tortured myself with endless food fantasies.

And then there was toileting. Desperate for a dump, I'd been obliged to walk to the nearest pub, during which time my target – DI Simmons – might have performed a top-hat and cane routine in the car park for all I knew. I'd also dozed off a couple of times with the monotony of it all, so he might have thrown in some juggling too.

But thank Christ, eventually I spotted DI Simmons leaving the station. Actually, 'leaving' is too mild a verb for the way he emerged from the building. 'Storming' is nearer the mark. He stalked towards his car, opened it, tossed some files on the back seat and slammed the door with such ferocity the sound echoed off the side of the cop shop. Then he began kicking the rear tyre over and over like it was someone's head, and even from thirty gust-filled yards away, I heard every syllable of his cursing.

'Fuckers. Bastards.' He pounded the roof of his car with his fists.

I locked up, crossed the road and reached into my jacket to check that the CD of voicemails was still there – that it hadn't somehow been sucked into a black vortex of boredom and now existed only in another dimension. I weaved my way through a few rows of cars, reaching DI Simmons' silver Volvo as he was firing the engine. I tapped on his window – I won't pretend not to have enjoyed that moment of role-reversal – and he wound it down and looked up at me.

'What the …?' he said, taking a moment to compute that, yes, it really was Llew Sabler staring down at him, proffering a CD.

'Detective Inspector Simmons,' I said, 'this doesn't look like a great time for you, but we need to talk about the Rollo Baer case.' I tapped the CD. 'I've got something for you.'

He blinked rapidly and held my gaze.

'Are you driving?' he said eventually.

I nodded.

'Meet me in the visitors car park in Eastney, out near the Marines barracks. In this weather, it'll be deserted.'

With that, he pulled away.

I returned to my car and made for Eastney. As I passed the barracks, I wondered how the landlord was progressing with meting out his personal brand of law enforcement to Jay the goon. It had been more than three weeks since he had plied us with tea and biscuits and there had been no word. Vigilante justice probably moves at its own pace, I told myself.

In exposed Eastney, the rain was wind-whipped and it stung the bodywork as the tyres crunched across the gravel car park. I reversed in next to DI Simmons, so that our driver windows were adjacent. It was a manoeuvre I'd seen in many of the same movies that made stakeouts seem borderline glamorous. We opened our windows.

'Talk,' he said. 'What's on that CD?'

I told him. He met my account with a poker face.

'And where did you come by those voicemails?' he asked.

I claimed that an anonymous source had sent them to me.

'S'funny,' he said, 'because I heard you were no longer on *The Tribune*.'

'That's right, yeah.'

'So where are you now?'

'JCN. I edit the staff newspaper.'

'You have some interesting sources for a man who writes a company newsletter.'

'Newspaper,' I corrected him. It might have been a piffling detail to anybody else but I would never concede that I'd sunk so low as to edit a newsletter. Newsletters were typically A4 or A5 format, whereas *Family First* was tabloid-sized. It might be a newsletter in every other regard, but at least its dimensions were that of a hard-hitting rag; I wasn't about relax my grasp on that particular straw.

'So why me?' he asked.

'Because I think you're *The Tribune*'s source,' I said, going on to remind him of his and DI Bull's anti-Masons turn when they'd visited Lucy's flat.

He nodded. 'I'm now the only non-Mason detective in the station,' he said.

'What about DI Bull?'

'He folded – went over to the dark side. Everyone thinks I'm *The Tribune* rat. Today I got busted down to uniform. Some trumped-up crap about not following due procedure.'

'That's why you were booting your car?'

'Something like that.'

'They're putting you back on the beat?'

'Worse. Transport Police. It's even more of a come-down than your move to a staff newsletter. Seems our careers are headed in similar directions.'

I chose not to correct him again. I still had some dignity, goddammit.

'So the long and short of it is,' he said, 'I don't know how much use I'm going to be to you. I'm a pariah. I've got maybe one option. Just one.'

I asked him with a look what that option was.

'There's a senior officer up at HQ. We were cadets at Hendon together. He's a nailed-on Catholic.'

'Ah,' I said. 'Catholics are anti-Mason, right? I've read that.'

'Correct,' he said. He looked away from me towards the road. 'Shit,' he said. 'That car over there? See it?'

I nodded.

'It's just pulled over. It's got no earthly business being here other than to follow me. I'm being tailed. And that means they're on to you now too.'

'They?'

'My Mason buddies.'

'Should I be worried?'

He gave me a look of bewildered amusement.

'We're talking about conspiracy to pervert the course of justice,' he said, 'and not just on the Rollo Baer case – this goes back years, to when Dakin beat a drug-smuggling rap. Two-and-a-half million quid was unaccounted for on that job. The court heard how the money was lying on the seabed somewhere off Cowes. S'funny though, because police divers found nothing, and neither have hundreds of treasure hunters who've been in search of it ever since. That's a lot of dough to just vanish. That kind of money could grease a lot of palms. Fifteen to twenty officers, say, plus a sprinkling of CPS lawyers and maybe a judge or two. And in the middle of it all, there's

Derek Dakin, a man who would slash his grandmother's throat in the dead of night if he thought it'd keep him safe. So yeah, Mr Sabler, I'd say you should be worried.'

I swallowed hard. So Larry had been spot on about Dakin all along. This thing was way bigger than Rollo's death.

'And one more thing,' DI Simmons said, pointing now. 'If I find out that those voicemails came from you – that you've been hacking phones – then I'm coming after you, understand? The law's still the law, whether I'm wearing white gloves or not.'

With that he wound up his window and drove off. I kept mine open and looked through the rain at the silver car that remained parked on the roadside fifty yards away. It was some kind of VW saloon. The driver's window was half wound down, and I could just about make out the silhouette of the driver. I watched DI Simmons pass the car. A few breaths later, the VW eased away in his wake.

I sat there looking out towards the invisible Isle of Wight. The rain-lashed Solent had coalesced with the sky to form a single slate-grey backdrop. Gusts of winds buffeted the car. I shivered, but not with the cold. Heart racing, I locked the doors and just sat there, riffling through scenarios, seeking one in which I didn't wind up dead, or damaged like Andy. I could find none.

The one scenario that would actually play out, no one could have seen coming.

THIRTY FIVE

'HE WANTS TO SEE ME, alone?' I said, parroting the words Larry had just spoken down the phone. 'Did he say why?'

'No,' he answered, 'and I didn't ask. I'm sure the landlord's got his reasons, and you'll find out what they are soon enough. He wants to see you this coming Saturday. Same drill – round the back, in the kitchen. Who knows,' he added, 'you might hit the jackpot this time, and get chocolate digestives.'

'I'm more of a Garibaldi man, actually.'

'Ugh. That stuff's like rat shit in Araldite. Anyway, once the tea party's over, head for the beach in front of the barracks. Me and Raffles'll be waiting there for a debrief.'

*

I knocked on the open kitchen door. There was no reply, so I eased my way inside.

'Hello?' I called. Still no answer.

On the table was a plate of concentrically arranged biscuits – the same selection as before. Would I be getting the Jammie Dodger this time? Being the sole guest, surely biscuit protocol would demand so – although I hoped not; I loathe them. I took a seat at the table. A kettle on the hob issued an asthmatic whistle and I heard footsteps on a flight of stairs.

'Ah, I see you let yourself in,' said the landlord, eating up the kitchen in a few strides. He didn't walk, he marched.

He opened a wall cabinet and took out the same china tea set as last time, handling it lovingly. He made a brew, opened a drawer and produced a knitted cosy. The knitwear depicted an exceptionally squat, naked, muscle-bound man who had a spectacular erection once the tea pot's spout was slotted into place. He hadn't used a cosy before, and I didn't know quite what to make of it.

'Little gift from an old Marine mate of mine,' he said, nodding down at the teapot. 'Standing joke.'

I forced a smile.

'Now,' he went on, 'the big question is, who gets the Jammie Dodger?'

'You have it,' I said. 'Really.'

'Don't mind if I do.'

He reached out and pressed the tip of an index finger into the biscuit's jam centre. He drew back his hand and the biscuit came with it, stuck to his digit. He manoeuvred it through the air as if the Dodger were some kind of improvised explosive device that would blow us to pieces were he to drop it. He reeled in his arm, held out the palm of his other hand, wiggled his index finger and caught the falling snack.

'Phew,' he said, puffing hard. 'That was a close one. Thought I'd lost her there for a second.' He glanced across at me. 'You're looking at me like I'm mad.'

'No, very good,' I said, wondering who the hell this man sitting before me truly was. I knew only four things about him for sure: he was a trained killer; he ran a pub; he abducted wrongdoers on a recreational basis and did God knows what to them; and he had a biscuit fetish. 'I've not seen that before,' I added. 'I'll have to try that.'

'In the officers' mess, first one to drop the Dodger bought drinks for the night, so you're talking a ton-fifty, which is a lot of dough to a soldier. I'm telling you, Dodge the Dodger was harder on the nerves than enemy action. Funny that, eh?'

'Yeah,' was all I could think of to say as I weighed up the relative pros and cons of facing a bar bill of one hundred and fifty pounds or being cut in two by enemy fire.

Rat-like, he nibbled at the biscuit, revolving it as he ate, until all that was left was the jam bullseye, which he placed on his side plate.

'Don't like the middle,' he said, removing the cosy and pouring tea. 'Right, grab a few biscuits and we'll get down to business.'

I selected one each of the choices on offer.

'Ah, the royal flush,' he said. 'Wise choice – man after my own heart. Okay, down to brass tacks. I ain't gonna fanny about, 'cos that ain't my style. Now, brace yourself. I asked you here today 'cos there's a contract out on your life, and I thought it best that you not learn that fact in front of your pals – you know, in case you start blubbing.'

I was thrown back in my seat like I'd been punched.

'You're in shock I see,' he said, reaching for a Custard Cream. 'S'what I'd expect.' He pried off the uppermost layer and, with more ratty nibbling, scalped it of its filling. 'Terrible habit, I know. I don't do it in polite company – no offence.'

He pressed the two sides of the biscuit together to form an empty sandwich. 'Now,' he said, holding it up. 'What would you call this?'

Even if my brain hadn't just been scrambled by discovering that someone wanted me dead, I'd have had no idea what the hell he was talking about.

'The custard cream's gone,' he said, by way of explanation. 'So now what's it called? It can't be Custard Cream, can it, 'cos there ain't any.'

I looked at him blankly, too bewildered to speak.

'No shame in not knowing,' he said, as if my self-worth had been dented at being stumped over what to call a Custard Cream minus its custard cream. 'No one's ever come up with an answer to that one, so you're in good company.'

He slotted both sides of the biscuit into his mouth and gave his jaw a workout. I was just grateful he kept his lips clamped.

'Anyway,' he continued, once his mouth was biscuit-free, 'as I were saying – that Jay scumbag, what we sorted out for your mate? Well, he told us *every*thing. Couldn't get it out fast enough. Shat himself, too, by the way. Most of 'em do, mind.'

'You're saying that Jay wants to kill me?'

'*Want* has nothing to do with it, son. He's being *paid* to kill you, by that boss of his. Wassisname? You know, the nightclub bloke.'

'Derek Dakin.'

'Yeah, him. Seems he's rumbled you. You went to see him, right, pretending you was working for some drinks firm or other?'

'Yeah, but—'

'Well, remember a while back your face was in the paper, when that Skinner bloke died?'

I nodded, and as I did so I saw Dakin's copy of *The Insider* sitting on his National Trust desk.

'I clocked it myself,' he continued. '*I knows him,* I says to myself when I sees you staring back at me from my morning rag. You look bang different with that beard, but the eyes was a giveaway. It's always the eyes.'

'Dakin wants to kill me because I conned him?'

No,' he said, leaning on the table, arms crossed, making his Popeye forearms even bulkier. 'He wants to kill you 'cos you've been talking to some police rat. Your man Jay? He told me Dakin showed him a photo of you and some copper in a car park. He said Dakin offered him five grand to take you out. So if I was you, my friend, I'd get gone, and I'd stay gone.'

He picked up a pink wafer and dunked it. I'd never seen anyone dunk a pink wafer before, and I chose to focus on that rather than on what he'd just told me.

'This ain't a new thing for you, is it, son?' the landlord said. 'Dakin ain't the first one to want you dead. That Skinner bloke, he came after you too, right? I remember reading about that'n all.' He formed a gun with his fingers and aimed it at my forehead. 'Seems like trouble follows you about like a bad smell. We had a bloke like you in the Green Berets. Whatever incoming we was facing – didn't matter if it were on exercise or in the field – everything always seemed to head straight for him like he was a magnet. Poor bastard.'

'What happened to him?' I had to ask.

'S'fucking dead, ain't he – that's the point. S'what I'm saying. You gotta take yourself outta the line of fire, else you'll be dead too, sure as eggs is eggs.'

'By leaving Pompey?'

'By leaving Europe. Indonesia – that's where I'd head. Over seventeen thousand islands. You could lose anyone there. No one'd ever find you. Leave it a few years till the heat's died down, then head back. Job's a good 'un.'

'I don't want to go to Indonesia. I don't want to go anywhere. I'm staying here.' No one was more surprised than me to hear the conviction in my words.

The landlord was about to pop a Bourbon in his mouth, but paused and gave me a hard stare. 'S'your funeral,' he said, wrapping his mouth around the biscuit and munching like a ruminant. 'At least I've bought you some time,' he added, before picking at his molars.

'Some time?'

'Well, Jay ain't gonna be killing no one.'

'You mean he's dead?'

'Nah, don't be soft. S'no need to kill a man when you've put the fear of death into him. He's fucked off, back up north to wherever he's from. We told him to get gone, else next time he saw us we'd be carrying shovels, and he'd be doing the digging. That always does the trick.'

'He's gone, for good?'

'Yeah, he's gone, but that don't mean nothing, 'cos Dakin'll just find someone else to do the job – only what with there being no hitman section in the *Yellow Pages* I reckon you got a bit of time. If you wanna use that time sticking about here, waiting for a bullet, that's up to you. Personally, I think you need your noggin looked at.'

'But … but … Dakin'll know that someone's got to Jay, won't he?' I said, hopefully. 'He'll be spooked, won't he? It'll be too risky, him still coming after me, won't it?'

The landlord held up his hands, seemingly in apology. 'I'll admit it, we fucked up on that front. As well as scaring Jay off, we shoulda had him warn Dakin that if he goes after you, then we'll come after *him*. But we wasn't thinking straight. Bit rusty on the old ops front, y'know. Anyway, long and short of it is, Dakin'll be in the dark about why his man Jay's vanished into thin air. My best guess is that Dakin is scratching about for someone else to do you in. As we speak.'

I coughed and pushed my chair away from the table, causing the legs to screech on the linoleum floor.

'If you're gonna puke, the bog's through there,' he said, pointing at a door.

Hand clamped across mouth, I raced across the kitchen. Vomit surged up and some trickled between my fingers. When I reached the toilet it gushed forth.

'Sorry about that,' I said, returning to kitchen. 'I got some on the seat. I cleaned it up.'

A glass of water was waiting for me on the table. I thanked him before rinsing and drinking.

'You alright?'

I told him yes. If I'd told him how I really felt, I'd still be there now.

'Listen,' he said, shunting the plate of biscuits away from him. 'There's another reason I wanted to see you on your tod today. I got a question for you.'

'You have?'

'Your mate, Andy.'

'What about him?'

'Does he, you know, like a bit of the other?'

'The other? The other what?'

'C'mon, y'know what I mean.' He held a clenched fist up in front of his face, and pumped it up and down. 'The *other*.'

'You mean women? Yeah, they love him.' *Had loved him*, I thought, before Jay slashed his features in two.

The landlord shook everything – head, hands, shoulders. 'Nah, nah, nah, s'not what I'm talking about. I'm asking if your mate, you know, maybe helps out when they're short-handed.'

'Short-handed? Helps out?'

He slapped the table, jangling both the china and my nerves. I might have whimpered, just a little.

'Oh, for fuck's sake. I'm asking you if he's gay – or bi, maybe. It's just he's got that manner about him.'

The landlord crossed his Popeye arms and gave me a curious look.

'S'funny,' he said, 'you look even more shocked now than when I told you there's a price on your head.'

'I … so … do you—'

'I'll make it simple for you. D'you think I've got a chance with your mate? Only I likes him, see. A lot. S'why I did what I did.'

'You mean to Jay? You did that so you could get a date with Andy? I thought it was because you wanted us to nail the MoD?'

'I do, but that's not why I did what I did. It was a cover story.'

I figured I was obliged to at least ask Andy. We owed the landlord that much.

'Okay, I'll ask him.'

'T'rrific.' He stood up and gave me a broad grin. 'Right, them lines ain't gonna clean themselves. I'd best get down that cellar – get things ready for opening. See yourself out.'

'Hang on,' I said to his back. 'What should we call you?'

He turned. 'Call me anything you like, son.'

'We've been calling you the landlord.'

He smiled. 'The landlord it is then.'

Mentally I gave The Landlord initial capital letters, now that it was his official name.

He marched from the kitchen. I heard him lift the cellar hatch and clamber down some wooden steps. I thought of the converted pub Emdel and I had lived in years earlier – the William the Conqueror, whose cellar had been the engine room of Rollo's porn empire. Listening to the faint echoes of The Landlord going about his business – among the kegs and casks under the floorboards – I had an overwhelming sense of déjà vu. I was back in my old Silver Street bedroom, pinned under the bedclothes by Herr Porno, while

Skinner's other enforcer, Freddie, approached the bed with a catering-sized roll of cling film. As I stood in The Landlord's kitchen staring at the half-eaten plate of biscuits, my heart kicked up some kind of crazy samba rhythm and I struggled to catch my breath.

Head swimming, I staggered outside. The Landlord had a small and orderly rear garden with a decrepit wooden shed at its foot. I stumbled towards it. The door was ajar. It creaked as I slid inside. I was met by the same iron-earth aroma that filled my dad's shed. There was a push lawnmower in one corner and sundry gardening equipment propped up in another. I nestled down in between them and curled up like a dormouse, settling down to outwait the sharp knifes of winter.

Eyes closed, I pretended it was my dad's shed, and that were I to step outside I'd be met by the sight of Dad watering his roses and Mum tending her vegetable plot. When I awoke, it was dusk and I truly did believe that the shed was Dad's. But then reality crashed down on me like a cartoon anvil, and my heart – calmed by sleep – fired up once more.

I tottered from The Landlord's garden, stiff and awkward, like the Tin Man, pre-oil. The swoosh of distant waves sang to me on the breeze and lured me to the coast.

It was a fresh night and I was stiff and cold from my time in the shed, so I walked the mile and a half to Southsea to warm up, and loosen up. The tide was out, and I followed the wave line as it washed up the firm, rippled sands. The Solent's soft, watery rhythms soothed my nerves, enough for me to ponder The Landlord's revelations without freaking. I would take his advice, I decided, and head for Indonesia – wherever the hell that was. I had some savings, enough to last a couple of years if I lived frugally.

By the time I was nearing South Parade Pier, the sun was so low that my shadow stretched long and thin across the sands, like I was an undernourished giant. Soon, the wan evening sun abandoned me to the night, and to the even longer shadows being cast by Derek Dakin and his Masonic mates.

THIRTY SIX

'YEAH, SO, HE'S NOT QUITE himself,' I heard Emdel tell Larry in the hallway outside my bedroom. 'He's kind of jumpy.'

Cheeky sod, I thought, despite being unable to think of any other way to describe my behaviour since discovering – over Custardless Creams – that Derek Dakin had a contract out on me.

'Too jumpy to take a phone call?' Larry remarked. 'I must've rung at least half a dozen times.'

'Yeah, about that,' said Emdel. 'See, he thinks the phone might be bugged, only I didn't wanna to tell you that down the line, just in case he's right.'

'*Bugged?* By who?'

I pictured Larry shaking his head in disbelief as he spoke the words.

'Ask him yourself, seeing as you're here.'

There was a knock on the bedroom door.

'Llew? It's Larry. Can we come in?'

We? Andy must be in tow. I gulped. How would I break the news that The Landlord had the raving hots for him? The entire thing was almost too weird to process. I mean, what the hell? The Landlord had abducted and tortured a man in order to woo Andy. Why couldn't he have bought flowers or an HMV gift token like a normal person?

'Here he is,' Larry said, pushing his way into the room. 'Holy shit' – he made for the window – 'it stinks of farts and old socks in here.'

He wound up the blind and swung open the double-glazed window. Light assaulted my retinas, prompting me to shield my eyes with a forearm. Fresh air also swept in, or at least the Southsea equivalent of it – a confection of fried fish and doughnuts, blended with a note of carbon monoxide, all carried on a fruity low-tide breeze. I think I preferred farts and old socks.

'Maybe he wants the blind closed,' said Andy.

'Yeah, maybe he does,' I said. 'Thanks, Andy.'

'*Wie geht es dir*, Llew?' he asked.

'*Ja, ja*, Andy. *Und dir?*' I'd learned more about foreign languages from Andy in six months than I had in a decade of schooling.

He nodded. My eyes hadn't yet adjusted to the light, and so Andy and Larry were largely silhouettes. I wondered if Andy's scar was any less livid than before. It would reveal itself soon enough.

'Whatever your woes, it's no good wallowing in a festering pit,' lectured Larry. 'I learned that the hard way, after Dad died.'

'I'm not wallowing,' I said, shovelling myself up the mattress until I was leaning against the wall. Prior to their arrival, I had been lying fully clothed on top of the duvet, staring into shadows and plotting my escape from Portsmouth. Again.

I'd fled the city years before, in the wake of John Skinner's attempt on my life. Now it was Derek Dakin. I couldn't stop thinking about The Landlord's comment – that I was somehow cursed, like the ordnance-magnet Marine he had once served with. The *dead* ordnance-magnet Marine. The longer I chewed it over the more I wanted to get gone, off island-hopping in Indonesia – seventeen thousand times, if that's what it took to save my skin.

'Well, it looks like wallowing from where I'm standing,' said Larry.

'He wants me dead,' I said. 'Dakin. He's got a contract out on me. That's why I'm holed up in here. I'm bloody petrified, Larry. I'm not wallowing.'

He fell back a half step like he'd tripped. 'Fuck! No wonder you're jumpy.'

'Hang on a second,' said Andy. 'Why does Dakin want you dead? How does he even know you exist?'

I explained it all – how Jay had told The Landlord that Dakin had not only seen my picture in *The Insider*, but that he also had photographs of my clandestine meeting with DI Simmons. That led me on to reveal that Simmons was their Deep Throat, and that he and I had been tailed by Mason cops to our car-park rendezvous, which was why I was worried the phones were bugged.

'What?' they said in stereo.

'That's not all.' I turned to Larry. 'The Dakin drugs trial?'

'What about it?'

'Remember you said you couldn't fathom how Dakin managed to wriggle off the hook? Well, get this. Over two million quid went missing from that cocaine haul, and Simmons says Dakin used it to grease palms. Lots of palms. Detectives, senior officers, CPS people and even a judge or two. This Masons thing is about far more than just Rollo. It's way bigger than that.'

Larry sat down on the bed – heavily as if his legs had gone.

'Now it all makes sense,' he said to himself as much as to me.

'What does?' I asked.

'Deep Throat's been in touch again. He says he's been suspended from duty for suspected phone hacking.' Larry turned to face me. My eyes had grown accustomed to the light and his dismay was plain to see. 'You handed him that CD of voicemails, didn't you?'

'I did, yeah.'

'And he took them to someone he thought he could trust.'

'He did – some high-ranking uniform at HQ who he said he'd been a cadet with.'

'Except he couldn't trust him. Simmons got screwed over,' said Larry. 'He's finished as a detective.' He threw his hands up in the air. '*We're* finished. There's nothing else anyone can do, not if they're brushing those voicemails under the carpet. It's the end of the road. Dakin's getting off scot-free. Rollo will never get justice.' Larry leaned across the bed and clapped a hand on my knee. 'And nor will you, fella, if you stick around here much longer.'

'I'm not sticking around. I'm heading for Indonesia. I've handed in my notice at JCN. I told my boss I've got some mental issues that I need to sort out. He said there was no need for me to work my notice – that I should head home right away, back to my folks.'

Geoff had been insistent that I not stick around. Mental health was not to be toyed with, he'd said, before revealing that he too had had a breakdown in his mid-thirties – when working for MI6.

'You were a spy? I'd asked, incredulity dripping off every syllable.

'No, a handler,' he said. 'But I'd no head for it, nor heart. I'd get attached to agents, I just couldn't help myself, and in that line of work you can't afford to get attached. I don't know how on earth I passed their psychometric tests. They went on for days. I must have just slipped through the net somehow. An anomaly.'

'Why MI6?' I'd asked.

'I don't know. At the time it seemed very exciting, and up to then I'd not had much excitement in my life.'

'My God,' I said. 'No wonder you like to be called Geoff. D'you know what, I'm gonna go one better than that – from now on you're Gezza to me, okay? Gezza,' I repeated with a note of deference, like it was a name to be worn with pride.

He'd smiled and patted my arm.

'You're not a bad lad, Llew but I do worry about you. You seem to lack judgement, and in life that can be a terribly dangerous thing – in truth, no less dangerous than counter-espionage in a hostile territory. Go home,' he'd added with another pat on my arm. 'Go back to your parents and let them do what parents do. It's the only way. Trust me. I know.'

Larry wore a look of surprise. 'So when're you off to Indonesia, wherever that is?' he asked.

I stood up. 'Soon, but listen. You're wrong. We haven't reached the end of the road, not just yet. We've got one more option.'

'Go on,' said Larry, inching forward on the mattress.

'Big Al.'

'What about him?' said Larry.

'We tell him everything, and I mean *every*thing. We give Al and Daphne the low-down on it all – us hacking Dakin, him wanting me dead, the drug money, Jay, The Landlord, DI Simmons – the lot. We'll let them decide if there's nothing to be done.'

'You mean see if Daphne's willing to call out the whole stinking lot of them in print?' Larry said.

'What have we got to lose?' I replied.

Larry turned to Andy. 'What d'you think, Raffles? Shall we speak to Al, first thing tomorrow?'

I took a good look at Andy for the first time since he'd entered my room; I was mindful not to sneak looks. His scar had dialled back from lurid scarlet to flushed pink, so that it no longer dissected his features but was more a part of them. The Landlord was spot on, I thought: Andy looked every inch the dashing Bond villain.

'I think Llew's right,' said Andy. 'We've got nothing to lose. Let's do it.'

'Alright,' said Larry. 'Why the hell not.' He extended a hand for me to shake. 'Listen, we'll be off. We've got a lot to sort out if we're to pitch this properly to Al. You stay safe, fella. Will we see you before you head off to sunny climes?'

'Of course. I'll give you a bell before I head out. You and Andy can drop by for a few jars.'

'Sweet,' he said. 'C'mon then, Raffles, let's leave him in peace.'

'Actually,' I said, 'I need a quick word with Andy.'

'Oh, alright,' said Larry, ignoring all the cues for him to leave.

'Alone, please.'

'Right, sure,' he said, arranging his features into an am-dram version of surprise. 'I'll see you outside, Raffles.'

'Is this about The Landlord?' Andy asked, a few moments after Larry had left the room.

I swallowed hard. 'Yeah, it is, and Andy? What I'm about to tell you is going to sound very, very strange, so just be prepared, okay?'

'Je suis prêt,' he said, with a half-cocked grin that creased his scar into the perfect picture of Bond villainy.

'I've no idea what that means, so I'll just come out with it. The Landlord wants to know if you'll, er, sort of, you know … oh, dammit. He wants to go on a date with you.'

Andy gasped. 'What? A date? You mean like a candlelit-dinner-for-two kind of date?'

'I think so, yeah – although he didn't mention dinner, candlelit or otherwise. I really don't know what he's got in mind. You've met him. He's a difficult man to read.'

Andy ran a hand through his light-brown locks and sat on the corner of the bed. 'He most certainly is.'

'And that's not even the weirdest bit.'

'Don't tell me he wants me in full gimp gear?'

I smiled. 'It's not that kind of weirdness.'

'Then what?'

'Get this. What he did to Jay, that scumbag who attacked you? That was his twisted version of making a play for you.'

Andy gave a short breathy laugh of shock. 'Are you telling me that he attacked my attacker in order to get into my drawers? Is that what you're saying?'

Drawers, I thought. Bless him. Only Andy would use a word like that in such a sick and twisted scenario.

'Yeah, pretty much. I did warn you it was weird.'

'Weird doesn't even scratch the surface. I can see why you asked Larry to step out. So this date? Is it a demand or a request?'

'A request, I think.'

'So I'm not obliged to say yes?'

'I don't think so.'

'I take it he thinks I'm gay then?'

Andy oozed feminine delicacy, and on first meeting him I'd wondered if he mightn't prefer men to women. I could certainly understand how The Landlord had thought he might be in with a chance.

'Does he help out when they're short-handed?' I said. 'That was the

question The Landlord asked me of you.'

'When who's short-handed? Help out how?'

'That's what I said.'

Andy got up and paced the room. 'I don't know what to think, Llew. This is just all so bizarre, and a little creepy too, actually.'

'I'm sorry to drop this on you, only I told The Landlord I'd ask. I thought it was the least I could do.'

'That's alright. It's not your fault. I just don't know what to think, let alone do.'

'Then just say no. You could maybe add that you're very flattered – you know, as a softener?'

'I don't think that's ever much of a softener, is it?'

He was probably right. I don't know why I thought the pain of rejection might not work the same way for gay ex-Marine vigilante pub landlords.

'Okay,' I said, 'then that's that decided. You can breathe again.'

'Yes, I can.' Andy stroked his chiselled chin. 'Only ... I wonder.'

He had a strange look about him all of a sudden.

'What do you wonder?'

'I'm just thinking ... maybe this thing The Landlord has for me is an opportunity for us to get to Dakin before he gets to you.'

I'd no idea what he was talking about but he had piqued my interest.

'Think about it,' he said, running a thumb down his scar, a gesture that seemed to have become something of a habit, as if he were checking that his disfigurement wasn't a product of a bad dream or his imagination. 'What if I *was* to go on this date? You know, play him a little – draw him in, ask him to do me a teensy-weensy little favour by having a gentle word with Dakin to discourage him from harming you.'

I stared at him, slack-jawed.

'What do you think?' he asked. 'You look like a gulping fish. Oh, Llew, old chap, those aren't tears in your eyes, are they?'

'I ... I don't know what to say, Andy, apart from I think that's the nicest thing anyone has ever offered to do for me. But ... but are you serious?'

'Listen, old chap, let me be honest with you. The Landlord is right about me. Sometimes it takes one to spot one. I actually don't mind helping out when they're short-handed, as he so delightfully puts it. Only now and again, mind, when the right chap comes along. And I do find him intriguing, The Landlord. He's quite handsome in his own way, don't you think? All those muscles.'

'But you have a girlfriend, right?'

'*Had*. We split up a while back. All very amicable. I think she understood that my heart wasn't really in the vagina business.'

'Oh,' was all I could summon in reply.

Andy crept to the door and whipped it open. Larry tumbled into the room.

'Er, yeah,' Larry said, dusting himself off and getting to his feet. 'I think you've got a touch of woodworm, Llew.'

THIRTY SEVEN

I HADN'T SET FOOT INSIDE *The Tribune* offices for an age, and as I made my way into the lobby the building felt at once reassuringly familiar yet also alien, as if I'd only ever seen it before in my dreams. My heart was also drumming some kind of Keith Moon solo at the prospect of seeing Thirza again. Daphne would be no cake walk either.

I stood before the newsroom door, my hand resting on its cold brass handle, which had been burnished to a pale gold by use. Blood hammered away in my ears and throbbed behind my eyes. I took a deep breath and pushed into the cavernous open-plan room. The air thrummed with the sound of news being gathered, finessed and placed. It was like slipping into a hot bath.

But the warm, woozy feeling didn't last for long, because up ahead was Thirza, and she was coming straight for me. I was rooted to the spot, like a buck in the headlights.

'What the fuck are you doing here?' she asked. 'And don't you look me up and down like I'm some piece of meat,' she added.

I hadn't been ogling at all, but rather checking that all items of her uniform-cum-armour were present and correct. Workmen boots? Check. Faded loose-fit jeans? Check. Outsized sweatshirt that fails to mask colossal breasts beneath? Check. Make-up-free face that's one of the most beautiful I've ever seen, or am ever likely to see, even if I live long enough to receive a telegram from the Queen? Check.

'You look well,' I said. And she did. She'd lost a little weight, and this elevated her cheekbones to the next level of elegance and refinement. Her beauty had a feline quality I'd not seen before.

'Yeah? And you look like a sack of shite. What's with the stupid fucking beard? Are you homeless or something?'

'I see you've mellowed, Thirza.'

'You didn't answer my question. What are you doing here?'

'Speak to Al after I'm gone. He'll tell you everything.'

I saw Larry and Andy weaving through desks on their way to Daphne's office. Larry signalled for me to follow.

'Gotta go,' I told Thirza. She huffed contemptuously and returned to her desk.

'Bandit,' said Big Al, nodding my way as I entered the room. There was no bookending of my shoulders between his palms, no shaking me so that my teeth rattled, no 'You lovely, lovely boy'. I owed him everything, yet how often had I let him down? What had he done to deserve me? I nodded back, sick with sorrow and regret.

He sauntered over and gave my beard a firm tug. 'What's with the facial furniture?'

'Ow.'

'He looks like wassisname, don't you think?' Al said, turning to Larry and Andy. 'You know, that DIY bloke off the telly – the one who's always hammering away at stuff.'

'Peter Sutcliffe?' offered Larry.

Everyone bar Daphne laughed.

'Llew, for the record, I've allowed you in here today under protest,' she said. 'I want you to know that.'

I could find no words in reply, so gave a little nod of uncomfortable acknowledgement.

Daphne poured herself a cup of coffee. 'Help yourself,' she said. 'I'm not a waitress.'

Her tone had a steel to it I'd not heard before, and her wardrobe had a sharper edge, I noted – more tailored, and composed of strong block colours, rather than the soft, swirly patterns that had once been her preference. Owning a daily newspaper probably does that to a person, I thought – especially if you own a paper with employees like hers.

'Okay, Larry,' she said. 'Off you go. Tell us everything, no matter how bad, no matter how shocking, and no matter how much you're worried I might fire your backside for stepping way out of line.'

She glanced from him to me as she spoke those last words, what with mine being the last backside she had fired for stepping way out of line.

The three of us had already agreed that we would say nothing of The Landlord. The situation with him and Andy was simply too mind-boggling for words. Not only that, but were we to reveal that we had sponsored a vigilante revenge assault on Andy's attacker – and that another abduction and assault, on Dakin this time, was in the offing – then we'd run the risk of blurring the lines between the good guys and the bad.

'Have you two actually tried saying out loud what we had him do to Jay, and what he'll do to Dakin?' Larry had asked Andy and me. 'Well, I tried it last night, and believe me it doesn't sound good. If we mention The Landlord, Daphne'll never give Al the green light to go after Dakin and those bent cops. She might even wonder if the paper oughtn't to be going after us, rather than Dakin and his Mason mates. And frankly, who could blame her?'

But The Landlord business aside, Larry told Daphne and Big Al everything else.

'Dakin wants Llew *dead*?' Daphne said – not entirely without concern, I was happy to note.

'It's why I'm off to Indonesia as soon as possible,' I said.

I still had every intention of fleeing, despite Andy's touching offer to have The Landlord scare Dakin off from killing me. I figured that in the time it would take The Landlord to execute such a plan – if it were even possible at all – then Dakin would have the opportunity to bump me off three or four times over.

'Bloody hell, Bandit,' said Big Al, shaking his head and sliding his third Consulate of the meeting from its packet. The room was already beginning to mist over. Everyone in the building had long since accepted that an occupational hazard of working with Big Al was the contraction of one or more respiratory diseases. 'You must be cursed. First Skinner, now Dakin.'

'You're not the first person to say that,' I said, thinking of The Landlord's bomb-magnet brother-in-arms.

As Larry spoke, Daphne allowed Big Al to ask the questions. She sat back, legs crossed, sipping coffee, looking at the floor, lost in thought.

'Is that everything?' she asked, looking up when Larry fell silent.

'Yeah,' he said. 'That's everything.'

Almost, anyway, I thought.

'Well, first up,' said Daphne, looking from Larry to me, 'it sounds to me like you've been busy breaking the law.' Then, to me: 'No surprise there. Computer hacking? Phone hacking? Deception? Are these now the tools of the trade for journalists?'

'No they're bloody well not,' shot Big Al, shunting his Michael Caine specs back up the bridge of his nose with an indignant finger. 'Not in my newsroom.'

'Desperate times call for desperate measures,' I said. 'What was the alternative? Letting Dakin off scot-free? No justice for Rollo, for Lucy? Not much of an alternative.'

'How can we hold others to account when we're not even on the right side of the law ourselves?' Daphne asked the room.

We were right not to mention The Landlord, I thought. Vigilante justice made a spot of hacking seem like small beer. Secrets and lies. Were they destined to follow me around for the rest of my life like a shadow?

Big Al padded across to an exterior window, which he opened. 'Bit smoky in here, even for me.' With that, he sparked up another Consulate.

'Al,' said Daphne, 'tell me: if we publish this story, what are the chances that Dakin will sue?'

'Depends, Daphne. If he's charged and convicted then we're okay, but if he's charged and found not guilty, then he'll sue. That's if he's charged at all, of course.'

'I need odds,' she said. 'Give me odds.'

'That he'll be convicted? Well, from what Larry says about that drugs case, it seems that Dakin's got a lot of people in his pocket – coppers, some CPS folk and at least one judge. So it's not just Dakin we're fighting here – it's the system. It's rotten.'

'Odds, Al? Please.'

'Twenty-to-one, minimum.'

Daphne stood up and made for the coffee pot. She poured herself a cup, took a sip and leaned against the wall. She looked into the middle distance as she cradled the mug in both hands.

'I'm being asked to gamble this paper's future on a long shot. If Dakin sues, we go under. That's just a financial fact.' She took one hand off the cup and pointed to the newsroom, invisible beyond the blinds. 'All those people out there? They'd be out of work, and so would we.'

'I take it that's a no then?' said Larry. 'You're not going to publish.'

Daphne took a few paces towards me.

'There's something in all of this that just doesn't quite fit, Llew.'

'Really?' I said, picturing The Landlord-sized hole in our story.

'Explain to me again how you discovered that Dakin wants you dead.'

'His voicemails,' Larry cut in.

'I didn't ask you,' she said. 'Llew?'

'It's like Larry said. We heard it on his voicemail.'

'So you're saying that Dakin arranged to have you killed via voicemail, and he mentioned you by name?'

Oh God. She's rumbled us. 'That's right.'

'It seems odd to me that he would incriminate himself in such a way, especially when he was so careful before – deleting messages and using two mobiles.' She sat down and crossed her legs. My eye was drawn to the expanse of naked thigh that fed into her maroon-and-black pencil skirt. 'And you say that the reason Dakin wants you dead is that he's discovered you're in cahoots with our very own Deep Throat?'

'Correct.'

'So answer me this: why would a careful man like Dakin incriminate himself in a voicemail when he knows it's never been more important to be careful? It doesn't add up.'

'It's all there, in the voicemails,' I repeated because that was the only move she had left me.

'I want to hear these voicemails. Have you got them?'

'I gave my only copy to DI Simmons,' I lied.

'Then run me off another. Can you do that?'

'Sure.'

'Good, because if I'm even to consider running this story then I can't afford to have a single doubt, and with you, Llew, all there ever seems to be is doubt. So until I hear Dakin saying the things that you claim he's said, there's nothing doing. Right, that's it. We're done here. Back to work.'

We began filing from the room.

'Llew,' Daphne said.

I stopped and turned around. The others continued on into the newsroom. Daphne shut the door on them.

'I think some of your behaviour has been shocking,' she said. 'Truly shocking. But honey, I like your Indonesia plan. Don't wait too long to go. She pecked my cheek. 'Take care, and send me those voicemails. ASAP.'

'Sure,' I said, knowing she didn't believe for a moment that they existed.

*

'Well, that's us well and truly fucked,' said Larry, slurping from a can of lager as he gazed out on South Parade Pier from the bay window in my living room. 'We can't give her the voicemails she wants because they don't exist, and without them she won't run the story. And without the story, Dakin gets off. For good. There's a very good reason why the bad guys never win in films. It feels all wrong and people fucking hate it.'

'Forget *The Tribune*,' said Andy, sipping delicately from his can and somehow making the act appear sophisticated, as if he were in a cocktail lounge, suited and booted. 'The story has gone – it's history. What matters now is Llew and his safety. At least we're still in control of that particular narrative.'

'Narrative?' said Larry, glugging enough lager to make his Adam's apple pump like a piston. He swiped away a dribble with the back of his hand. 'Raffles, even when you speak the Queen's English I struggle to follow you sometimes.'

'The Landlord, you buffoon,' said Andy with a little grin that animated his scar in an evil-plan-for-world-domination kind of way. 'I'm meeting him tomorrow night,' he continued. 'Some little French bistro in King Street. He's found someone to run the pub for the evening.'

'Holy shit, Raffles,' said Larry, cracking open another can. 'You're a right box of surprises you are. So tell us – what's the plan?'

'Simple. I have The Landlord take care of Dakin.'

'Hang on,' said Larry. 'You don't mean, like, you know ... have him killed, do you?' He placed the full can back on the table carefully, as if it might otherwise slip from his grasp.

Little finger cocked, Andy took a sip of lager. 'I didn't say that.'

'But did you mean it?' Larry asked.

'All I know is that we need to protect Llew. He can't be expected to spend the rest of his life in Indonesia.'

'Llew,' said Larry. 'You're very quiet over there.' What's on your mind? What're your thoughts?'

I looked from one to the other. 'Andy, I haven't got the words to thank you enough for what you're thinking of doing.'

'Not just thinking, old chap. *Doing*.'

'Yeah, see, that's the thing,' I said. 'I don't want you to. What do we actually know about The Landlord? He says he scared Dakin's man off, back up north, by tying him to a tree. But do you buy that, really? I find it hard to believe that goons like Jay are so easily scared.'

'Are you saying what I think you're saying?' asked Larry.

'I'm saying that we haven't the first clue what The Landlord's capable of. The guy's way-out-there weird, and he's got some kind of dark agenda. Plus he's a trained killer to boot. Maybe Jay's dead, maybe he isn't. We don't know. This has gone far enough. Don't meet him, Andy. Call it off, please.'

'But what about Dakin?' Andy said. 'Where does that leave you?'

'In Indonesia,' I said. 'Dakin'll forget about me soon enough. I think The Landlord's right about that.'

'Don't kid yourself,' said Andy. 'You'll forever be looking over your shoulder. Do you really want to live like that when you don't need to? I can get The Landlord to scare off Dakin. I'm certain of it.'

'I'm telling you, forget it! I mean it! Enough! This whole thing is madness – complete fucking madness!'

'Hey, hey, fella,' said Larry, patting the air with flat palms. 'Calm down. Jesus! There's no need to scream. We hear you. Andy won't go tomorrow, will you, Raffles?'

'Hang on a second,' said Andy, stroking his chin. 'Llew's right. We don't know anything about The Landlord, but here's the thing – we're involved now, whether we like it or not.'

'Your point being?' said Larry.

'That we need to find out as much about him as we can, starting tomorrow night. I'll make this dinner date a fishing expedition. I won't mention Dakin at all. All I'll do is winkle as much from him as I'm able.' Andy wiggled his eyebrows. 'You know, using my charm. Then we'll have a better idea of who and what we're dealing with. What do you think? Llew?'

I rose from the settee. 'This is all wrong. It's always been wrong. It's like we're talking about some game or other. This is no game. Look, Andy, I'm asking you not to meet him, but you're a free man – do what you think's best. But I'm sick of it all. I just want a normal life.

I'm going to bed. I'm so tired you've no idea. See yourselves out. And for the record, I don't want to talk about any of this stuff ever again. Okay? I'm done with it.'

'The trouble is, old chap, Dakin's not done with you,' Andy said. 'That's my point.'

I brushed past him, out of the room. From my bed, I heard them leave. Neither spoke, at least not within my earshot. I lay there, lost in the shadows, and sighed. It came from a deep place unknown to me. As the night sucked me further in, I found myself wondering if a bullet to the brain was really such a bad thing.

THIRTY EIGHT

NO ONE TRULY WANTS TO die – not even people with disgusting diseases whose suffering is so unbearable they would happily blow their skull apart were someone to hand them a firearm. No, what such people really want is to be healthy again, and to go back to the business of living and loving – only they've been denied that option, and so the sole path left to them is death's cold embrace. Even in suicide, death is not a choice in the truest sense, but rather the perceived absence of viable alternatives. Death is *reductio ad absurdum*: it becomes our truth only when life has reduced every other possible outcome to ashes and dust.

So although the prospect of being killed by Dakin had come to fill me with a preternatural calm, this did not mean I *wanted* to die. It's just that every conceivable outcome I envisaged ended either with Dakin actually having me killed, or with me fearing that he would. Andy was right: I could spend ten years in Indonesia, but when I returned home still be wide-eyed with terror that around the next corner lay my fate.

I mean, Jesus, I still fretted about John Skinner somehow getting to me and he was dead, so what chance did I have of ever being free of the fear that Dakin would kill me? None, I decided, and so I stopped caring about death – and that's when the magic started to happen.

It was utterly liberating. I felt more free than at any other point in my life – including back when Emdel and I were kids, running riot without a care in the world. The act of welcoming death, while not actively seeking it, turned me into someone else, someone better – someone who could bear to hear the truth. This was a new thing for me, mainly because, historically, the truth and I were often to be found in different postcodes.

Anyway, the upshot of it all was I chose not to flee to Indonesia. Instead, I worked out my notice at JCN and in the evenings did what normal people do: I shopped, I went to the cinema, I enjoyed meals out, I watched TV and I read. At weekends it became my habit to head off for long walks around the coastlines of Portsea and Hayling Island. I also explored the Isle of Wight, travelling via ferry, and once or twice staying overnight. It was wonderful, and I did it all alone because no one wanted to be with me when Dakin's hitman came out of nowhere and popped a bullet in my skull, and maybe theirs too. Emdel was so freaked out he began sleeping at Glenn's.

People gave up trying to persuade me to get the hell out of Pompey: Emdel, Larry, Andy, Daphne, Big Al – even Thirza, sort of. She and I bumped into one another in a supermarket, and she called me a 'twat' for sticking about. It gave me a real lift, knowing that at least she didn't detest me enough to want me dead.

The thing is, I didn't miss any of them, for I'd never been happier in my own company or skin. More than once I felt that Dakin had done me a favour by sponsoring my death. It was almost a transcendental thing. Indeed, were it not for the fact that the experience comes with the guarantee of a violent, bloody end, I might recommend assassination as a vehicle for self-growth. 'The hitman self-discovery experience: death is the new life.' It's a tough sell, but it worked for me.

The one thing that really stung, however, was knowing how devastated my folks would be that I was no more. But what can I do? I asked myself. I'm ready for death, and that's all there is to it.

C'est la mort, as Andy might say.

*

'I was going to phone,' said Thirza, sipping her tea, 'but I thought fuck it, I'll go see him – tell him in person. You're staring again. Can you stop it. It's freaking me the fuck out.'

'Sorry,' I said. 'I just still can't quite believe you're here. I thought I'd seen you for the last time. I didn't think you'd visit – not in a million years.'

She sighed, shook her head and looked at me with sad eyes.

'Why have you given up, Llew? If your life's really in danger, why are you just sitting here like a sitting duck?'

I smiled, tutted and wagged a finger. 'That's two sittings.'

She returned my smile. 'God, we used to do that all the time, didn't we? Sub-edit each other's conversations.'

'We used to do a lot of things all the time.'

Her smile faded. 'You were always the better sub,' she said matter-of-factly. 'Why do men love subbing so much? I think there's some kind of autistic shit involved there. All that obsessive detail.'

'Why did you come here, Thirza? It wasn't to relive the past, I know that much. Those days are long gone – more's the pity.'

Another sigh.

'Okay, fair enough. I'm here because you should know that Lucy was in the office yesterday. I thought someone else might've told you, but it seems not. People're almost too scared to phone you now.'

'Yeah, well … anyway, tell me about Lucy.'

'So she was sort of okay when she came into the newsroom. We were all so glad to see her. She was kind of muted and distant – not the same Lucy at all. Then she had a sit-down with Daphne. Not long, just ten minutes or so. She stormed out of there, and I mean fucking *stormed*. I tried talking to her but she shoved me out of the way – almost knocked me over. And her face? It was twisted all the fuck up, like she was possessed or something. I'm telling you, it was freaky.'

'Daphne must've told her there was nothing doing on running the Dakin story,' I said.

'She did. I went in to see her after Lucy left. She said Lucy had a right to know that she'd probably never get justice for her father.'

'Maybe, but Jesus – what the hell's she meant to do with that information?'

Thirza shrugged and coughed. 'She said something else, Daphne. She said she might've published, had you lot convinced her you'd been straight with her. What did she mean by that?'

Secrets and lies. Well, no more. Not with Thirza. Not with anyone.

'That's why you're really here, isn't it?' I said.

'Kind of. I don't expect the truth from you, but I do like to think you're still capable of it.'

'Daphne knows we're hiding something from her – me, Larry and Andy. That's what she meant about lies.'

Thirza plonked her cup on the coffee table that lay between us. 'Go on.'

She sat there, stock still and disbelieving, as I told her about The Landlord – his military background, his attack on Jay and his infatuation with both Andy and biscuit selections.

'What the *fuck?*' she said eventually.

'I know, I know. It beggars belief. I'm aware of that.'

'Did Andy actually go on a fucking *date* with Mr Psycho Marine?'

'I'm not sure. It's possible. I tried talking him out of it. I told him we had no idea what The Landlord's capable of, but I've not spoken to Andy or Larry since.'

'What the fuck were you all thinking? Vigilante justice? This isn't some Charles fucking Bronson movie. You're newspaper journalists, for fuck's sake. And Emdel? What's he playing at? Does he think this is some kind of fucking game? And that landlord freak? He did-in Andy's attacker just to get into his pants? Jesus, fuck, that's too twisted for words. It's off the charts. He's a bigger fucking psycho than Dakin and Skinner combined.'

'I think we just got caught up in it all – the frustration, the anger, the feeling of impotence that Dakin and the police could do whatever they pleased. We wanted to hit back.'

'Well, at least you've been honest. So tell me something else – why are you still here? Why aren't you running? Do you want to die? Is that it?'

I tried explaining, but I couldn't make her understand. It's a quicksilver concept, a person's acceptance of death, especially when it seems to others that life is a viable alternative.

'Well, *you* might be happy to die but what about the rest of us?' she asked pointedly. What are we meant to do when your brains are splattered all over Clarence Parade?'

'Thirza, what are you saying exactly? I'm a bit confused. I thought you hated me.'

She looked to the heavens, before leaning forward to pick up her tea. She took a sip and pulled a face.

'S'fucking cold.'

'D'you want another?'

'Got anything stronger?'

'I've sort of given up drink.'

'A fat lot of fucking use you are. You must have something?'

'I think Emdel might have a bottle in his room.'

'Then what the fuck are you sitting there for?'

I returned with a full quart of Jack Daniels. We drained our cups of cold tea and I poured us both a stiff measure.

'I've got a bit of dope,' she said, spluttering on liquor fumes. 'Fancy a spliff, for old times sake?

'Go on then.'

She skinned one up.

'So tell me,' she said, passing me the trumpet-shaped joint. 'When did you last see Lucy?'

'Ages ago. She doesn't want to know me. I suppose you could say we're estranged.'

'But you'll go see her now, right? To check up on her?'

'I think it might be better if you went. She'd be more receptive to you. We didn't part on great terms last time round, her and me. I'm not sure there's anything I can do or say that'll make much difference.'

'Okay, I'm happy to go if you think it'll help. Talking of help, d'you think she needs any? Medical help, I mean.'

'Maybe. There's this neighbour, some old crone who's known her all her life. She's convinced Lucy should be sectioned. She thinks history's doomed to repeat itself – you know, her mother, in the bath.'

'D'you think she's right?'

'Before I'd have said no. But now with it looking like Dakin'll never answer for Rollo's death? I'm not so sure. I worry that the hopelessness might be too much.'

'Jesus, fuck, I better drop in on her later tonight then. I'll let you know what happens.'

'Thanks. Remind me to give you my key to her place before you go.'

After that, we passed the joint back and forth in silence and slugged the rest of the Jack. It was like old times. All we needed was for Emdel to join us, but there was scant chance of that. He was still kipping on Glenn's sofa, fearful that living with me was some kind of death sentence by proxy. At least he rang every day to check I was still alive.

Thirza took one last drag on the spliff and stretched her arms above her head, as if she had just woken up. Her chest jutted out in all its magnificence.

'Don't look at the floor,' she said. 'Look at me. C'mon. I won't bite.'

I glanced up. Her lips flickered into a playful grin. She grabbed the hem of her sweatshirt in both hands, her arms forming an X across her body, and then she whipped off her top. Her breasts were heaved together in a lacy black bra, her cleavage rising to a point just below the start of her collar bones.

'Don't look away, Llew.'

'This is some kind of trick, right?'

She glided towards the sofa I was sitting on and stood between my splayed thighs, looking down on me. She knelt on the sofa – first one knee, and then the other – so that she was straddling me. She reached down a hand and gave my crouch a squeeze. I gasped.

'Better open these before they ping off,' she said, unbuckling my belt before working each button free. She slipped a hand inside my boxers and massaged me until I thought I might pass out from the pleasure.

'I … I don't understand,' I said. 'Why—'

She put a manicured index finger to my lips.

'Shh,' she said, before bending down and clamping her mouth on mine. She tasted of spliff and Jack, and it was like getting stoned and drunk all over again only much, much nicer. I fumbled with her bra clasp. It must have been some kind of heavy-duty number, with a big wide strap to take the load. I undid two clasps but still the thing remained in place. She smiled, reached behind her and finished the job for me. Her breasts tumbled free and surpassed everything I'd imagined them to be: breathtakingly full and exquisitely pendulant, topped by taut nipples that rose from saucer-like areolae that faded almost into nothing. I plunged in greedily and became lost in them, in her.

Even now, I wonder if the next hour or so truly happened – if it wasn't just another of the Thirza fantasies I once had on an almost hourly basis. Our lovemaking was as close to being a religious experience as I am ever likely to have. I shall forever hold it as sacred. There will be no self-pleasuring over it. That would be sacrilegious.

Why did Thirza do what she did? I can only think that it was her way of saying goodbye. *Fuck his brains out before they get blown out.* If all goodbyes were like this, I'd never stop leaving. Ever.

*

'Llew,' said Thirza down the line a little breathlessly. I wondered – hoped – that she might be about to say she wanted to do it all over again, but no. 'Lucy's gone,' she continued. 'That neighbour of hers? The witch? She hasn't seen her for days. There's no sign of her. She's disappeared. Vanished. What should we do? I'm worried for her.'

THIRTY NINE

WE SHOULD HAVE FELT FREE to report Lucy missing, but what was the point? The cops who'd be probing her disappearance were the very people who had caused it in the first place, by cheating her of justice for her murdered father. And so it was left to those who cared about her to drive public awareness that she was missing.

Big Al placed her front and centre in people's minds by publishing a full-page cut-out-and-display 'missing' poster every day for a week. He used the same photo the paper had taken when applying for her press pass. In it, she was beaming, so proud and happy to be joining *The Tribune*. That smile back-lit her bewitching eyes with vitality and passion, and those same eyes stared out from windows all over the city. For a time, she became the best-known face in Pompey, but as days became weeks, hope slowly gave way to despair and then anger.

The Tribune turned its anger on Dakin and his Mason mates. Although the paper couldn't accuse anyone of anything in connection with Rollo's murder – not without being sued out of existence – Big Al did the next best thing. He produced a second poster using the photos I'd taken of cops arriving at their lodge meeting. In one hundred-point type, above a rogues' gallery of images, sat a single word: SHAME. At the foot of the poster was the following: *These men are serving police officers, many of them senior. They're also*

Freemasons. If you don't want your city policed by a secret society, stick this poster in your window.

The Tribune ran the poster for a week, and on the facing page, every day, was Lucy's poster. It was a masterstroke of juxtaposition. It screamed at Dakin and the Mason cops: 'We know exactly what you've done.' Hundreds of householders across the city displayed the posters side by side. It was as if the population of Portsmouth was also pointing the finger.

Dakin and the Mason police must have been squirming, and while this knowledge made us feel a little better about things, it didn't bring us any closer to finding her. She had simply vanished. I did my best to ignore the nagging feeling in the pit of my stomach that she was dead by her own hand. The one thing I kept falling back on for reassurance was that if she really had committed suicide, then where was the body? You can't hide your own corpse, even if you walk into the sea.

So if not that, there were only two other possibilities: she had been abducted and killed, or she'd fled some place. But had someone really murdered her? Was that very likely? Okay, she was connected to the same conspiracy that was set to claim my life, but Dakin had no reason to want her dead. Might it have been a sex attack then? She's an attractive girl, and vulnerable. It was an outside chance, and only time would reveal if that had been her dreadful fate.

So it seemed to me she must have fled. But she couldn't have gone overseas because I'd found her passport in the flat, bumping into Mrs Matthews in the process. She'd been at her Hammer Horror worst.

'Just upped and left,' she said, arms folded, lips pursed, leaving me in no doubt where things were headed.

'You *saw* her leave?' I asked.

'Not as such, but she's not here, is she. I warned you,' she added, pointing to *The Tribune*'s 'missing' poster in her window. 'I told you that that girl needed doctoring, but would you listen?'

And there it was: it was all my fault. I could have slapped the self-satisfied look off her sour old face.

'When did you last see her?' I asked instead.

'Two days afore she went missing,' she said. 'Things seemed normal, or what passes for normal with that one.'

'So how did you know she was missing?'

She pulled a vinegar face. 'It were when that brassy friend of yours turned up here like a bad penny. She found the place empty, and it's been empty ever since. I go in every day – just to check that she's not come back, you understand.'

Yeah, and to have a good old rummage, you vile old sow.

So passport aside, none of us knew anything useful in the hunt for Lucy. All we could do was wait, and hope.

*

That day started much like any other. I awoke to the thought that today might be my last, and so I had better make the most of it. The clocks had recently gone back, and so the first sign of dawn was leaking into the sky shortly after 6 a.m. I was out of the front door by half past, and out on to a murky, deserted esplanade with only the sound of gulls and a milk float for company.

I was headed for Farlington Marshes, an area of marshland at the top of Langstone Harbour, an inlet enclosed by Portsea Island to the west and Hayling Island to the east. I'd decided that Farlington Marshes was the perfect place to die, being both desolate and yet so very beautiful, and so I had started visiting it more and more often – up to three times a week. On a clear day you could see for miles in three directions because everything was at sea level. To the north, in all weathers, Portsdown Hill loomed large, its chalky slopes full of old forts and battlements. With the exception of an occasional dog walker or birdwatcher, I was nearly always alone in the marshes.

So if anyone was going to kill me there, I would see them coming from a way off. I liked that thought – not because I knew I'd have ample opportunity to run, but rather because I'd have sufficient time to prepare properly for the end. As my killer closed in, I would stand there on the walkway that fringed the marshes, eyes closed, breathing in its perfume – salty and fresh at high tide, rich and tangy at low.

I would be at one with the world, and then … I would be no more.

You might think me obsessed with death, but in truth most of the time I didn't think about it at all, especially not when out on the marshes. I simply drank everything in; not literally, obviously – I can't see marsh water ever flying off the shelves. No, I just felt supremely connected to my surroundings, far more so than in any other place.

The day began no differently to any other that involved a visit to the marshes. I walked the seven miles from Southsea to Farlington at a leisurely pace, hugging the coastline – first through Eastney and then up past the scrubby expanse of Milton Common, before crossing the road-causeway that joins Portsea Island to the mainland.

By this time I was growing peckish, and that's when I realised I'd left my knapsack at home; I had nothing to eat. So instead of turning east for the marshes, I continued on into Farlington itself for provisions. Its marshes might be remarkable but Farlington itself? Less so. In fact, it's so unremarkable that its two longest roads are named First Avenue and Second Avenue, as if the town planners themselves lost interest before Farlington was even finished. My plan was to get in and out as quickly as possible. When the clock is ticking on your life, every moment is precious.

I found a mini-supermarket just beside a bus stop and went in. I was queueing at the till, gazing idly out of the window, when I saw her – Lucy. I was certain it was her, even if this girl looked profoundly different. She was sporting a board-stiff green Mohawk hairdo and wore heavy black eye make-up, kind of like Siouxsie Sioux. She was standing alone at the bus stop. At one point she turned to face the shop, giving me a good look at her. The Landlord was right: it's always the eyes. I saw a bus approaching the stop and ran for the exit, clutching the water and sandwich I had yet to pay for.

'Hey,' the woman on the till shouted. 'Come back here, you.'

I paused. Quite why in the circumstances I would care if people mistakenly thought me a thief, I'm unsure, but care I did. I cast about for somewhere to jettison my shopping, tossing it into a bargain bucket of out-of-date crisps. By the time I swung my attention back to the bus, its doors had closed and the girl was aboard. I darted forwards but the bus was pulling away just as I reached it. I slapped its coachwork and windows, shouting for the driver to stop, but being a miserable bastard he didn't. As the back windows of the bus slipped past me, my eyes met Lucy's. Her jaw dropped.

I stood there I've no idea how long for, dumbstruck. Had she had some form of breakdown? That didn't quite add up. Dressing as a punk didn't strike me as go-to breakdown behaviour.

I thought long and hard about her punkiness. It can't have been random, I decided. Everyone knows how a new hairdo changes one's appearance more than anything else – a trim, even, let alone a six-inch bottle-green Mohawk. Then there was the mask-like make-up. It was like she was hell-bent on not being recognised. If so, why had she gone to the bother of disguising herself so spectacularly when she could have been instantly anonymous simply by going anywhere other than Portsmouth with all its posters of her? From who – or what – was she hiding? What the hell was she up to?

FORTY

THE EARLY DECEMBER MORNING SUN sat low in the sky. The tide was turning in Langstone Harbour, the sea slowly submerging the shimmering mudflats. Sunlight burned brightest on the waters of the artificial lagoon, fashioned from the remains of an old oyster bed. I stared at its dazzling waters, half closing my eyes to create a blur of beautiful golden lens-flare patterns that danced and swirled. The light show was cut with the soundtrack of the marshes, which I had grown to love: the calls of terns, gulls and wading birds, overlain on a sibilant sea breeze as it swept through nearby grass banks and reed beds. I simply couldn't imagine being any place else.

I opened my eyes, and my vision remained bleached for a time by the brilliance of the lagoon. Slowly, my sight was restored. On the coastal walkway – maybe five-hundred yards off – a figure emerged. At first I thought it was unmoving, but after a minute or two it grew larger and more distinct, until the shoulders told me it was a man. He had no dog, so he must be a birdwatcher, I thought, here to observe the oystercatchers and redshanks before the muds were interred by the tide, obliging them to snack elsewhere. But it became clear soon enough he was not a twitcher; he had no binoculars. Over one shoulder was slung a bag, and in one hand he clutched something long and grey. Gun-metal grey. I swallowed hard. So this was it. It was time. I might have expected my heart to start gunning the engine, but if anything it slowed. I found myself experiencing full-blown relief – that finally, it was over: the worry, the drama, the lying, the upset. All of it – soon to end, along with me.

I closed my eyes and listened to the birds, the wind. These would not be the last sounds I would hear, of course, but by then it wouldn't matter. I thought of my parents and how hard this would be on them. I said goodbye, and that brought a tear to my eye. I thought of Emdel and Big Al and smiled. I wished them well. Next came Lucy – punk rocker Lucy, whose secrets I would never know. I kissed her farewell. The man's footsteps were audible now, and heavy, like he was wearing military boots. Finally, I turned my attention to Thirza, and a warmth radiated out from my stomach and percolated through every part of me. I had no thought of her at all; rather I felt her, and that's when I knew I was ready.

The footsteps were upon me. They stopped. I spread my arms, like an eagle floating on a thermal, as the last of Thirza left me. There was a metallic click. I flinched. Then silence. Nothing. I opened one eye to peek. The man was fiddling with something.

'Bloody thing,' he said.

It seemed that Dakin had hired a duffer. If I'd been so minded, I might easily have snapped out a kick at his knee or groin, but instead I just stood there, waiting. Still there was nothing, other than some ill-tempered muttering from the worst hitman in the northern hemisphere. In the end I had no choice but to take a proper look at him. In his hand wasn't a gun but a microphone – one of those big furry ones they use in TV. Over his shoulder was slung a tape recorder, and around his neck he wore a set of headphones.

'Typical,' he said. 'Forgot to charge the bloody battery. My editor's going to kill me.'

'Your editor?'

'Yeah,' he said. 'It's for a wildlife documentary on seabirds. She wants me to capture an hour of bird call, free of wind, and today's the stillest it's been for yonks. She'll go bloody Garrity.'

My shoulders sagged. Having invested so much into preparing for the end, I felt cheated – cheated out of dying.

Death can be so cruel sometimes.

I'd no idea what to do. I ought to have been supine on the coastal walkway, my blood and grey matter being sucked into the mud and sand. But I wasn't. I was very much alive.

The supreme Zen state I had achieved in readiness for the end was shot to pieces, possibly never to return. Dying seemed to have lost its allure, perhaps for good. Life suddenly felt priceless. My parents beamed lovingly at me, while Emdel and Big Al gave me the thumbs up. Lucy kissed me, slow and warm, on the lips, while Thirza called me a twat. But she was smiling, which was good.

'Fucking idiot,' I said without quite knowing who I was addressing – myself or the hapless sound engineer.

'There's no need for that,' he snapped.

I turned my back on him and headed for the Live and Let Live. I wanted a drink, I decided. Lots of drink. And biscuits. I needed biscuits more than at any other point in my life. I'd even eat a plate of Jammie Dodgers if I had to. Whatever it took.

As I made my way across the causeway back to Portsea Island, my mobile started buzzing in my pocket and it didn't stop. On and on it went. I had relented and bought one. My expecting to die had compelled me to be contactable, just in case someone wanted to bid me farewell. Was one person calling me lots of times, or were lots of people calling just the once? Whichever, I had no desire to speak to anyone about anything, so I switched it off and picked up the pace.

Each of the many hundreds of miles I had walked in recent months had been leisurely because the journey had been the thing, not the destination. But now it was different. I speed-walked down past Milton Common, and by the time I neared Eastney I was doing a light jog and breathing heavily. Sweat condensed on the inside of my waterproof jacket. I stripped it off and tied it around my waist. Then my jumper. By the time I was nearing the Live and Let Live I was down to a white vest, with my shirt now also wrapped around my burgeoning waist. I must have resembled a cricket umpire.

I stopped to catch my breath outside a corner shop, fingers interlaced atop head. My eye was drawn to a sandwich board advertising that day's issue of *The Tribune*. It was sideways-on, so I wasn't able to read the headline. Big Al always wrote the teaser heads for the newsagent boards, and they were never less than compelling. I took a few steps forward so I could enjoy his handiwork, and stood there staring at it forever. I shook my head and checked the board again to make sure I wasn't dreaming. *Mason club-boss found dead*, it said. I darted into the shop and bought a copy of *The Tribune*.

Derek Dakin really was dead. His wife had found him on the kitchen floor the previous morning. The piece, by Larry, made it sound like natural causes. Natural or unnatural, I didn't really care. I felt alive again – more alive, even, than when I'd been about to die just a couple of hours earlier on the marshes.

I just hoped that Lucy would read the same headline and that it might bring her back to us – that enough of her anger would be cooled by Dakin's death for her to at least begin thinking of the future.

Future. The word sounded so good, better than ever before. I took a deep breath, closed my eyes and exhaled. Tucking the paper in my backpack I set off again, at a pedestrian pace now. The Live and Let Live came into view. I walked towards it and then right on past. I wanted to go home, not to my Southsea flat but to Wycombe to visit my folks. I'd hold them close and tell them I loved them – even though I knew that when it came to it, I would do neither. But it's how I felt, and that's all that mattered. And when I was done seeing my parents, I'd return to Pompey, and if Lucy was still lost, I'd go find her and I wouldn't stop until I had.

After finding Lucy, I would visit Thirza – you know, just in case she fancied saying hello the same way she had said goodbye. Imagine that. Then I could die a happy man, all over again.

FORTY ONE

I SPENT A BLISSFUL WEEK with my parents. Normally, I found being treated like a ten-year-old teeth-grindingly irritating, but this time around I loved it; it was just what the doctor ordered. Having everything done for me was wonderful, as were the teenage-style lie-ins, which were completely uninterrupted, save for the cooked breakfast Mum would bring in every morning, after which I'd drift back to sleep.

Even having to fit into their regimented routines caused none of the usual aggravation. They'd only ever had the one telly, and as I grew up, some of our biggest rows had been over their refusal to buy another so I didn't have to watch all the crap they liked. (Mum had a soaps problem while Dad was a quiz junkie, so there'd been no shortage of flashpoints.) Now, the real entertainment was to be found in sitting with them and enjoying the minutiae of a twenty-nine-year marriage.

Mum: 'Stocktons have a special offer on turkey mince.'

Dad: 'Too dry, turkey. Unless it's thigh. I do like a bit of thigh.' Cue conspiratorial and theatrical wink in my direction.

As I had suspected might be the case, I neither told my parents I loved them nor gave either of them a hug. Instead, our welcomes and farewells followed the set patterns of a lifetime: a quick peck, a firm handshake and then into the small talk. That was all I needed, and all they would have expected. Bless them.

Back in Portsmouth, my top priorities were finding both Lucy *and* a job. As it turned out, I didn't have long to wait for either.

After a few days I landed myself a new career … as a postman. Before I knew it, I was up and out in the morning in my crisp pale-blue Royal Mail shirt, off to the sorting office and then out on my round. I would finish at two in the afternoon, head home to change and then drive up to Farlington in search of Lucy.

I hadn't told anyone about having seen her; I was worried that people mightn't believe me, especially when I threw in the punk details. Sometimes I wondered myself if I had seen only what I wanted to see, but deep down I knew it was her and so I went on looking. In the end it was she who found me.

I was in my car about to set off for Farlington when there was a tap on the glass and Lucy's face filled the window. Her head was shaved and she wore no make-up. She winked. I got out.

'Did you tell anyone you saw me in Farlington?' she asked.

Too stunned to speak, I shook my head.

'Thank God. Promise not to say anything just yet – please?'

I nodded. 'Lucy, what the hell's going on? People've been sick with worry. You must've seen the posters.'

'I can't say anything right now, okay? I'm heading abroad for a time – a year, maybe two. I need some time, some space.'

'Where are you going?'

'Around the world. I'm not short of money. Thanks Daddy.' She blew a kiss skywards.

'I don't understand.'

'I'll tell you one day, promise. Wait about a week before telling people you've seen me. Say I had to get out of town for a while and that I'd no idea I'd caused all that trouble, what with people looking for me and everything. And say thank you to Big Al and Daphne for the posters. They made me feel cared for.'

'You *are* cared for, Lucy. *I* care about you. You know that, right?'

She leaned into me and planted a kiss on my cheek.

'Of course I know. I'm sorry for how I was to you. I feel better now. Not mended or anything like it, but better. Definitely better.'

From a shoulder bag she produced a pair of outsized sunglasses that covered half her face. They were followed by a black beret, which she positioned, Gallic-style, on her shaved head.

'I've gotta go. Take care, Llew.' She gave me another kiss, on the lips this time. 'I'll write. Try not to move house.'

She glanced over her shoulder, crossed the road and was gone. She didn't look back.

*

A week into the new year, the same coroner who had dealt with Rollo's death announced an open verdict on Derek Dakin. Toxicology reports revealed that he'd had a fatal anaphylactic reaction after ingesting the proteins arachin and conarachin, found most commonly in peanuts and peanut products. The only other detail of note was that he had a sizeable contusion on the temple, which the coroner ruled was the result of Dakin striking his head when he collapsed on the tiled floor of his kitchen.

'Incredible, isn't it,' said Larry after the inquest. 'A peanut managed to do what none of us could – get justice for Rollo. A fucking peanut.'

FORTY TWO

'HERE HE IS – POSTMAN PAT,' called Larry, striding across the newsroom. 'D'you sleep in that uniform or what?'

'Yeah, real funny. I've come straight off my round,' I said, nodding hello to countless former colleagues who were waving or smiling, a number of them quizzically at the sight of my uniform. 'So what's with all the text messages? What's so urgent that I've got to be here? Hello, Thirza,' I added, as she waltzed past. I tried hard to dial down my excitement at being near her again.

'See you in there, twat-face,' she said, pointing to Daphne's office.

'C'mon,' said Larry, addressing Andy and me. 'Let's head in.'

'What's going on, seriously?' I asked.

'Dunno,' Larry said. 'Something big, that's all we know.'

I followed them into the room to find Big Al chatting amiably to DI Simmons, who was coughing amid a billowing blue cloud of Consulate smoke.

What the hell?

'Here he is, Postman Pat,' said Big Al, beaming.

'Larry beat you to that one, Al,' I said. 'And just about every schoolboy in Portsmouth I meet on my round beat Larry to it.'

'Fair play, Bandit, you lovely boy.'

I'm a lovely boy again! It's official.

'I think it's great, this new job of yours,' he went on. 'Keeps you out of trouble, I'll wager. Talking of which, we've a very special visitor,' he added, gesturing at DI Simmons.

'Detective Inspector,' I said, nodding as he and I shook hands.

'Detective *Chief Superintendent*,' Big Al corrected me.

'Wow,' I said. 'Congratulations. That's, er … unexpected.'

'How are you, Mr Sabler? The new job keeping you fit? It must be a bit like pounding the beat, only with a heavy old bag.'

'He's had a few heavy old bags in his time,' quipped Larry, drawing a smirk from Big Al but a scowl from Thirza, which soon wiped the smile off both their faces.

'If you don't mind,' said Daphne, giving Larry a steely look over the rim of her coffee cup. 'The Chief Superintendent hasn't come here for your saloon-bar humour.'

'Thank you, Miss McNair,' said Simmons, who took a few steps forward, then turned to face us. 'I can see just how surprised you are to see me, so I'll not keep you in suspense. I'm here to tell you that there have been developments in the Derek Dakin case – significant developments – and I thought it only right and proper that *The Tribune* be party to these, given all that you've done in that area.'

'What kind of developments?' I asked.

'It seems we weren't the only ones who were fighting injustice and corruption in Her Majesty's Constabulary,' he went on. 'Have any of you ever heard of ghost squads? Well,' he added when his question was met with silence, 'a ghost squad is special team of people whose remit is anti-corruption. It's made up of trusted former detectives, ex-Ministry of Defence police and financial experts – because in corruption cases, one always follows the money.'

'Is this going where I think it's going?' Larry said.

'If you'll let the Chief Superintendent speak,' Daphne chided.

Simmons nodded his thanks, and continued. 'Some years back, a ghost squad was set up to investigate the acquittal of Derek Dakin in relation to drugs smuggling charges, as well as the disappearance of over two million pounds in drugs money, and suspected links between that money and certain members of the police force and the judiciary. After years of painstaking work, building a case that they could prosecute, they were about to make their move when all that business with Rollo Baer happened. Because Dakin was tied to Baer's death, they decided to hold off and see if they mightn't catch a few more rotten fish in their net. And so they did, thanks in no small part to yourselves. It was *The Tribune* that alerted the ghost squad to the role that Freemasonry has played in all of this, both with regards to the drugs money and to how justice was denied Mr Baer. So on behalf of all honest and decent police officers everywhere, thank you.'

His words filled me with the same warm feeling I'd experienced in the seconds before being gunned to death by the sound engineer's furry microphone.

'So what happens now?' I asked.

'People are being arrested as we speak. Twenty-three serving police officers, three CPS lawyers and two circuit judges.'

'And what about the scum involved in Rollo's death?' asked Larry.

'Taken into custody by Wearside police this morning.'

'And my attacker?' said Andy, stoking his scar in a Blofeld kind of way.

'Unfortunately, we don't yet know the identity of that person,' Simmons said. 'But we're hopeful that when the questioning starts, others will be implicated.'

Andy nodded and looked from Larry to me. *You're a smart cookie*, I thought. He knew it might have appeared odd had he not asked the question, given the severity of the attack on him and its clear links to Dakin.

'And as you can see,' Simmons said, smiling and tapping one of the red epaulettes on the shoulders of his uniform, 'I have been promoted.'

I slapped the Royal Mail insignia on my chest. 'So have I.' The room rang with laughter.

'Why are you all still here?' said Simmons with a look of faux surprise and the trace of a grin. He paused, as we eyed one another in confusion.

'Haven't you got a story to write?' he continued, reaching for an attaché case on Daphne's desk. He slipped a wadge of papers from the case. 'Here, these might help. These are press statements that are due to be released once all the arrests have been made public. You'll be the ones to break this story, but you're not to publish anything until I give you the say-so. Do you understand?'

We assured him, flamboyantly and earnestly, that we did.

'I know what you journalists can be like – don't I, Mr Sabler.'

More laughter.

'What *can* you mean, Detective Chief Superintendent?' I said, shrugging. 'I'm just a humble postie.'

*

Larry, Andy and I met at 5.30 p.m. in the American Bar of the Savoy Hotel in London as arranged. We looked one another up and down. It was the first time any of us had worn dress suits. Larry and I scrubbed up well enough, but Andy was off the charts.

'Raffles,' said Larry, placing his hands on Andy's shoulders, 'you make me sick. I almost want to go to bed with you myself. The Landlord was spot on about that scar.'

'That's not all that he was spot on about,' said Andy with a sly smile.

'I still can't get my head around it,' said Larry. 'You've got skirt queueing up round the block gagging for it, yet you end up with him – a tattooed grunt with a biscuit problem and a penchant for abducting—'

'Okay, Larry,' I cut in. 'Let's change the subject, shall we. The others'll be down soon, and The Landlord's hardly a topic for public consumption.'

'Yeah, unless you happen to be Thirza,' he said sourly. He still hadn't forgiven me for telling her of our involvement with The Landlord.

She had taken Andy and Larry to one side and given them both barrels. Later, Andy told me that he'd been close to tears by the time she'd finished with them. He'd gone on to reveal that he and The Landlord were getting on famously and were officially an 'item'.

'One doesn't choose love,' Andy had said. 'Love chooses one.'

'Are you seriously telling me you love him?' I'd asked, having first caught my breath.

'Well, maybe love's a little strong, but there's a palpable connection. I felt it, and so did Timothy.'

'Timothy?'

'Don't mock, Llew. It doesn't become you.'

'So you're serious, then, about The La … about Timothy?'

'Avoir un coup de foudre pour quelqu'un.'

'I'll take that as a yes,' I'd said.

Andy had nodded, and now – in the American Bar – he pointed. 'Here they are,' he said. 'The lovely ladies.'

Daphne and Thirza sashayed towards us, smiling and waving. Daphne had plumped for a tight-fitting pea-green number with sequins. It gave her the air of a ballroom dancer, I thought. Thirza, meanwhile, was an essay in sophistication, wearing strappy heels and a black cocktail dress with a plunging back. I'd rarely seen her in anything other than boots, jeans and sweatshirt. I couldn't take my eyes off her.

'Wind your tongue in, Llew, or you'll trip over it,' said Larry. 'Good evening, ladies,' he continued, when they were almost upon us. 'Drinks?'

While Larry was at the bar, Big Al emerged through the crowd, a glowing Consulate glued to his bottom lip.

'You look very handsome, Al,' said Daphne, adjusting his bow tie. 'So, give me some odds. What are our chances of winning, d'you think?'

'Which award?' he asked.

The Tribune had been nominated for two prizes in that year's National Press Awards: Exclusive of the Year, and Newspaper of the Year, both for the Dakin-Masons exclusive.

'Even-money on the exclusive,' he said. 'As for best newspaper? Well, the last time a regional won that was over twenty years ago, so … five-to-one.'

'Al,' I said, 'there's five papers nominated, so our chances are quite literally five-to-one.'

He blew a cloud of smoke in my face. 'Bandit, sometimes I wonder if we did the right thing having you back.'

'So do I,' said Thirza.

'Me too,' added Larry.

Daphne gave me a funny little look. She'd called me in to the office a few weeks earlier, 'for a quick word' and offered to have me back. 'You'd be working under Larry,' she'd added, 'and there'd be conditions.'

The conditions were that I was never, ever, *ever* to break the law again in the course of my job under *any* circumstances. And I was never, ever, *ever* to mislead her, or anyone else, ever again about anything. Ever.

I agreed on the spot. I'd enjoyed being a postman, and was sad in some ways to give it up, but nothing came close to being a newspaperman. I was a news junkie and I needed my fix.

*

'We woz robbed,' Larry slurred in my ear as the ballroom throbbed to the sound of dance music.

The last time I'd been around such sounds I'd been high on E in Rollo's club. I thought of him in that moment, shuttling back and forth between his garages. I also saw him being suffocated by heat and smoke, as he dragged himself across the floor in a blind panic.

What a dreadful way to die.

I wondered where Lucy was and what she was up to. Did she have a boyfriend, or maybe even a girlfriend? I wouldn't put anything past that girl. She'd been gone five weeks and I'd heard nothing from her.

'I said we woz robbed,' Larry bellowed in my ear.

'Jesus Christ, there's no need to perforate my eardrum.'

'You were off with the fairies again. What was it this time?'

'Look, we got Exclusive of the Year, so just be happy with that. Besides, we don't need awards to tell us we did a good job. We know what we did.'

'Cheers to that.' He and I clinked glasses. 'Right,' he added, straightening his tux. 'I'm off for a shit.'

'Yeah, thanks for that Larry.'

I watched him go before winding my way back to *The Tribune*'s table. Big Al and Daphne were deep in conversation, while opposite sat Thirza, tapping her foot to some rave number.

'Mind if I join you?'

She patted the seat next to her.

'You enjoying it?' I asked.

'Yeah, despite the tossers. Tabloid pigs. I've already had words with one prick. He won't be squeezing my arse again in a hurry.'

'Is he still alive?'

She smiled. 'Let's just say it might be Tuesday before he catches his breath.'

'Solar plexus?'

'You got it.'

'Thirza, you do know that your mouth is by far your deadliest weapon, right? You reduced Andy to tears, remember?'

'Oh, come on. Kermit the Frog could reduce Andy to tears.'

'But you properly shook Larry as well – you know, over that business with The Landlord.'

'Yeah, well, he needed shaking. You all did. I still can't believe you lot got involved with him. You're fucking crazy, and as for Andy? What the fuck is he playing at, dating the guy?'

'It's no different to you and Blanche.'

'No different?' she scoffed. 'Are you fucking kidding me? I don't have to worry that Blanche'll kill me and bury me in woodland.'

'Andy insists that Timothy is actually very sensitive.'

'*Timothy*?'

'Yeah, and it seems the pair of them are head over heels.'

'Spare me.'

'So how *is* Blanche? We don't see you two out and about much.'

'David sends his best,' she said, side-stepping the question with practised ease – forever her way with matters personal. 'He says he still misses the times when you and him'd watch musicals together, above the Barley Mow.'

'Really?' I said, recalling those seemingly endless nights of top-hat-and-cane hell, which – although utter torture – had cemented our friendship. 'That's nice of him.'

'He and Max are looking to open a restaurant in Edinburgh.'

Max. God, I hadn't thought about him in an age. Years earlier, when he was still a serving Catholic priest, Max had taken the rap for my altar-defecation stunt, copping a suspended sentence and months of community service.

I ought to be silently giving up thanks to him every day.

'Edinburgh?' I said, snapping back into the moment. 'Why there?'

'The Festival, dumbo. It's the gayest city in Europe.'

'Well, wish them luck from me.'

'Will do. Right,' she said, standing up. 'I'm off to bed. I'm all in.'

I reached out and laid a hand on her arm. 'Thirza, about before. You know, when you came round to see me that time. We haven't had a chance to—'

She put a finger to my lips and slowly, gently shook her head.

'Goodnight, Llew,' she said.

I tracked her every step as she left the ballroom, transfixed by the giant pink V revealed by the dress, knowing it would be the last of her flesh I ever saw.

I sighed. Would I ever get that girl completely out from under my skin? I decided probably not, and that I should just be happy we were friends again. At least I could, and would, share everything with her, which is more than can be said for many lovers, wives and husbands. She and I would have both love *and* intimacy. Okay, so there'd be no sex, but what was sex, ultimately? She had Blanche for that, and I bet even Blanche didn't tell her everything.

'What're you grinning about, Bandit?' said Big Al. 'Come and join us.'

I did, and we talked newspapers, joyously, until the music stopped. Not long after, Savoy staff began ushering us to our rooms, all paid for by Daphne. That night, I slept the sleep of the blessed.

FORTY THREE

'I JUST CAN'T SHAKE THE image of him burying Andy in some woodland,' said Thirza as she studied Andy and The Landlord at the other side of the public bar sharing an intimate moment across the ale pumps.

'Well, Blanche told me earlier how wonderful she thinks The Landlord is, so there you go,' I said.

'Yeah, that's because it's him she's got to thank for her first night off for fuck knows how long,' countered Thirza, taking a slug of white wine. 'If he was Fred West she'd still be giddy with excitement.'

'Fred West has been dead four years,' I reminded her.

'Mood she's in, that'd make no difference.'

We were at David and Max's farewell drinks to mark their Edinburgh adventure. Originally, Blanche had been set to host the night at the Mow, but when The Landlord heard from Andy about what was going down, he insisted it be held at the Live and Let Live instead and volunteered to work behind the bar. 'He's so thoughtful,' Andy had added rather dreamily when he explained it to me earlier.

'Here's what I don't get,' said Thirza. 'They both run pubs yet Blanche gets, like, one day off every six months and yet *Timothy* seems to be forever out and about.' Her eyes were locked on Andy, who was now leaning across the bar and whispering something into

The Landlord's ear. The pair of them laughed. 'What does he do when he's away from his pub? I bet he's out hunting victims.'

'That's a little fanciful,' I said.

'Is it? What about Dakin, then? How d'you explain that? Think about it. Landlord fancies Andy, so offers to sort out Jay. Jay tells Landlord Dakin wants you dead. Andy dates Landlord, and then, bingo! Dakin's dead. Coincidence? I think fucking not.'

'Peanuts killed Dakin,' I said. 'Not The Landlord.'

'And how'd those peanuts get inside him?'

'He ate something he shouldn't have. That's the coroner speaking, by the way, not me.'

'Jesus, fuck, Einstein, the coroner doesn't know about Dakin's hacked voicemails, does he. But Andy knew about them all right, including the one about Dakin's peanut allergy. So Andy, desperate to save your sorry arse from Dakin, tells The Landlord about the peanut thing, and because he's so fucking smitten, he uses his Marines bullshit to somehow get peanuts down Dakin.'

'How, exactly?'

'Tied him to a tree, forced them down his throat and then dumped him in his kitchen. How the fuck should I know? I'm not a trained killer.'

'The autopsy would've shown signs of struggle.'

'He had a great big bruise on his head, for fuck's sake.'

'He hit it on the floor.'

'Really? You reckon?'

'Besides, there was no sign of forced entry.'

'Come on, his job was to break into fucking countries and kill people, so I can't see a house being much of a challenge.'

'Look, Thirza, to be honest, I don't wanna talk about this any more. He's dead. That's all I care about. I've moved on.'

'So you don't care that one of your mates is probably dating a serial killing psycho vigilante publican fuck?'

'Look, I—'

'Or that Andy could be an accessory to Dakin's murder?'

'Jesus Christ, give it a rest will you. My head's hurting.'

'Fuck your head. I'm telling you right now for nothing: you've not heard the last of this. You mark my words.'

'Okay, they're duly marked. Are we done now? Can we go back to having a good time, like everyone else?'

*

Bill, bill, bill, bill, I thought, as I rifled through yet more dreary mail. Then I gave a little a gasp. I was holding a slender envelope with a red and blue border. It was air mail, and it bore an Australian frank. *Lucy*. I looked at my watch. It was time to leave for work. I'd read it on my way. The toaster popped. I stuck the letter in my trouser pocket, dashed into the kitchen, buttered a slice of toast, grabbed a coat, locked up and slipped out into another day.

Barely thirty seconds down the esplanade I'd finished the toast, hardly bothering to chew, and fished out the letter. I stopped to open it, so as not to tear any of the writing, and eased open the glued flap. The envelope concertinaed out into a three-panel letter.

Lucy had dreadful handwriting. I'd only ever seen it before on notes she'd left me when we'd been on *The Tribune* together, and I had struggled to read those, so this was almost a job for Bletchley Park. Yet after a few minutes' reading I had begun to unpick her scribble patterns. She was in Sydney, in the King's Cross area, and was staying at some hostel. She'd made a few friends and was planning to buy an old van with them and travel through the outback.

I was virtually at work by the time I had decoded that much. I straightened out the paper to read the final panel and stopped dead in my tracks. Behind me, a woman with a baby buggy crashed into my ankles.

'Oh, sorry,' she said. 'Are you okay?' She looked from me to the letter as her baby girl chomped on a teething ring, saliva dripping from her chops.

'Yeah, fine. Thanks,' I said.

I waited for her to move off before re-examining the letter. I stared at it, transfixed by the small portion of a photograph that Lucy had cut out and glued to the bottom of the page: a bottle of groundnut oil. There was an arrow pointing to the image, along with her handwritten caption: *That's what they call peanut oil here. It's little things like this that remind me I'm a long way from home.*

Up ahead was a newsagent. I went inside and bought a box of matches. Up ahead was a potholed access road leading to a row of garages. I turned into it and walked for fifty or so yards before ducking into an area of woody shrubs and small trees, sliding sideways between the leafless branches. I took out the matches, struck one and applied the flame to one corner of Lucy's letter. I held it long enough for the flames to singe the hairs on the back of my hand, and then let it go. It floated to the ground like a burning kite and expired on a bed of dead, soggy leaves.

But the cut-out picture of the groundnut oil remained intact. I picked it up and tore it into tiny pieces. Then I placed them on the flat of my hand and blew them into the air.

As I set off across the road to work, I was aware that no matter how long I toiled in a newsroom I'd be lucky to unearth a story one tenth as shocking as the one I had just torched in those bushes.

FORTY FOUR

'WHEN'RE YOU GONNA SHAVE THAT crap off your face?' asked Larry as he tapped away at his keyboard.

'Why?' I said. 'Does it offend you?'

'You've got half a croissant stuck in it. Again.'

I gave the beard a rub and watched crumbs tumble into my lap.

'I want to see how far I can take it.'

'You mean like ZZ Top?' Andy asked.

'Well, maybe not that far. I was thinking more, you know, Brian Blessed.'

'No wonder your love life's non-existent,' said Larry. 'It must be like kissing a baboon's arse.'

'Baboon's arses are bald,' I said. 'And blue. That's a terrible simile.'

'Orangutan,' said Andy.

'What's that, Raffles?'

'It has a hint of ginger, Llew's beard. So of all the primates, it most closely resembles an orangutan's arse.'

'Try saying *that* in German,' I quipped.

'Es hat einen hauch von ingwer, Llew's bart. Von allen primaten ähnelt es am ehesten dem arsch eines Orangutan.'

'The man's a genius,' I said. 'He's wasted on us.'

'So what language d'you whisper at night in Timothy's ear?' asked

Larry. 'English, French or German?'

'French, of course – not that it's any of *your* business.'

'Everything's his business, Andy. He's a right nosy bastard. Remember that time when ... Lucy,' I added, trance-like.

'Remember that time when Lucy *what?*' asked Andy.

'No,' I said, pointing. 'Lucy. She's here.'

'Hello, gentlemen,' she called, waving. 'I thought I'd surprise you. Seems to have worked, on Llew anyway.

Andy and Larry stood up. Lucy went first to Andy and gave him a hug.

'That scar is so cool now,' she said. 'You look like a cross between the Milk Tray Man and, er—'

'Edward Scissorhands,' said Larry, arms open. 'Come here, you. Lovely to see you.'

They hugged, and then she turned to me.

'Can you spare him for an hour or two?' she asked Larry and Andy. 'I need to borrow him.'

'Have him for as long as you want,' said Larry. 'Just watch out for the beard. Half his breakfast's still in there, and yesterday's tea.'

Lucy smiled, and beckoned me up out of my seat.

'Shall we?' she said, offering me her arm as if we were a promenading Victorian couple.

Both Big Al and Thirza dashed towards Lucy as she led me from the newsroom. Their excited chatter and bonhomie was lost on me. I was in some kind of dream – present, yet absent – and it was hardly any different once we were outside the building.

'Where are we going?' I said eventually.

'The beach,' she replied. 'Where else.'

'I got your letter.'

'You didn't write back, and I gave you a poste restante address and everything.'

'I didn't know what to say. Well, actually, that's not true. I knew exactly what to say, only I thought it better not to – you know, just in case.'

She nodded. 'Probably wise.'

'We *are* talking about the same thing here, aren't we?' I said, as the sense of unreality swept over me once more.

'I don't know, Llew. Why don't you tell me what you're talking about and then we'll know for sure, won't we.'

I glanced over my shoulder to check no one was within earshot. We passed the access road to the garages near where I had burned her letter almost exactly a year earlier.

'The peanut oil.'

'Yes, we're talking about the same thing, but let's save it for the sea, shall we. No flapping ears there.'

*

'I wasn't going to tell you,' she said as we walked along the hard wet expanse of sand exposed by the turning tide. 'But I had to. Hence that picture of cooking oil. I think it was a confessional thing – you know, like you Catholics have. It's no small thing, killing a person, even if that person deserved to die, twice over, slowly and horribly, and in agony.'

We walked and she talked – all the way up the coast past Milton Common and back again.

I mostly listened, speaking only occasionally, either to seek clarification or if the shock – and admiration – at what I was hearing became too much.

'You rented a flat in Farlington, so you could case Dakin's home?'

'You taught yourself to pick locks?'

'You spiked his cooking oils with peanut oil?'

'No way? He came down for a fried-egg sandwich when you were still in the kitchen?'

'You clobbered him with a leg of defrosting lamb when he was choking, to stop him fetching his wife?'

By the time we got back to Eastney, the tide was drawing in and we were reduced to navigating a narrow strip of sand between the sea and the stones.

'So now you know everything,' she said after we had walked in silence for a time. 'What will you do with the information, d'you think?'

'What *can* I do with it?' I asked, nonplussed.

'Well, me telling you kind of makes you an accessory after the fact, doesn't it? Will you go to confession or something – to offload?'

'No, I don't believe in all that crap, and besides, I don't need to offload because I don't think you did anything wrong. He killed your dad and he was going to kill me. What you did was … heroic. There it is. You're my hero.' I stopped and took both her hands in mine. 'Truly, you are. You saved my life.'

'It's heroine, actually,' she said, smiling.

Her words left me with a strong sense of déjà vu.

'Spoken like a true sub,' I said.

We began walking again.

'Talking of work,' I added, 'what'll you do, now that you're home?'

'Well, I didn't tell you, but I've written a novel. I've got an agent and everything. I did tons of writing in Australia. Often there wasn't much else to do. I loved it. Anyway, my agent says the book's great, but raw, and so I've tons of editing to do.'

She went on to explain that her book was based on the prize-winning short story she had written as a schoolgirl that had prompted our first ever meeting all those years ago.

'Wow. I look forward to reading it. I bet it'll be brilliant.'

'It's quite intense, I suppose. *Write what you know*, and all that.'

'Are you sticking around Pompey in the meantime?'

'For a while at least. I've got a lot to sort out – not least the flat. I'm selling up. Too many memories, and who wants Mrs Matthews as a neighbour.'

'Quite. So where will you go?'

'Oh, I don't know. More travelling maybe. That's the great thing about writing – you can do it anywhere. And you? What're your plans?'

'I'll stay here for a good few years yet, I think. Things are good. Quiet, but good.'

'I'm happy for you, Llew. Truly. You mean so much to me. D'you know, I think that in another life you and I might've got married and been really, really happy together.'

'But not in this one?'

She shook her head and gave me a wistful little smile.

'No, not in this one.'

She leaned in and we kissed – properly this time, tongues dancing. She pulled me to her, real close. It was heavenly. Then, gently, she eased away.

'Bye, Llew. Love you. Take care.'

As I watched her go, I knew I'd not see her again.

Maybe she'll write about us one day. Maybe she'll give us the happiness we'd have had in another world. That would be nice.

I turned to face the incoming sea, which by now had claimed the last of the sands. A sharp winter wind gusted along the seafront. I breathed in deeply. The air was clean – far cleaner than in the summer. I much preferred off-season Southsea. The roads carried only a little light local traffic, and the esplanade was free of all that endless snacking and pig-headed determination to have a bloody good time, come what may. The place had grace, and dignity.

I looked across the water to Ryde and wondered if the sense of serenity I felt in that moment was coming from without or within.

Does it really matter?

I smiled and set off back to the newsroom. That story about the one-handed pianist with eight children by nine mothers wasn't going to write itself.

THE END

AUTHOR'S NOTE

While *Splash* is a work of fiction, some of its references are drawn from real-life events – in particular, freemasonry's hold on the police.

For the Masons-police plotline I would like to thank the late journalist and author, Martin Short, whose explosive and exhaustive 1993 book *Inside the Brotherhood* shone a light into the dark recesses of Freemasonry and its shadowy influence on those in British public life.

As a result of his book, Short was an expert witness to the parliamentary select committee on Freemasonry in the police and the judiciary in 1996.

Inside the Brotherhood focuses on the Metropolitan Police. For *Splash*, I used Short's devastating research on this front as the basis for the fictitious Derek Dakin plotline.

THANK YOU

Writing books is a lonely endeavour, but it's not possible to succeed at it without the help of friends, family and talented professionals.

So thank you to my editor, Averill Buchanan. First you helped me find my writing 'voice', then you gave that voice clarity. Thanks also to Rebecca and Andrew at designforwriters.com for their stunning cover.

Also of huge help were Neil Ashcroft and Christopher Dean, who helped weed out typos and inconsistencies. (If you spot any we missed, please let me know: sean@sgmashcroft.com).

Writing books can also be a terribly selfish endeavour, and so the biggest thank you by far is owed my wife, Naomi. You have been patient, understanding and long-suffering. Without your support I could never have followed my dream.

REVIEWS PLEA

Thanks so much for reading *Splash*. Although sales are the ultimate vote of confidence, reviews come a close second. So if you enjoyed this story, might you leave a review on Amazon? That would be brilliant. They help drive sales and I'd appreciate it massively.

To leave a review:

1. Search for 'SGM Ashcroft' on Amazon.
2. Click on *Splash*.
3. Scroll down to customer reviews and click the button that says 'Write a customer review'. (See below).

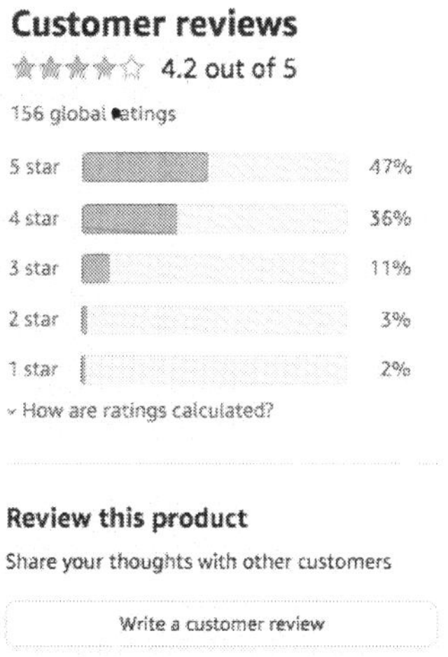

ABOUT THE AUTHOR

In a 35-year career, Sean Ashcroft has worked on local, national and international newspapers as well as on newsstand magazines. Since 2005 he has been helping businesses tell their best stories (zyzzyva.co.uk). *Splash* is his second novel. He lives in west London with his long-suffering, patient and understanding wife, their two children and Pip, their dog.

Printed in Great Britain
by Amazon

84270474R00137